HELL ON EARTH

Machetazo did not pull the brand out until it was nearly extinguished. Mewing pitiably, Tarleton doubled over and retched, his features twisted in acute torment.

"Any clever comments to make, *gringo*?" The Beast mocked his misery. "Any more lectures on what it means to be perfect like you?"

"So this is why you lured most of the soldiers from Fort Fillmore," Susannah said, tears streaming down her cheeks.

"Precisely. While most of the garrison is away, I will help myself to enough rifles and revolvers to outfit the rest of my army." Machetazo touched his cap. "If you will excuse me, duty calls."

Practicing the same care he had on his descent, Fargo crawled back up the hill. For once Juanita was right where he had left her. The tears moistening her face told him she had witnessed the whole thing.

"That devil's cruelty, his wickedness, are an affront to all that is decent in us. If I could, I would kill him with my own hands," Juanita said.

"You'll have to wait your turn." Fargo tried to dispel her gloomy mood. "His days are numbered. He just doesn't know it yet."

A GIANT

TRAILSMAN

ADVENTURE

NEW MEXICO
NIGHTMARE

by

Jon Sharpe

A SIGNET BOOK

SIGNET
Published by New American Library, a division of
Penguin Putnam Inc., 375 Hudson Street,
New York, New York 10014, U.S.A.
Penguin Books Ltd, 80 Strand,
London WC2R 0RL, England
Penguin Books Australia Ltd, 250 Camberwell Road,
Camberwell, Victoria 3124, Australia
Penguin Books Canada Ltd, 10 Alcorn Avenue,
Toronto, Ontario, Canada M4V 3B2
Penguin Books (N.Z.) Ltd, Cnr Rosedale and Airborne Roads,
Albany, Auckland 1310, New Zealand

Penguin Books Ltd, Registered Offices:
Harmondsworth, Middlesex, England

First published by Signet, an imprint of New American Library,
a division of Penguin Putnam Inc.

First Printing, February 2003
10 9 8 7 6 5 4 3 2 1

The Trailsman

Beginnings . . . they bend the tree and they mark the man. Skye Fargo was born when he was eighteen. Terror was his midwife, vengeance his first cry. Killing spawned Skye Fargo, ruthless, cold-blooded murder. Out of the acrid smoke of gunpowder still hanging in the air, he rose, cried out a promise never forgotten.

The Trailsman they began to call him all across the West: searcher, scout, hunter, the man who could see where others only looked, his skills for hire but not his soul, the man who lived each day to the fullest, yet trailed each tomorrow. Skye Fargo, the Trailsman, the seeker who could take the wildness of a land and the wanting of a woman and make them his own.

New Mexico Territory, 1861—
Where ambition and bloodlust
make for an explosive mix.

Prologue

Esteban had to be careful. He did not like the idea of being hacked to death, which was the punishment in store for anyone caught doing what he was about to do. When evening fell over the encampment he went about his duties as he normally would. He joked and laughed with his *compadres*. He made coffee and helped hand out their meager suppers. Later, he sat in on a dice game. The one thing he did not do was act the least bit excited, although inwardly he bubbled like a volcano. No one must suspect.

The summer night was uncomfortably warm, but Esteban didn't mind. He would rather be too hot than too cold. His loose-fitting cotton shirt and pants were not much protection from the elements. Nor did it help that he was too poor to afford shoes. His well-worn sandals were little better than going barefoot.

Esteban had never complained, though. Poverty was his family's lot in life, as it was every *peón*'s. He had been content with his beloved Dorotea, their modest hut, and their small plot of ground. It wasn't much, but it was theirs, and he was happy. Then came the day when he was in the hut sharpening a sickle and his wife shouted his name. The fear in her voice filled him with dread, and he had rushed outside thinking it must be Apaches. But no, winding up the dusty excuse for a road had been a column of *soldados*. Not uniformed *Federales* on sturdy horses, but unkempt men in dirty clothes, marching on foot in ragged formation. All were armed with machetes at their sides, and perhaps every man in three had a gun and a bandoleer.

The sight of the machetes had filled Esteban with terror; each was snug in a long black sheath.

"Mother of God, preserve us!" his wife exclaimed.

"Quiet, Dorotea, or they will have our heads," Esteban had cautioned. Smiling, he moved to meet the soldiers, saying, *"Buenos días, señor—"*

"Capitán, if you please," the man at the front of the column said gruffly. "Captain Ruiz, of the People's Army for the Liberation of Mexico." He was squat as a cactus and had a neck as thick around as a bull's. "You will provide water for my men, and be quick about it."

Esteban's well was his pride and joy. He had slaved many days to dig it, and while it barely produced enough water to irrigate his plot, it enabled him to fulfill his dream of being his own master and not having to work for someone else. "Right away, Captain," he said, eager to please. The sooner their thirst was slaked, the sooner they would leave.

First, Esteban shooed Dorotea into the hut. She was not the most beautiful of women: her hips were too stout, her waist too broad, her face quite plain; yet that did not stop several of the Black Sheaths from hungrily eyeing her and licking their parched lips.

Filling the wooden bucket and taking their battered tin dipper in hand, Esteban went from man to man. Most rudely grabbed it and gulped, spilling as much as they drank. He approached the captain last.

Ruiz sipped slowly, studying him over the dipper's rim. "What is your name?"

Esteban told him.

"You call this dung heap a farm?"

"I do the best I can." Esteban knew better than to let his resentment show. He admired his rows of corn.

"It is not much, I grant you, but my wife and I are happy."

Captain Ruiz snorted. "So are pigs in a trough. It never ceases to amaze me what some people are willing to settle for in life. But be honest, dirt farmer. Don't you ever yearn for something better?"

"Who doesn't?" Esteban said without thinking.

"You are just like us, then," Ruiz said, gesturing at his men. "We look for the day when those who hoard the wealth of our land no longer do so; when the leeches in Mexico City have been overthrown."

Esteban had no argument with the government. It left him pretty much alone, which was exactly how he liked things. He thought his taxes were too high, but then, who didn't? "I do not give much thought to politics."

Captain Ruiz took another slow sip. "How old are you?"

"Forty-three."

"Are you in good health?"

"Yes, thank God." Esteban did not see what that had to do with anything.

"Do you own a gun?"

"No, sir, I could never afford—" And Esteban had stopped, a horrible insight knifing through him. "Please, sir," he quickly said. "You cannot be thinking what I think you are thinking. As you say, I am a simple farmer, not a soldier."

"You *were* a farmer," Captain Ruiz amended. "We are on a recruiting drive. You are now a member of our grand army, and will fall in at the rear when we leave. I grant you two minutes to say good-bye to your wife."

Forgetting himself, Esteban cried, "You can't do this!"

Ruiz's machete leaped free and the tempered edge swept to within a whisker's width of Esteban's throat.

3

"Never tell me what I can and cannot do, dog. I act on the authority of General Machetazo himself."

Despair filled Esteban. Machetazo was a self-styled revolutionary whose fervor was matched only by his cruelty. The fiend had cut a swath of blood and destruction across northern Mexico, leaving countless innocents dead in his wake. His nickname was the Beast, and if ever a man deserved the title, it was he.

"I could take your head if I wanted," Captain Ruiz was saying, "but we are in need of able-bodied men, and you qualify whether you like it or not." In a fluid, practiced swing, he slipped the machete back into its sheath.

Esteban noticed several soldiers had ringed him, their hands on the hilts of their own machetes. To resist was to invite certain death. He wanted to curse, to rail at them, to punch them, but he dared not. "If you do not mind my asking, how long will I be away from home?"

"That is for the general to decide." Ruiz removed his sombrero and wiped a sleeve across his sweaty brow. "The important thing is that you do as you are told at all times. And never, ever, try to desert. The punishment for desertion is death by machete."

One of the other men snickered. "You would be hacked to bits, farmer, screaming like a stuck pig the whole while."

"Go say good-bye," Captain Ruiz commanded. "We do not have all day."

His legs leaden, Esteban had shuffled inside and broken the news to Dorotea. She wailed and clung to him, begging him not to go, but what else could he do? When the captain bellowed, he went out and took up at the end of the column. His heart felt as if it were being crushed and his eyes blurred with tears. The last he saw of his wife, she was on her knees by the well, her arms outstretched to the heavens.

That had been two months ago. Two months of hell:

of bad food and little water; of being made to drill, morning and afternoon; of standing guard every third night from sunset to sunrise; of being bossed around by the officers and the sergeants; and of often wishing he were dead.

Esteban saw the Beast only a few times. The first was when he and the other new conscripts arrived. General Machetazo addressed them personally. A tall, stern-faced man with a thick black mustache and a scar on his left cheek, he clasped his hands behind his back and regarded them much as a cat might regard a bunch of mice. His voice was low and deep and rasped like the growl of a jaguar.

"Welcome to the People's Army, gentlemen. From this day on your life is dedicated to the greater good of Mexico. Tomorrow morning you will be issued your machetes. Wear them with pride. To be a Black Sheath is an honor."

That was it. General Machetazo stalked off, and Captain Ruiz led them to their companies. Although calling eight men a "company" was more than a little ridiculous, in Esteban's estimation, he did not say so.

Rumor had it the Beast's army numbered many thousands. Esteban was amused to discover there were only a couple hundred. Half had been recruited as he had. The rest were dregs: cutthroats and killers who joined for the slaughter and the plunder, not out of any great notion of liberating their fellows.

As promised, Esteban received a machete in a custom black sheath—but no gun. There were not enough to go around. Sergeant Gonzales told him it might be months before he was given one. Gonzales also said something else—something that set Esteban to pondering the unthinkable.

One night around a fire, a soldier mentioned that federal patrols had been seen in the area, and that they would be leaving for the mountains in a few days.

"Our poor general must sleep with one eye open

all the time ever since the government placed such a hefty bounty on his head," Sergeant Gonzales had commented. "Ten thousand *pesos* just for turning him in! More than most of us see in a lifetime."

"Only a fool would be tempted," said a man from Hermosillo.

"*Sí,*" agreed another. "Our leader is never without his bodyguards. I hear they are pledged to hunt down anyone who betrays him."

Someone spotted Captain Ruiz strolling toward them, and Sergeant Gonzales whispered, "Quiet, you simpletons! Let him hear one word of such talk and he will have us dragged before the general."

A different subject was brought up but Esteban no longer listened. He could not stop thinking about the money. Ten thousand *pesos* was a fortune to a man who had only less than five to his name. He and his wife could buy a bigger home—a nicer place, with a wood floor and a better well.

Esteban tried to cast the seed from his mind but it had taken firm root. He found himself spending every waking moment plotting how he might do it and not be caught. The best way was to sneak off after everyone turned in, go get his wife, and hurry to the nearest garrison. The *Federales* might insist that he personally lead them back, but that was fine by him. For ten thousand *pesos*, he would gladly lead them to the flap of General Machetazo's tent.

Now the time had come. Tomorrow the army was to depart for the mountains. Esteban had sentry duty, and he waited for the camp to quiet as he paced the stretch of south perimeter that had been assigned to him. Sentries were not permitted to sit down, and perish the thought that they should ever doze off. The consequences were not worth the extra rest.

Not that Esteban could sleep if he wanted to. His blood was racing faster than a hare. He noted the rise of a crescent moon with disfavor since it increased the risk, but he refused to change his mind.

By midnight only a few of the rougher element were still up, and they were at the other end of camp.

Esteban neared a boulder that served as the east marker of his section, and was taken aback to see the man from Hermosillo coming from the other direction.

"So, it is your night, too, eh, *amigo*? And tomorrow we will be on the march all day. No rest for the weary."

Esteban walked to the boulder and did an about face as he had been taught. Of all the men in camp, why did it have to be the one whose gums never stopped flapping?

"Where are you off to? What is your rush? No one is breathing down our necks. Stop and talk awhile."

"Later," Esteban said. The last time the two of them shared sentry duty, they spent half the night chatting.

"Are you bucking for colonel? In case you haven't heard, we already have one."

Colonel Fraco was his name, and he scared Esteban even more than General Machetazo did. "It is too early yet," Esteban said over a shoulder. "Wait until all the fires are out."

The west marker was a stunted tree. Esteban did another about face. One hundred paces and he was back at the boulder. So was the man from Hermosillo whose name he had never bothered to ask.

"So tell me, *amigo*, were you able to get word to your wife like you wanted? I asked to have a letter sent to my family but the captain refused. He said they do not have the paper to spare." The man swore.

Esteban pointed at the flickering flames of the last fire. "We will talk when that goes out and not before. I wish you would get that through your head. Didn't you see what happened to poor Pedro?" A fellow

7

peón conscript, Pedro had made the mistake of not taking his sentry duty seriously enough. He had been stripped to the waist, tied to a wagon wheel, and whipped until his back was raw meat.

"Oh, very well," the man from Hermosillo grumbled, and walked off.

Esteban returned to the boulder four more times, always contriving to get there after the other. Midway to the stunted tree, he broke off and bolted to the south, running as he had never run in his life. Country born and bred, he was fleet for his age. In no time the camp was out of sight. Smiling, he congratulated himself. A few seconds later he sensed someone was behind him, and a glance confirmed the worst. Several shadowy figures were hard on his heels, loping after him like wolves after a buck. Their speed put his to shame.

A strangled cry rose unbidden from Esteban's throat. *This couldn't be. Not so soon.* He exerted himself to his utmost and beyond, yet still his pursuers steadily narrowed the gap. Whoever they were, they made no sound whatsoever. Were he superstitious, he could be forgiven for believing they were otherworldly specters. But he suspected the truth well before they overtook him, and his guess proved a good one.

At the last Esteban decided to stand and fight. His very life was at stake, and while he was not violent by nature, he would not give in like a lamb to the slaughter. Stopping and whirling, he drew his machete and girded himself.

They were on him in a twinkling, the three of them striking in concert. One sprang for Esteban's right arm even as he swung, while the other two tackled him, one about the waist, the other down lower. He felt the ground jar his spine, felt a blow to the chin that caused the stars to spin and dance, and then he was in twin grips of steel, being ushered to the last place in the world he wanted to go.

One of his captors went on ahead. All the officers were waiting when Esteban arrived: General Machetazo, Colonel Fraco, Captain Ruiz, and both lieutenants. The fires had been rekindled, and Gonzales and the other sergeants were assembling the men.

In a state of shock, Esteban hardly resisted when he was stripped and tied belly-up to a wagon wheel. He was aware of the troops gathering around but all he had eyes for was the Beast, General Machetazo, who stood next to the wheel, a machete in hand. "Please," Esteban softly pleaded.

"Do you hear him?" the Beast roared to his army. "This craven coward begs for his life. He put us all at risk by running off and leaving our southern flank open to attack. And now he has the nerve to ask to be spared. What say you, my soldiers? Who among you thinks he deserves to live?"

The silence was deafening.

"Very well." The Beast raised the glistening machete.

Dorotea's kindly features swam before Esteban, and he had to swallow to clear a lump from his throat. "I never asked to join your army, General. I have a wife, a home. This is not fair."

"Life itself is not fair, fool."

Esteban was a long time dying.

1

For the better part of the morning Skye Fargo had been winding steadily to the south along a rutted track that served as the main link to civilization in that neck of the country. The Territory of New Mexico was mostly rugged, untamed wilderness, sprinkled here and there with settlements and a few small towns. It boasted two cities, and only two: Santa Fe and Albuquerque.

Nowhere was its raw, wild nature more apparent than along its southern border with Mexico. Here, roving bands of Apaches, gangs of cold-blooded outlaws, and Mexican bandits fond of killing and robbing *americanos* made life a living hell for the few souls brave enough—or foolhardy enough—to take up homesteading or ranching.

Fargo loved the land, regardless. It was stark; it was arid; it was inhospitable. Menace lurked around every bend. Yet it was exactly the kind of place where he felt most at home. He had been raised in the wild, so to him the dangers were a normal part of life, to be taken in stride like drought and snowstorms.

Big and broad-shouldered, Fargo had piercing lake-blue eyes and a face women found more than pleasing. Buckskins molded to his muscular frame like a second skin. In a holster on his right hip was a Colt; in his saddle scabbard, a Henry rifle. And tucked in his right boot, strapped in an ankle sheath, was an Arkansas toothpick—his ace in the hole when he was in tight spots.

To Fargo's left flowed the Rio Grande, low and sluggish at that time of year. To his right reared foot-hills, stepping-stones to the mountain haunts of the fierce Apache. Fargo had been in those mountains be-fore and knew them well, and he had a hunch that before his stay was done, he would have cause to visit them again. The message that had brought him to New Mexico had not stated why he'd been sent for, except that the commander of Fort Fillmore was in desperate need of his services.

From around the next bend came a sudden shout. Fargo instantly reined up, his right hand dropping to his revolver. Someone cursed mightily, and a commo-tion followed. Since none of it was directed at him, Fargo felt safe in kneeing the Ovaro forward. What he saw caused his jaw to involuntarily clench.

A pair of canvas-topped wagons were stopped beside the road. The pilgrims who owned them were gathered around a husky, bearded brute who had an Indian boy on the ground and was slapping the tar out of him while an Indian girl vainly tried to pull the man off.

"—teach you, you mangy redskin!" the man was raging. "I'll knock your stinking red teeth down your rotten throat!"

The girl leaped and grabbed a brawny arm but she was like a reed pitted against an oak. With hardly any effort, the man flung her off. She landed on her side in the dust, hurt but still game. Rising, she went to throw herself at him again, but just then another man and a woman seized her by the arms and held her fast.

No one noticed Fargo until he was right on top of them. Drawing rein, he demanded loud enough to be heard above the ringing slaps, "What's going on here?" All eyes swung toward him, and without wait-ing for a reply, Fargo said, "Let that boy up."

Surprise gave way to resentment. The broomstick

of a man holding the girl snapped, "Who the hell are you, stranger, to come waltzing in here like this, telling us what we should do? You've got your gall."

"That's right!" barked the woman. "This is our get-out, not yours. Go poke your big nose somewhere else."

The husky slab beating the Indian boy had paused with his calloused hand upraised. Now he sneered and growled, "You heard 'em. Light a shuck before I learn you some manners." He tensed to strike the boy again.

The Colt seemed to flash from the holster of its own accord, and at the metallic click of the hammer, everyone froze. Fargo leaned over his saddle horn. "Go ahead and hit him if you want, but every time you do you'll lose a finger."

The man rose like a riled grizzly set to charge. "Are you a damned Injun-lover, mister? Is that why you're buttin' in? Because if you are, I'm tellin' you here and now: The only thing I like less than Injuns are whites who cotton to 'em."

The boy didn't move. His mouth was bloody, and more blood was trickling from his nose and a gash in his cheeks. In addition, he was laced with welts that would turn into bruises.

"Do you have a name, bigmouth?" Fargo asked the bigot.

"I'm Tyrel Owensby," the man stated as if it should mean something. "These here are my kinfolk. We're from Georgia, on our way to Mesilla to hook up with my brother." He jabbed a thumb as thick as a railroad spike at the two Indians. "We stopped to rest a spell and caught these no-account Apache brats tryin' to steal vittles from one of our wagons." Owensby clenched his huge fists. "We're well within our rights to give these heathens a lickin', and that's exactly what I aim to do."

"You've already beaten the boy enough," Fargo

said, the Colt's barrel fixed squarely on Owensby's broad face. "And these aren't Apaches, you lunkhead. They're Pimas."

"Who?"

"Pimas," Fargo repeated. "One of the friendliest tribes west of the Mississippi. They make their living by farming, and they've never raised a finger against a white man. Fact is, they help the whites in these parts fight Apaches from time to time."

Tyrel blinked. "How the blazes was I to know? We're new to these parts." He paused. "Besides, if these sprouts are tame Injuns, why'd they try to steal from us?"

"Probably because they're hungry." Dismounting, Fargo twirled the Colt into its holster and stepped up to the boy. Owensby took a stride toward him, and for a moment Fargo thought he would have a fight on his hands, but the Georgian stopped and lowered his fists. Sinking onto a knee, Fargo helped the boy sit up. "Anything busted inside?"

The boy merely stared. He had long dark hair and wore a breechcloth and moccasins typical of his tribe. Not much over fifteen, he was lean of build and limb.

"Don't you speak English?" Fargo asked. Many Pimas did, thanks to missionaries trying to convert them. His own contact with the Pimas had been limited but he knew a few Pima words. He used one now. Touching his chest, he said the Pima word for "friend."

All the boy did was keep staring.

"Estamos amigos," Fargo tried, but that failed to spur a reaction, as well.

The woman and the broomstick were still holding the Pima girl. Rising, Fargo gave them a hard stare and they let go.

The girl ran to the boy. They were enough alike to be brother and sister. She was older but her exact age was hard to tell. Pimas did not show much sign of

14

aging until well into their middle years. Looping an arm around the boy's, she boosted him to his feet. Then off they went into the brush, without a word or a backward glance.

"Good riddance, I say," one of the women said. "I don't rightly care if they are peaceable. Indians can't be trusted. No way, no how."

Fargo swung onto the Ovaro and lifted the reins.

"One thing before you go, stranger." This from Tyrel. "Don't ever meddle in my affairs again. I excused it this time. But I won't be so charitable if you think you can make a habit of it, you hear?"

"I give you a year," Fargo said.

"A year for what?"

"To live. In this country bullheaded bastards like you don't last long." Fargo lightly applied his spurs and trotted on down the road. If he never ran into the Owensby clan again, it would suit him just fine.

The sun was approaching its zenith when Fargo reached Mesilla, a sleepy hamlet that showed more Spanish influence than American. Northeast of it a short ways was Las Cruces, another fledgling settlement. Southward six miles lay Fargo's destination—Fort Fillmore, the southernmost post in all New Mexico—and forty miles beyond was the border.

Fargo rode down the dusty main street to a hitch rail in front of a cantina. He could use a bite to eat and some rotgut. The last drink he'd treated himself to was in Albuquerque and he had a lot of trail dust to wash down. Welcome coolness bathed him as he strode inside and over to a poorly stocked bar. At that early hour the place was practically deserted. Other than a couple of old-timers swapping tall tales at a table and a morose-looking Mexican nursing a drink, the place was deserted.

The bartender was also Mexican; a portly, friendly sort who greeted Fargo with a warm *"Buenos tardes, señor. Como esta usted?"*

"Thirsty," Fargo responded, and slapped a coin down. "Give me a glass of your best whiskey."

"*Sí, señor*. Most gladly." The bartender produced a bottle from under the counter and opened it. "This came all the way from St. Louis."

Since the wrapper was missing, Fargo was skeptical. But one sip brought a smile. "Damned good coffin varnish, friend."

"Did I not say so?" The man offered his pudgy hand. "I am called Chico. If there is anything else you are in need of, all you have to do is ask." Chico gave a sly wink.

"How about some grub?"

Chico chuckled. "That is not exactly what I had in mind, *señor*. I was thinking more of companionship, as they say. But I can have my wife make some *tortillas* and *frijoles*, if you like. And there might be some *pollo*, some chicken, left from last night. All for only a dollar."

Fargo savored another swallow and relished the liquid warmth that flowed down his throat into his belly. "Kind of steep, isn't it? I can get a full-course meal at a fancy restaurant in Denver for that much."

"But you are not *in* Denver," Chico said amiably. "And I have eleven small mouths to feed." A drawn-out sigh fluttered from his lips. "My wife, she can never keep her hands off me. Even now, after all these years, I am lucky to get a wink of sleep at night." He looked down at his big belly. "I cannot decide if she is blind or *loco*."

Fargo couldn't help laughing. "I know men who would give anything to have a wife like yours."

"They only think so because they never get enough," Chico said. "But too much is just as bad."

"If you say so." Fargo had never indulged in that luxury. He had to enjoy his where and when he found it. Which reminded him: "You mentioned companionship?"

"Sí, señor." Chico winked again and nodded at a short flight of steps. "Up the stairs and to the right. *Bonitas señoritas.* You can take your pick from two of the prettiest young women anywhere."

Fargo had heard claims like his before, and more often than not the women in question turned out to be considerably less than advertised. "Your wife doesn't mind you having them under the same roof?"

"It was her idea. We get ten percent of all they make. Which, in a town this size, is hardly enough to cover the cost of feeding them. Who would think *putas* could eat so much?" Chico sighed. "Are you interested, *amigo?*"

"I reckon a look wouldn't hurt." Fargo polished off his whiskey. He hadn't enjoyed the company of a woman since Colorado, and it might be a while before he was afforded another chance. Ambling upstairs, he discovered two young women seated on a bench, whispering.

Jumping to their feet, they beamed and clutched his shirt.

"You want some fun, *gringo?*" one asked.

"Muy hermoso," said the other, and giggled.

To Fargo's considerable amazement, they truly were lovely. The one who knew English had full ruby lips and a winsome figure. The other was more amply endowed but she was half a foot shorter. Both weren't much over twenty. "I get to take my pick?" he said, ogling one and then the other.

"A hard decision, no?" said the tallest, grinning.

Fargo was slightly partial to her but he flipped a coin to decide the outcome. Heads, it would be the tall one; tails, the short woman. It turned out tails. "Lead the way," he said, and motioned to demonstrate.

"Just my luck," the taller woman groused. "We finally have a handsome man show up, and Maria gets to have all the fun."

"I expect to be back this way when my work is

done," Fargo said to pacify her. "Next time you'll have the honor."

The taller one grinned. "I will hold you to that, *gringo*. And if you do not show up, it will break my heart." She pealed with mirth.

Maria's room was small but clean. A bed took up half the floor space. Sashaying over, she stood with her hands on her hips in an enticing pose, her tight blue dress leaving little to the imagination.

Fargo removed his gun belt and placed it on a dresser. His buckskins were caked with dust, and out of courtesy to her he started to strip off his shirt, but he barely had it hiked to his chest before she was flush against him, hungrily rubbing her warm palms over him.

"Musculoso hombre! Nervudo." Maria turned his back to the bed and gently pushed him backward until he fell on top of it. Tittering, she reached behind her to undo the clasp on her dress.

"Allow me," Fargo said, pulling her down on top of him. Maria's mouth found his and her silken tongue glided between his parted lips. She tasted sugary. He sucked on her tongue as he would hard honey while his hands rose to cover her breasts. She squirmed deliciously when he squeezed them. Soon her nipples were jutting against the sheer fabric, and when he pinched one, she cooed deep in her throat.

Rolling Maria onto her side, Fargo pressed flush against her and cupped her bottom. In response she ground her hips against his, the friction sparking a fire in his groin. He ran his left hand through her rich, lustrous hair and roved his lips to her neck and ear.

"Apasionado," Maria breathed, her tapered fingernails digging into his shoulders. *"Me gusta."*

Fargo slid his right hand around her neck and deftly unfastened the clasp. Below it was a row of small buttons leading down to her waist. As he undid the last one, the dress parted, revealing her lacy undergar-

18

ments. The swell of her bosom was too enticing to resist. Fargo kissed and licked the tops of her breasts, his fingers busy lower down, divesting her of the barriers to her charms.

At last Maria was bared in all her sensual allure, stretched out with one leg hooked and with a lusty smile on her cherry lips. She crooked a slender finger at him, her eyelids hooded.

Stripping off his shirt and boots, Fargo renewed their coupling. He kissed her mouth, her cheeks, her shoulder, then fastened his lips on a hard-as-nails nipple and tweaked it with the tip of his tongue. For her part, Maria inserted a knee between his legs and rubbed it up and down along his inner thigh. Every so often her knee would gently stroke his manhood in a manner designed to heighten his carnal hunger. For her age, she was a wily temptress, versed in the secrets that made men lose themselves in her velvet pleasures.

Fargo was so hot, his skin prickled as from a heat rash. He switched his mouth to her other breast and let his hand knead the one he had forsaken. Her fingers were roaming up and down and back and along his ribs, eliciting pleasant little ripples. Kneeling between her legs, he licked her stomach, her navel.

Maria mumbled in Spanish, something about wanting him inside.

Glad to oblige, Fargo gripped his pole and rubbed it up and down her moist opening, tantalizing her with what was to come. Then, inch by inch, he fed his manhood in. She cried out, her arms rising to loop around his neck, her mouth fusing to his own, her inner walls clinging to him like a satiny glove. The heady musk of her womanly scent filled the room.

Fargo began the ages-old rocking motion inbred into man since the dawn of time. Maria matched the tempo of his thrusts, their bodies performing as one. Over and over and over he thrust up into her, adrift in their mounting rapture. Under them the bed creaked with rising urgency.

Maria began tossing her head from side to side, and moaning. Her fingernails were buried in his biceps hard enough to hurt, while her legs were a vise about his middle.

Fargo was trying to pace himself but it had been a while and his body wasn't to be denied. He could feel the explosion building at the base of his spine but did his best to hold back the deluge as long as he could. It was Maria who triggered the inevitable. She abruptly rose partway off the bed, her eyes wide, her nostrils flared. Her whole body shook and she cried out louder than before.

Seconds later Fargo crested the summit. The bed and the ceiling seemed to change places, and his whole body exploded like a keg of black powder. The room receded into a blur. He spurted and spurted and spurted some more, lost in the sweet ecstasy of mutual oblivion.

Together they sagged onto the quilt and Fargo rolled off Maria and onto his back. A dreamy lassitude came over him and, although he wasn't very tired, he dozed off and napped until someone rapped on the door.

"*Señor*? Sorry to disturb you, but Chico, he says your food is ready and you can go down any time."

Fargo rose onto his elbows and was puzzled to see Maria on her side, staring at him with a peculiar expression. *"Que quiere?"*

Maria's gaze drifted below his waist. *"Es grande,"* she said softly.

Swinging his legs off the bed, Fargo began to dress. Maria watched him through hooded lids, curling and uncurling strands of her hair. When he turned toward the door, she slid off the bed and gave him a hug. He asked her how much she wanted, paid a dollar extra, and went out. From the other room came sounds that told him where her friend had gotten to.

Chico had the meal, including the bottle of whiskey, ready at a corner table. "I trust everything was to your liking?"

"Couldn't be better." The aroma set Fargo's stomach to growling. Easing into a chair with his back to the wall, he poured himself a drink.

"Should there be anything else you want, you only have to ask. I will let you eat in peace."

"I'd rather have some company," Fargo said. "Bring another glass and we can talk. The drinks will be on me."

"*Gracias, señor,* you are most kind."

It had been Fargo's experience that when it came to learning all the latest news anywhere on the frontier, a bartender was worth his weight in newspapers. So after Chico made himself comfortable, Fargo revealed, "I'm on my way to Fort Fillmore to do some work for the Army. Anything I should know about what's going on in these parts before I get there?"

"You do not look like a soldier, so you must be a scout, eh?" Chico treated himself to a swallow of redeye. "If you don't mind my saying so, you would be wise to turn around and go back to wherever you came from. This is dangerous country, *señor*. Even more so for those in uniform, and those who ride with them."

"Tell me something I don't know," Fargo said between bites. "The Apaches and the Navajos have been spilling blood for years."

"True, *señor*, but they cause more and more trouble as more and more whites show up. The Mescalero Apaches have let it be known they intend to drive every white-eye from their mountains. And the Navajos say the only way they will move to a reservation is if they are buried there." Chico shook his head sadly. "Many lives have been lost; many scalps taken. I fear many more will be before it is done."

Fargo wondered if Colonel Blanchard had sent for him to help track down the renegades.

"But that is not all," Chico continued. "*Bandidos* have been raiding the *rancheros* and holding up stagecoaches. The Army has tried to catch them but cannot."

"American or Mexican bandits?"

"A little of both, *señor*. It is a new bunch made up of killers from both sides of the border. They are led by a *gringo* named Pike Thornton. Maybe you have heard of him, yes?"

"Yes," Fargo said. Thornton was a hellion from Texas with a string of murders and robberies to his credit that stretched back a decade. The last Fargo heard, the Texas Rangers had made it too hot for Thornton in his home state, so he'd drifted elsewhere. Now Fargo knew where.

"Then there is the Beast," Chico gravely intoned. "General Machetazo." Finishing his drink in a single gulp, he crossed himself and declared, "May you never run into him, *señor*. He is worse than the Mescaleros, the Navajos, and the *bandidos* combined."

Fargo found that hard to believe. "I've never heard of the gent," he admitted.

"There must be a thousand souls in hell who wish they could say the same." Chico glanced around the room, then lowered his voice. "We first heard reports of him about six months ago. Rumor had it he was gathering an army. With it, he plans to topple the government and take over all of Mexico."

"Another would-be dictator," Fargo remarked. Mexico had seen more than her share. Ever since winning her independence from Spain, one government after another had risen and fallen.

"*Sí, señor,* but Machetazo is the worst. They do not

22

call him Bestia for nothing." Chico refilled his glass. "He delights in making others suffer in the most horrible ways he can think of. When he demanded food for his army from a small village and the villagers refused, he had every man, woman, and child put to the machete. But he was not content to slit their throats. Not him. He had them chopped to pieces." Chico paused. "I have many friends south of the border, *señor,* and they told me that grown men who saw the remains broke down and wept."

"Why haven't the *Federales* stopped him?"

"It is not as if they haven't tried. But the general always stays one step ahead of them.

It is said his Black Sheaths have the help of evil spirits."

"Black Sheaths?"

"My apologies, *señor.* That is how his soldiers are called. They wear black machete sheaths so everyone will know who they are."

"Has this general ever strayed north of the border?" Fargo had become so absorbed in their talk, he was neglecting his meal. He remedied that by digging in to the mountain of *frijoles.*

"There have been rumors to that effect, *sí.* But I would not really know. He is not fond of *gringos*, from what I hear. I would—"

Chico stopped. Someone had flung the door open so hard, it smacked against the wall. In tromped five men Fargo had hoped to see never again. In the lead was Tyrel Owensby, his shirtsleeves rolled up, exposing arms as thick as tree trunks. He marched straight to the bar and pounded it with a ham-sized fist.

"Where the hell is the bartender? What's a coon have to do to get a drink around this dump?"

"Perdón," Chico said, and hurried around.

As yet the new arrivals had failed to notice Fargo,

but it was only a matter of time. Sliding his chair back a few inches to give himself more room to move his arms, Fargo loosened the Colt in its holster.

"How may I help you gentlemen?" Chico asked. "Whiskey, perhaps? I have some of the best. Just ask my friend over there." Then, as innocently as could be, Chico pointed at the corner table.

Tyrel Owensby glanced over a broad shoulder and stiffened. "Well, well, well. Look who it is, boys. Our old friend, Mr. Big Nose himself. Let's go pay our respects, shall we?"

2

Skye Fargo never went out of his way to seek trouble. He never went out of his way to avoid it, either. His philosophy was that when it reared up and bit him, he sure as hell was going to bite back. So as the five smirking Southerners ringed his table, he looked their leader in the eye and said bluntly, "Don't start something you can't finish."

Tyrel planted himself, laced his fingers together, and popped his knuckles with a loud crack. "You must have me confused with some puny Yankee. I've yet to meet the jasper I can't lick."

The broomstick who had held the Indian girl was also there, and he snickered viciously. "Stomp him into the floor, Ty. Show this meddler what for."

"I have half a mind to do just that, Elwin." Tyrel leaned on the table and sneered in rank contempt. "I held off earlier because the women and kids were there, but it's just us menfolk now. So what say you get up, and let's get this over with?"

Fargo slowly rose, his right hand brushing the Colt. "Whenever you're ready."

Tyrel nonchalantly placed his big hands on his hips. "In case you ain't noticed, mister, I'm not heeled. I don't go in for none of that fancy gunplay. When I fight, it's man to man—the way it should be."

Not until that moment did Fargo realize that not one of them was armed. And shooting unarmed men went against his grain.

"Well?" Tyrel taunted. "I dare you to unbuckle that hogleg. Or are you all gurgle and no guts?"

Fargo was past the age where insults could provoke him into a fight. He had nothing to prove to himself or to anyone else. But he had to admit he liked the idea of taking the man-mountain down a peg or three. He was about to undo his gun belt when there was a low whistle from the bar.

Chico had taken a double-barreled shotgun from under the counter and was pointing it at the Georgians. "There will be no fighting in my cantina, *señores*," he announced. "The first one to start anything is the first one I blow a hole in."

"Damn you, Mex, you have no call to butt in," Elwin grumbled.

"I beg to differ, *señor*." Chico thumbed back one of the hammers. "I paid for everything you see with years of hard work. If you bust it up, who will buy me new tables and chairs? You and your friends? I think not."

Tyrel glowered in resentment. "Doesn't anyone in this stinkin' territory know how to mind their own damn business?" He took a step toward the bar.

"I wouldn't be hasty, *señor*," Chico warned. "If you think I will not shoot, you are very much mistaken."

From out of a side door came a heavyset woman wearing an apron and holding a pistol in one hand and a meat cleaver in the other.

"Permit me to introduce my wife, Rosita," Chico said. "She, too, would be most upset if you did damage to our fine establishment." He wagged the shotgun at the entrance. "So maybe it is best if you leave. *Pronto.*"

For a moment Fargo thought Tyrel would launch himself into the twin muzzles of the hand cannon. But then, cursing a mean streak, he stormed on out.

Elwin was last to leave, and he paused in the doorway. "Don't think you've heard the last of us, mister.

Or you, Mex. We're skinning out now, but us Owensbys weren't brought up in the woods to be scared of owls." With that, he was gone.

Chico's bushy eyebrows puckered. "What was that about owls?"

"It's a saying down South," Fargo explained. "It meant they're not afraid of us." The threat past, he sank into his chair and renewed his assault on the mountain of *frijoles*.

Rosita said something to her husband and went back into the kitchen. Chortling, Chico came over, bringing the shotgun. "That woman of mine. She says she would like to use her meat cleaver on that big one and separate him from his *cojones*." Taking a seat, he leaned the shotgun against his chair. "I believe the skinny one spoke the truth, *amigo*. You have not heard the last of them."

"Maybe so," Fargo agreed, but he wouldn't lose any sleep over it. In his wanderings he had run into a lot of troublemakers like Tyrel; bullies with more brawn than brains, who took perverse pleasure in picking on others. Most ended up on Boot Hill because they tended to overlook an important fact: Thanks to the invention of the six-shooter, all men were now equal, and some more equal than most.

Chico was having similar thoughts. "That is the problem with this border country. There are too many *bastardos*. Sometimes I think it would be better to pack up and move my family to Santa Fe. They have a marshal who keeps a tight rein on things."

Fargo didn't blame him. Easterners took law and order for granted but in the West it was as rare as hen's teeth. Only big towns and cities could afford the services of a full-time lawman. Places like Mesilla had to get by pretty much on their own. Occasionally a U.S. marshal would stop by or a cavalry patrol pass through. But as everyone liked to joke, they were never around when they were needed most.

"Another ten years or so and it will be different," Chico was saying. "Father Justin over at the mission believes so many people will move here, the day of the gun will be a thing of the past."

Some frontiersmen scoffed at the notion of the West ever becoming as tame as the East. Fargo wasn't one of them. Not all that long ago the land east of the Mississippi had been unexplored wilderness, a pristine land teeming with game and Indians. Now most of the game had been killed off and the Indians had been uprooted and forced onto reservations—those who hadn't been wiped out, that was.

Fargo would hate to see the same thing happen to the prairies and mountains he loved so much. Were it up to him, he'd have a great wall built like the one he had heard about in China, a wall stretching along the west bank of the muddy Mississippi from Canada clear down to Mexico. Emigration from the States would dry to a trickle, and the West could go on being as it always had been.

Chico was speaking. "Better be careful when you ride out, *amigo*. I would not put it past that big ox and his *compañeros* to lie in wait and ambush you."

Neither would Fargo. "I'll keep my eyes skinned." He always did. It was one of the reasons he was still alive. He'd learned at an early age that all it took to become wolf bait was a moment's carelessness.

They made small talk until Fargo pushed back his plate and stood. "If I eat another bite I'll bust a gut. Tell your wife she should move to Denver and open her own fancy restaurant. You'd be rich inside a year."

"She is a great cook, is she not? But then, she has had a lot of practice. Eleven kids eat a lot of food."

"As much as those doves upstairs?"

"You poke fun at me, but I tell you, no one eats as much as a hungry whore unless it is another hungry whore."

Fargo paid his bill and shook Chico's hand. "If I make it back this way again I'll be sure to stop by."

"You better. Rosita will be anxious to show you she can work the same magic with *tamales* and *atole*."

Rested and well fed, Fargo emerged into the harsh glare of the afternoon sun. The Ovaro was dozing. So were half the horses in sight, as well as a sizeable percentage of the adult population. Down the street at the blacksmith's the two prairie schooners were parked. Their owners were nowhere to be seen.

Unwrapping the reins, Fargo forked leather. He was almost to the end of town when a sharp shout drew his attention to an alley between a general store and an adobe house. A lithe figure in a plain buckskin dress was in full flight, with a clerk from the store in angry pursuit.

"Stop, thief! Bring those back!"

The middle-aged clerk was no match for the culprit and gave up before he reached the far end. Turning back, his eyes on the ground, the clerk was so caught up in muttering to himself, he nearly blundered into the stallion.

"My word! I didn't see you there."

"What did she take?" Fargo inquired.

"You saw her, did you?" The clerk muttered some more. "She stole a bottle of Professor Flegalman's Celebrated Cure-all Bitters and Essence of Life. I noticed right away that she was acting nervous, and kept glancing at me out of the corner of her eyes." The clerk was one of those who could talk the ears off a politician. "She picked up every bottle of patent medicine in stock. Reading the labels, I reckon, so she must be well educated. Strange, isn't it? I never had an Indian steal from me before. Say what folks will about them, they're as honest as the day is long. Well, except the Apaches. They're the trickiest devils this side of Purgatory. Why, I've heard—"

Fargo guided the Ovaro past him into the alley.

"Are you going after her, mister? Better be careful. She might have a buck with her. And if they're desperate enough to steal, could be they're desperate enough to kill."

A thought struck Fargo and he drew rein and twisted. "How much for the medicine?"

"Huh? You want to pay for it? Whatever for?"

"I know that girl," Fargo said, which was an exaggeration. He had seen her only once, and then only briefly.

The clerk shook his head. "There's no need. I'm not about to complain to the Army over one measly bottle." He turned to go inside. "Besides, I figure if she needed it so badly she has to steal it, someone must be feeling awful poorly. Hell, if she'd asked, I'd probably have let her have it. On credit, of course. I'm not one of those who dislikes Indians on general principle, like some folks I could mention."

The alley opened onto thick brush. Although the ground was dry and hard-packed, the Pima's tracks were plain. She had been running, and the slap of her moccasins had left clear impressions in the dust. Fargo brought the Ovaro to a trot. In a quarter of a mile, when the girl had been convinced no one was after her, she had slowed and entered a dry wash that ran from north to south. Her tracks pointed north. In another hundred feet she'd left the wash, jogging east.

Fargo rose in the stirrups but didn't spot her, so he halted. She couldn't have gotten that far; she had to be somewhere close. His hunch was confirmed a few moments later when he heard her voice. Dismounting, he shucked the Henry from its scabbard and advanced as quietly as a Comanche on a moonlit raid.

The Pimas were in a hollow. The boy was on his back in the shade of a shoulder-high boulder, while the girl was on her knees next to him, trying to get some of the patent medicine down his throat. She was tenderly coaxing him in their language but he wouldn't cooperate. He just lay there, his blank eyes fixed on the sky.

"What's wrong with him?" Fargo asked.

The Pima girl spun, fear lighting her bright eyes. Recognition flared, and she blurted in English, "You again!"

Fargo walked down the incline. "The clerk isn't going to report you for the theft. I offered to pay him but he wouldn't accept any money."

"Why would you do that for us?" the girl demanded. A wary uneasiness had replaced her fear. She was like a doe that wanted to bolt but wouldn't leave a stricken fawn.

"I've spent a lot of time among Indians," Fargo said, and let it go at that. Now that he had time to study her up close, he saw that she was older than he'd thought—twenty, maybe twenty-two. Her breasts, though small, jutted like ripe melons against her buckskin dress. He had to stop himself from thinking about them, and asked, "What's wrong with him? Is he hurt from the beating he took?"

"Culazol was like this before the big white-eye caught us taking bread," the girl said. "I would not have done it but we were starved and my brother was weak."

"You're both a long way from Pima country," Fargo remarked. It was well to the west, past the mountain haunts of several Apache bands.

A wistful look came over her. "I would give anything to be back among our people. Our parents made a mistake in leaving."

The boy's arm moved at this juncture, and the girl immediately bent and cradled his head on her legs. "Culazol? Culazol? It is Lieta, your sister. Please speak to me."

Her brother's face was a blank slate.

Introducing himself, Fargo hunkered. "I'm no doctor but I've tended sick and wounded before." He felt

Culazol's forehead, then pressed his thumb against the boy's wrist, over the veins. "He doesn't have a temperature and his heartbeat is steady."

"There has been no change since we were attacked by outlaws," Lieta said, mirroring deep sorrow.

"Maybe you'd better start at the beginning."

It was a few seconds before Lieta complied, her voice husky with strained emotion. "Two winters ago a new missionary came among us: Reverend Winslow. He converted my father and mother to the white man's religion, and my father and he became friends. A moon ago, when the reverend was told to start a new church in Las Cruces, he asked my parents to go along."

That struck Fargo as strange, and he said as much.

"The reverend thought it would help convert Navajos and others if they met Indians who had given up the old ways. He called my father and mother his 'sterling examples to heathens everywhere.' "

"You didn't see it that way?" Fargo commented.

"I am not white. I am Pima. The ways of my people are my ways, not the ways of Reverend Winslow." Lieta looked at him. "I will never understand why my father let himself be baptized. Mother did it only because he did. Secretly, she still believed in our own religion."

"How does all this account for your brother?"

Lieta's eyes welled with tears. "Five sleeps ago Reverend Winslow asked us to go with him to visit a band of Navajos. We never got there. Nine men came out of the hills and stopped our buckboard. They wanted money, and when the reverend told them all he had was a few dollars, they became angry."

"Any idea who these men were?"

"As they were riding up, Reverend Winslow told us to sit very still and not say anything. He called them the Thornton gang. Five white men and four Mexicans. Their leader was an ugly man with one cheek missing and a bent nose as flat as an arrowhead."

Pike Thornton, Fargo recollected, had been kicked by a horse years ago and severely disfigured. It was said one look at his face was enough to give the faint of heart nightmares.

Lieta had gone on. "The ugly one climbed down, pulled Reverend Winslow off the seat, and beat him. My father stood up to help the reverend and Thornton drew a pistol and shot him. When my mother screamed, he shot her. My brother tried to catch her as she fell, and Thornton hit him with his gun barrel." Lieta touched a spot on Culazol's temple, near the ear. "That night when he opened his eyes, he was as you see him now."

"I'm surprised Thornton didn't finish him off," Fargo said. And kill her, as well.

"He would have, I think. But he saw me holding my father, and he started to climb into the buckboard with that gleam in his eyes men have when they want a woman." Lieta stopped and shuddered.

"If you'd rather not say any more—"

"No. It is all right. Nothing happened. Reverend Winslow stood up and called down the wrath of the white Lord on their heads. He said if they touched me, they would burn in hellfire forever."

Fargo couldn't see that discouraging an animal like Pike Thornton.

"The ugly one laughed. But one of the Mexicans said it was not right to abuse a man of God. He said they had done enough harm, and they should go."

"How did Thornton take that?"

"He was mad. He cursed the Mexican. They had their hands on their guns, and I thought they would shoot one another. But another Mexican agreed with the one called Cipriano, and Thornton said 'To hell with it' and they rode off."

The Pima girl had been incredibly lucky, Fargo reflected. If not for this Cipriano, she would have been brutally raped, perhaps repeatedly. "You didn't stay with the minister, I take it."

Lieta was a while in answering. "He is a good man, but with my mother and father dead, I had no reason to stay. I want to go home. I want to be among my own people."

Fargo didn't blame her. "So you struck off on your own with your brother in the shape he's in?"

"I thought it would pass and he would be his normal self again. But he will not speak, will not move, unless I take him by the hand and lead him. I was afraid to leave him alone, even to hunt for food. When I saw the wagons, I made a mistake and tried to steal some. For that I am sorry." Lieta tenderly lowered her brother's head to the ground. "But the big white-eye should not have beaten him. It was not right."

Fargo took the bottle of patent medicine from her hand. Like most, the gaudy label boasted that the concoction could cure just about every ailment under the sun. "For diseases of the heart, stomach, kidneys, liver, and bowels," he read aloud. "Effective for fever of the brain, colic, nervous disorders, and menstrual cramps. Will also kill lice and their nits."

"I thought it might help Culazol," Lieta said. "I remembered the store from when the reverend took us to Mesilla."

"There's only one thing this stuff is good for." Removing the cap, Fargo upended the contents.

Lieta reached for it but drew her hand back. "I do not know why, but I trust you. So tell me. What *will* help my brother?"

"He needs a doctor. There's one at Fort Fillmore, which is where I'm headed."

"The army post? Why would they help a couple of Indians?"

"Because you need it," Fargo said simply. "I'll fetch

34

my horse and we can head out." He stood, and she did likewise. But as she straightened, her eyelids fluttered and she swayed, and she would have fallen if he hadn't caught her. "When was the last time you ate?"

"Three sleeps ago I killed a small snake."

"That's it? Then we're not going anywhere until you and your brother are strong enough to travel." Fargo eased her down. "Stay put and rest." Their eyes met, and Lieta smiled and squeezed his wrist. He could still feel the soft pressure as he hastened out of the hollow.

Retrieving the Ovaro, Fargo removed his saddlebags. In one was a bundle of pemmican. "Here. Eat your fill." He gave her a handful, but she gave no thought to her own hunger. Instead, bending over him, Lieta forced her brothers lips apart.

"Please, Culazol, chew this."

The boy stared right through her, his mouth unmoving.

"Let me get a fire going," Fargo proposed. "I think I know how we can get some food into his belly."

Tears again rimmed Lieta's eyes. "I will be grateful. I cannot bear to lose him, too." She bowed her chin. "I wish my father never brought us here."

"Eat some of that pemmican," Fargo urged. "You'll feel better." Taking his coffeepot from his other saddlebag, he hiked toward a line of cottonwoods. Beyond flowed the Rio Grande, which looped eastward just north of Mesilla and then curved south again. He had filled the pot and was climbing back up the bank when fate smiled on them. A rabbit was nibbling grass not fifty yards away. He downed it with one shot.

Lieta was sleeping the sleep of total exhaustion when Fargo returned. As quietly as he could, he collected firewood and started a fire. He filled a large pan with some of the water and put it and the coffeepot on to boil. Skinning and butchering the rabbit took only a few minutes. Presently, the delicious aroma of boiling stew and percolating coffee laced the air.

Fargo stripped his saddle and saddle blanket from the stallion and tethered the pinto to a picket pin. Not that it would ever wander off. He did it to make it that much harder for any Apaches who happened by to indulge their fondness for horse stealing.

The sun was well on its downward arc when Fargo shook Lieta to awaken her. He had to try several times before she stirred. Sitting up, she sleepily sniffed a few times, then scooted to the pan and licked her lips in anticipation. "How soon will it be done?"

Fargo produced his battered tin plate and a spoon. "It's done now." He ladled a heaping portion and sat back, watching her devour it with wolfish intensity. She was so famished, she didn't look up until she had scraped the plate clean. She saw him watching her, and blushed, but whether from embarrassment or some other emotion, he couldn't say. "Feeling a little better?"

"Very much so, thank you."

Accepting the plate, Fargo began to fill it again. "For someone who isn't fond of white ways, you speak our tongue better than most whites."

"I learned at the missionary school. Of all the students, my grades were always the highest." Lieta said it with a touch of pride.

"You have a knack." Fargo envied those who had a natural aptitude for learning new languages. He always had to work hard at it.

"Permit me," Lieta requested when he moved toward her brother, and snatched the plate and spoon. Dipping the latter into the thick broth, she let the liquid trickle between Culazol's parted lips. His throat bobbed, and for the first time since Fargo met them, he saw the boy's eyes blink.

"Did you see?" Lieta exclaimed.

Fargo examined Culazol's temple for a wound or swelling but found neither. The blow had done inter-

36

nal damage of some kind. It was important the boy be checked by a sawbones, and soon.

Turning to pour himself a cup of coffee, Fargo heard the Ovaro nicker. The pinto had raised its head and was gazing toward the Rio Grande with its ear pricked.

The Henry in hand, Fargo moved to the rim. At first he saw nothing to account for the stallion's alarm. Then a line of riders materialized to the north, paralleling the river on the near side of the vegetation. He counted nine, and when they were closer, he was able to tell that five were whites. Sombreros, *calzoneras*, and Spanish-style saddle rigs pegged the remaining four as Mexicans.

The lead rider happened to gaze toward the hollow. His face, even at that distance, was hideous—the kind that would terrify small children.

Only one person in the whole territory had a face like that.

"Damn," Fargo said. But he wasn't overly concerned. The trees were a good fifty yards away. His fire wasn't giving off any smoke, and the outlaws couldn't see the Ovaro. Odds were they would ride on by, none the wiser.

Pike Thornton unexpectedly reined up and turned in the saddle to talk to an older Mexican with a gray-flecked beard. Thornton gestured at the trees. From the look of things, either he wanted to water and rest their dust-covered mounts, or else he was considering making camp early.

Fargo hoped they would just ride on.

A couple of their horses were staring toward the hollow. The breeze, Fargo realized with a start, was blowing in their direction, and the animals had caught wind of the Ovaro. They didn't whinny, though, and in another few seconds Pike Thornton shrugged and headed south again.

Smiling, Fargo let himself relax. But he did so too soon, for Lieta chose that moment to shout his name.

"Come see my brother! Culazol is sitting up on his own!"

3

Nine to one weren't odds to crow about. Add to that
the fact that the Pimas didn't have mounts and could
easily be chased down and slain, and it was easy to
understand why Skye Fargo didn't want the outlaws
to come any closer. When they wheeled their horses
and started toward the hollow, he sprang into the open
and trained his rifle on Pike Thornton. "That's far
enough!"

Thornton and the others reined up. A few dropped
hands to their hardware but no one wanted to be the
first to draw as they all knew that whoever did was
bound to be the first one shot.

"Keep on riding."

Pike Thornton placed his hands on his saddle horn.
"That ain't very neighborly of you, friend."

"I'm not your neighbor and I'm sure as hell not
your friend," Fargo retorted. He heard footsteps coming up the slope behind him and said quickly but quietly so only Lieta would hear, "Stay down! We don't
want them to know you're here."

"Who is it?" she whispered. "I've heard that voice
before."

It wouldn't do Fargo any good to lie. He had to
hope she wouldn't let the deaths of her parents cloud
her judgement. "It's Thornton's bunch. If he sees you
he might decide to take up where he left off."

Pike Thornton had the eyes of a hawk. "Who are
you talking to there, stranger? Got some friends hid,
do you?"

Fargo sighted down the Henry. He wanted dearly to squeeze the trigger but if he did it would stir the others into attacking and he couldn't guarantee the safety of Lieta and her brother. "I won't tell you again."

"Sure, mister, sure." But judging by the look on Thornton's travesty of a face, he didn't like it, not one bit. "We'll mosey right along." He motioned to the others and reined to the south. They went about twenty yards, then abruptly turned into the trees.

Fargo hopped into the hollow and crouched. Lieta was staring after the outlaws, her whole head above the rim. Grabbing her by the shoulder, he hauled her back down. "I told you not to show yourself."

Pimas were reputed to be the most peace-loving Indians on the planet, but no one would know it by the hatred Lieta radiated. "Why didn't you shoot? You could have killed him but you didn't!"

Fargo glanced at her brother. Culazol had sat up and was staring at them with eyes only slightly less blank than they had been before. "I couldn't guarantee I could protect the two of you from his friends."

Lieta softened and sheepishly rested her hand on his. "I am sorry. Anger clouded my thinking. You were right to put my brother's welfare before all else."

"And yours," Fargo stressed. He was rewarded with a faint pinkish tinge in both her cheeks. "But we're not out of danger. They didn't leave."

"How can you be sure? I cannot see them."

"I'm sure." Just as Fargo was positive that once the sun went down, the outlaws would encircle the hollow and sneak in close to pick him off. "We can't stay here."

"You go on alone," Lieta advised. "By yourself you can escape. We would slow you down too much, and my brother and I do not want your death on our conscience."

Her brother, Fargo refrained from pointing out, was

in no shape to care. "We're leaving together and that's that." They had an hour or more of daylight left—plenty of time to prepare. "Keep watch while I saddle my horse. Give a holler if they show themselves." He started toward the bottom but stopped when she grasped his wrist.

"Thank you."

Their eyes met again, and Fargo smiled. "You can thank me proper if we all make it out of this alive." Which, at that point, remained to be seen. After hastily throwing on his saddle and tightening the cinch, he wolfed a plate of stew and downed two cups of black coffee. Culazol watched him with interest, much as a two-year-old would. It was an improvement, but not much.

"I see men moving!" Lieta excitedly whispered.

Fargo was by her side in a flick of the pinto's tail. Shadowy shapes were fanning out through the underbrush. Thornton was an impatient cuss, but Fargo still believed they wouldn't try anything before dark. "I'll keep watch now. Try and get more food into your brother. He'll need it."

For a while all was still. Then Fargo noticed several branches high in a tree shaking as if to a strong wind—only there wasn't a lick of breeze. He scanned the foliage and spied a Mexican peering back. Instantly the gunman slid around to the other side of the trunk and shimmied to the bottom like an oversized squirrel. Now the outlaws knew the girl was there, if they hadn't already.

Culazol was chewing on his own but Lieta still had to spoon-feed him. Every now and then he would move his head, another encouraging sign.

Half the sun was gone when Fargo hurried to the bottom. "Gather up all the grass and weeds you can find and make a pile." He had an idea but he had to time it just right or it wouldn't work. He stuffed the pan, plate, and spoon into his saddlebags but he held off with the coffeepot. It was half full, more than enough for his purpose.

The shadows lengthened as the sun gradually relinquished its aerial throne to encroaching twilight. Lieta had a knee-high pile and was scouring for more when Fargo told her that was enough. "Give me a hand with your brother."

Together they hoisted Culazol into the saddle. He wanted to sit up straight but Fargo had Lieta bend him low over the saddle and keep him there. Then he ran to the rim for another look-see. Some of the outlaws were visible, readying for the rush.

Fargo returned to the Pimas. "Your turn, Lieta."

"What about you?"

"I'll have hold of the reins until we make it into the trees. After that, we'll see." Fargo gripped her waist. For a moment their bodies touched and her hair brushed his face. He breathed deep of her womanly scent, his manhood twitching like a Thoroughbred eager to be quirted out the starting gate. Then he swung her up and the moment passed.

Fargo watched the western sky. When the twilight deepened to purple and he could barely see the rim, he kicked the pile of grass and weeds onto the fire. Wisps of smoke bloomed, giving birth to fingers of flame. The fingers became fiery swords. At that crucial moment Fargo poured the coffee onto the blaze, smothering it, and in the process created a thick cloud of smoke that rapidly expanded to fill the hollow.

Swiftly, Fargo shoved the empty coffeepot into his saddlebags. A faint breeze had arisen, and the smoke cloud was drifting to the southeast. He moved with it, leading the pinto and whispering to the Pimas, "Take small breaths and try not to cough," which was easier said than done.

They came to the crest. Fargo couldn't see his hand at arm's length, which was exactly how he wanted it. The breeze pushed the cloud toward the river and he went with it, moving slowly although his every instinct was to do the opposite.

To their left, boots thudded, and Pike Thornton hollered, "They have to be in this smoke somewhere! Find them!"

More feet thumped the earth, and to Fargo's right a dark outline appeared amid the smoke—the outline of a man with a drawn revolver. They spotted each other at the same split second. Fargo fired first, from the hip. The Henry boomed and bucked and the figure was knocked back into the smoke as if kicked by a Missouri mule.

"They're over here!" someone bawled.

Hauling on the reins, Fargo broke into a run. A gun cracked several times but none of the slugs came close.

"Watch where you're spraying lead, damn it!" Thornton roared. "Those shots almost nailed me!"

Too bad they didn't, Fargo thought. His right heel snagged on something and he nearly fell. It was a small bush. Near it was a tree. They had reached the vegetation but they weren't safe. He angled to the south, walking faster, anxious to get out of the smoke. Culazol picked that moment to have a coughing fit.

"Over here, you jackasses!" an outlaw yelled.

"Over where?" responded another. "I can't see a damn thing!"

Someone shouted in Spanish, "This *gringo* is most clever!" then laughed, as if being outfoxed were hilarious.

A tree limb pierced the gloom and Fargo ducked barely in time. Veering wide, he steered the Pimas clear. The boy started coughing again and Lieta put a hand over his mouth in a vain effort to stifle the noise.

Brush crackled to the passage of a hurtling form. "This way! This way! I can see them!"

Fargo saw the gunman, too: a tall drink of water in chaps and a leather vest, holding a Sharps rifle. The outlaw banged off a shot and a leaden hornet fanned

43

Fargo's ear. He answered in kind. His shot cored the man's shoulder and spun him halfway around. Fargo levered in another round to finish the killer off but the smoke thickened and he couldn't see him.

Drawn by the racket, other outlaws were rapidly converging. Fargo was about to slap the Ovaro on the flank and send it galloping off with the Pimas when a horse whinnied close at hand, and in a few more steps he came up on the outlaws' horses. They had been left with their reins dangling, and the smoke and uproar was making them skittish.

Snagging the reins to a claybank, Fargo wheeled, grabbed Culazol, and switched him from one animal to the other. The boy glanced about in wide-eyed confusion, his fingers entwined in the claybank's mane. Lieta began to climb down but Fargo grabbed her and in a twinkling had her behind her brother. "Hold on to him," he directed, thrusting the reins into her palm.

A rifle barked and a slug splatted against a branch.

Gripping the Ovaro's saddle horn, Fargo vaulted onto the hurricane deck. He went to race off, then saw a panicked look on Lieta's face. "What's wrong?" he asked, conscious that any moment might be their last.

"I have never ridden a horse before."

Fargo had forgotten. The Pimas were a poor people. They lived in simple dwellings and tilled small plots of land. Their possessions were few. Owning a horse was practically unheard of. They went everywhere on foot.

The rifle cracked again. So did a pistol, the shots uncomfortably near.

Lunging, Fargo caught hold of the claybank's reins with the same hand in which he was holding the Henry, cried "Hang on!" and trotted southward. He'd wanted to scatter the other mounts but he dared not delay.

"They're gettin' away!" Thornton sounded furious. "After them!"

A glance revealed several outlaws already at the horses. One paused to fan his revolver but all he did was waste lead.

Fargo had gone from the smoke into the frying pan. With the claybank burdened as it was, there was no hope of outdistancing their pursuers. And with the Pimas such inexperienced riders, there was a very real chance one or both would take a spill if they weren't almighty careful. He summed up his appraisal of the situation with a vehement "Damn!"

The sun had been completely swallowed by the horizon and night was falling fast. Fargo concentrated on avoiding obstacles and hoped to high heaven the Pimas held on. The undergrowth was heavy enough that if he could gain ground on the outlaws, he could lose them.

Then the claybank began to lag. Every outlaw mount had appeared worn out from long hours on the go, and the claybank's stamina was at a low ebb. Fargo firmed his grip on the reins but that was a temporary solution. Exhaustion, in man or beast, could not long be denied.

Out of the deepening murk reared a stand of saplings, their slim boles so close together Fargo was forced to rein from a trot to a brisk walk. Threading through them was akin to threading through a maze. It didn't help that the claybank constantly balked. Fargo lost precious time. As he came out the far side he heard the outlaws entering the other.

To Fargo's left high weeds flanked the Rio Grande. Coming to a halt, he leaped down, lowered Lieta and her brother to the ground, then gave the claybank a slap that sent it trotting off in the direction in which they had been going.

"Bring your brother," Fargo instructed Lieta, and

45

with the Ovaro in tow, he barreled into the weeds and on down a short bank to the river.

Hooves thundered west of them. Fargo hiked the Henry but held his fire as a knot of riders raced after the claybank. With any luck it would be a while before they caught up and discovered they had been tricked.

"We're safe!" Lieta whispered.

"Not by a long shot." Fargo plucked at her sleeve and headed north. "Keep close and don't let that brother of yours make a sound."

"Why are we going back the way we came?"

"Because it's the last thing they'll expect. While they're searching the country south of here, we'll circle around to Mesilla and I'll rent a room for the night." Fargo doubted Thornton would risk coming into town. The killer was a wanted man, his likeness plastered from Texas to California.

"Stay in a hotel?" Lieta made it sound as if he had proposed they camp out on the moon.

"What's wrong with that?" Fargo rejoined, one ear cocked for sounds.

"I have never slept in a white man's bed. I have heard they are too soft, and they make a person weak and sluggish. I would rather—"

Fargo silenced her by thrusting a hand over her mouth. Voices wafted through the trees; among them, that of the scourge of the territory. And from the sound of things, he wasn't in a pleasant frame of mine.

"Stay here and keep your brother quiet," Fargo whispered into Lieta's ear. He didn't have far to go. In the clearing where the outlaw mounts had been were Thornton, the Mexican with the gray beard, another white on horseback, and two men on the ground. One was dead. The other was the gunman Fargo had shot in the shoulder.

Thornton was raving: "—like a passel of chickens with their heads cut off! Two Injuns and some jackass

46

in buckskins, and they slip away right under our noses!"

"The others will catch them," the gunman on horseback declared.

"I wouldn't be so sure," said the Mexican. "That business with the smoke was clever. A man that shrewd will not be taken easily."

Thornton spun. "Leave it to you, Cipriano, to always look at the dark side. There are times when you're mighty tiresome, old man. A word to the wise, if you savvy me."

Cipriano had been lounging against an oak. Now he unfurled and said menacingly, "Was that a threat, *gringo*? Any time you think you are faster than me— you are welcome to shut me up—if you can."

"Who are you trying to kid?" Pike Thornton snarled. "You're past your prime, Mex. That's why you're hiding out north of the border. All those young *pistoleros* willing to gun you down for your rep down Mexico-way have you plumb scared."

"One day you will cross the line," Cipriano said.

The wounded man had been listening in rising impatience. "Will you two quit your damn bickering for two minutes and have someone bandage this wound before I bleed to death? I can't do it myself."

"Quit your bellyaching, Dinsdale," Thornton said. "You act as if you've never been plugged before."

Fargo slowly backed away. They would be there awhile yet, which would give him the opportunity he needed. He crept to where he had left the stallion and the Pimas, and couldn't credit his senses. They were gone! Bewildered, he cast about in the reeds for sign but it was too dark. A sudden snort to the south brought him around with his finger on the trigger but it was only a buck he had spooked.

Fargo reasoned it out. The Pimas wouldn't try to cross the Rio Grande in the dark. And they hadn't gone west or he would have spotted them. That left

north. He jogged over twenty-five yards and was beginning to think he must be wrong when the Ovaro
loomed as large as a buffalo.

"Skye? Is that you?" Lieta was fearfully clutching
both the reins and her brother, whose cheek was on
her shoulder.

"What got into you, leaving like that?" Fargo demanded more harshly than he'd intended. "I told you
not to budge."

"I heard something in the underbrush and was
afraid they had found us."

The buck, Fargo guessed, then was taken aback
when the girl released Culazol and pressed against
him, her fingers on either side of his neck. Until that
moment he hadn't appreciated how scared she was.
The loss of her parents, having to fend for her brother,
stranded in a strange new territory—they all must be
taking a toll. He stroked her hair. "Let's keep going.
It's a long way to town yet."

The night was quiet. The gunfire had cowed all the
coyotes, owls, and other creatures of the wild into
silence.

Fargo stopped frequently to look and listen but all
he heard was the sigh of the wind. The route he chose
would bring them out on the main road well north of
Mesilla. Culazol was walking on his own but much too
slowly; he shuffled along like a five-year-old. To speed
things along, Fargo once more swung him onto the
Ovaro. He offered to do the same for Lieta but she
said she would rather walk.

Under other circumstances, Fargo would have enjoyed a starlit stroll with a beautiful woman at his side.
As it was, now and then he found himself dwelling on
how well she filled out her dress and how soft her hair
had been to his touch. Each time, he derailed his train
of thought to concentrate on the matter at hand.

They had covered about half the distance to Mesilla

when Lieta cleared her throat and asked, "Is it safe to talk?"

"It should be." Fargo hadn't seen or heard any sign of the outlaws since they'd left the Rio Grande.

"I am puzzled. Twice now you have come to the aid of my brother and me, putting your life at risk. Yet you hardly know us." Lieta looked at him. "I would like to know why."

"Whites have a saying. Maybe you've heard it." Fargo saw some lights to the southwest that had to be the town. "Never look a gift horse in the mouth."

"Do not think poorly of me. I just want to understand. Few of your kind would do as you are doing. Many whites do not like my people. Or Indians in general. You are a mystery I cannot solve."

"Don't make more out of it than there is. I saw a man beating up a kid, so I stopped it. I'd have done the same no matter what color the kid was." Fargo seldom gave much thought to why he did the things he did. Usually, it just seemed right at the time. "As for saving your hide back at the hollow, Thornton's outfit would just as soon have gunned me down as you and your brother."

"You ask me not to make too much out of it," Lieta said, "and in the next breath you make too little. You are an unusual white man, Skye Fargo."

"Maybe that's your answer. I don't see people as red or white or black. I just see them as people."

"Then you are more remarkable than you know. Most whites—and, I must admit, most of my own kind—see only as deep as the color of a person's skin."

Fargo shrugged. "There are more like me than you imagine. You just haven't met them yet."

"The missionaries told us all men are brothers, and said they want white and red to live together in peace and harmony. Yet their idea of harmony is for the red man to become white. To adopt the white religion and take up white ways. For all their fine talk, they are no different than those who hate us. They cannot see past the color of our skin, and would change it to match their own." Lieta frowned. "I refuse to be something I am not. I refuse to live in a way not my own. Is that so wrong?"

Fargo thought of his own life: of his endless wanderlust; of always wanting to see what lay over the horizon; of all the women, and the whiskey, and his fondness for cards. Shameless vices, some folks would call them, and brand him a sinner and a scoundrel. But it was how he liked to live his life, and he would be damned if he would change to suit those who walked around with their noses in the air. "No, it's not wrong."

Warm fingers enfolded Fargo's free hand. "There is something you should know, Lieta. When my work at the fort is done I'll be moving on."

"What is your point? As soon as my brother is up to it, we are going back to our own people."

"Just so we understand each other."

Fargo suddenly halted. South of them rose the drum of hooves. Riders were heading west toward Mesilla.

"It must be Pike Thornton," Lieta said with a touch of anxiety.

"Or some of his men. Maybe he's figured out we'll try for town and sent them to stop us."

"What will we do?"

"Exactly what we're doing." Fargo didn't feel they were in any immediate danger. But from then on he exercised more caution, his senses strained to their limits, and didn't say another word until they came over a low rise onto a strip of ground that was a welter of ruts and hoofprints. "It's the road."

At that hour no one else was abroad. It wasn't considered safe to do much traveling after dark, an outlook Fargo didn't share since Apaches and Navajos rarely attacked at night.

On a trip back East a couple of years earlier, Fargo had learned it was the same thing there. Except for those in big cities, people generally stayed indoors late at night. So maybe it wasn't fear of the Apaches so much as it was fear of the dark that left roads like this one empty.

Most whites would have been amazed to have found out that most Indians were the same. The Blackfeet, the Cheyenne, the Crows—they all preferred the safety of their villages once the sun went down. In many other respects white and red were a lot more alike than they were willing to admit.

Fargo bent his steps toward town. It had been a long day and he was looking forward to some rest. And possibly something else, should Lieta prove willing and they could be alone for a while.

Out of the blue she turned to him and asked, "Are you sure it will be all right for us to stay at the hotel?"

"Why wouldn't it be?"

"Some white establishments do not allow Indians inside. They have signs in the window saying NO RED-SKINS ALLOWED."

"I didn't see any signs like that in Mesilla." And if the hotel did have one, Fargo would persuade them to make an exception in his case. Whether they wanted to or not.

Hooves drummed again. The riders were much closer than before, and coming directly toward them.

"Hide!" Fargo said, and veered toward the brush bordering the west side of the road.

"Too late!" Lieta cried.

That it was. Nine or ten horsemen swept out of the darkness. In a span of heartbeats Fargo and the Pimas were completely surrounded—the center of a ring of leveled carbines—and one of the night riders declared, "What do we have here?"

4

Practice made perfect. In Skye Fargo's case, he could draw and fire his Colt in the blink of an eye, so he could easily have shot four or five of the riders before they cut him down. Instead, he held his hands out from his sides to show he wouldn't resist, for even in the dark their uniforms were plain to see. The rattle of accouterments added proof the men were exactly what they appeared to be: soldiers.

A young lieutenant with his hand on a saber nudged his mount closer. "Who are you, sir? And why are you skulking about in the dead of night with a pair of Apaches?"

"Pimas," Fargo corrected him.

A grizzled trooper wearing the insignia of a sergeant major also moved his mount forward, his eyes widening in wonder. "Begorra! Can't it be? Here we thought we might have caught us some hostiles, and it's the lord of the wild manor himself."

"How's that, Sergeant McDermott?" the lieutenant asked.

McDermott lowered his carbine and smiled down at Fargo. "This here tall drink of water, sir, is a card-playing, woman-chasing, whiskey-guzzling devil, and the only mother's son ever to drink me under the table, and that's a fact."

"You know this man, Sergeant?"

"I should hope to God I do, and proud I am of the acquaintance. We've whiled away many an evening. Fort Riley, Fort Laramie—he shows up all over the

52

place, like the bad seed he is." Laughing, Sergeant McDermott extended his right gauntlet. "How are you, boyo? Have you been keeping out of mischief?"

"I try," Fargo said, shaking his hand. He had met a lot of soldiers in his travels, but few he liked more than the burly Irishman.

"Like hell," McDermott said, grinning. "You've got wildness in your veins, and that's for sure, Skye Fargo, whether you'll be admitting to it or not."

"Fargo!" the young lieutenant exclaimed. "Not the scout Colonel Blanchard told us to be on the look-out for?"

Sergeant McDermott's neatly trimmed beard bobbed. "One and the same, Lieutenant Jurgenson, sir."

Jurgenson went as rigid as a ramrod. "Sling carbines!" he barked at his men. Dismounting, he stiffly offered his own hand, saying, "Lieutenant Jurgenson, Detachment H, Third Cavalry, at your service. If you're willing, I would be honored to have the privilege of escorting you and your friends to Fort Fillmore."

"I don't suppose you have a horse to spare for this lady and her brother?" Fargo requested.

At the mention of "lady," Jurgenson glanced quizzically at Lieta, then bawled, "Private Rickert, you will relinquish your mount and ride with Private Fleming. On the double, if you please."

While the switch was being made and Fargo was busy helping Culazol down and over to the cavalry horse, Jurgenson chattered on.

"Colonel Blanchard has been expecting you for days. He was worried something might have happened to you, what with the Apaches on the warpath and the Navajos acting up again. I swear, why our government doesn't just round them all up and ship them off to Florida is beyond me. How many more whites must die before Washington comes to its senses?"

Reminding himself that junior officers like Jurgenson were usually new to the frontier and as ignorant as newborns, Fargo commented, "I haven't seen any sign of hostiles, but I did have a run-in with Pike Thornton."

"The outlaw? I have standing orders to take him into custody so he can be turned over to civilian authorities for a proper trial and a proper hanging. Where did you encounter him?"

Without going into a lot of detail, Fargo related what had happened, and made special mention of the attack on the minister and the murder of Lieta's and Culazol's parents.

"Thornton beat a man of the cloth? What kind of depraved animals would do such a thing?" Jurgenson was more upset about that than about the deaths of the Pimas.

"The worst kind," Fargo said. Holding on to the cavalry mount's reins, he climbed onto the Ovaro. "Whenever you're ready."

Lieutenant Jurgenson insisted they ride at the head of the column with him. In due course the patrol passed through Mesilla, drawing curious stares from doorways and windows, and continued on the six miles to the post at a trot.

Fort Fillmore was typical of most in the territory. There was no palisade, and no fortifications to speak of other than a pair of cannon emplacements. The buildings, constructed of adobe and brick, were spread out around the perimeter of a central square where the troopers drilled daily. A long, low barracks and the mess hall were on one side, the officers' quarters and the sutler's on the other. Storehouses, a stable, and an armory made up the rest.

Lieutenant Jurgenson escorted Fargo and the Pimas to a small house reserved for the commander. Colonel Phil Blanchard was a seasoned, no-nonsense officer highly respected by his peers and well-liked by his men—which accounted for his presence at a crucial post like Fort Fillmore. The Army needed one of its best to maintain order in a land rife with violence and bloodshed.

Too much desk work had put excess pounds on Blanchard's waist, but otherwise he was a bulldog of a man with a salt-and-pepper mustache and thick gray sideburns. He greeted Fargo warmly, gripping him by the arms and declaring, "Thank God you've made it! I'm told you're the one man I can rely on to prevent another war."

Fargo's curiosity was piqued. But he held his tongue and filled Blanchard in about the Pimas. The colonel ordered Jurgenson to take them to the fort physician so Culazol could be examined.

Lieta was reluctant to go. Pulling Fargo aside, she whispered in his ear, "Are you sure it is safe?"

"No one will harm you," Fargo assured her. "And the doctor might be able to help your brother."

"Will we see you again?"

"As soon as I'm done here I'll head over to the infirmary." Fargo squeezed her hand and received a peck on the cheek.

Left alone on the porch with Blanchard, Fargo asked, "Now, what's this about a war?"

"Come inside, why don't you?" the colonel suggested. "Sometimes the night has ears."

Fargo was guided into a modest parlor where he was introduced to Blanchard's wife, a kindly woman with doleful eyes who brought him a cup of coffee and a biscuit, then politely excused herself.

"Now, then," Colonel Blanchard began, seated in a rocking chair across from the settee. "Let's get down to brass tacks, shall we? I sent for you because every officer I've consulted says you're the most capable man for the job."

Fargo bit into the biscuit, which Mrs. Blanchard had smeared with butter, and washed it down with some of her piping hot, sweetened coffee. There were definite benefits to tying oneself to a good woman. "What job would that be?"

"Ever heard of a butcher who calls himself General Machetazo?"

Fargo remembered his talk with Chico in the cantina. "Just today, as a matter of fact. Has he been causing you trouble?"

Colonel Blanchard had a habit of tugging at his sideburns when he was agitated, "Has he ever! The bastard has been skipping across the border into the U.S. whenever Mexican federal troops nip too close at his heels. Once they withdraw, he slinks on back into Mexico. Rumor has it he holes up somewhere in the mountains southwest of here, but so far we haven't been able to find out exactly where. That's where you come in."

The assignment sounded simple enough, and Fargo said so.

"There's more at stake than you realize," Blanchard stated. "You see, there are certain factions in our country who would dearly love an excuse to start another war with Mexico."

Fargo took a bite of biscuit. The last war, as he recalled, had ended a dozen years ago after a long and bitter conflict that had cost both sides thousands of lives. "Why would anyone want another war, when we won?" Mexico had been forced to give up California, Texas, New Mexico, and other parts of the Southwest. In the end the United States wound up with a third more territory than it had possessed at the outset.

"Some highly placed people, in both the military and the civilian sector, were unhappy with the terms. They thought the U.S. should take over Mexico—lock, stock, and barrel—and not just some of its territories."

"Make Mexico part of the United States?" Fargo had seldom heard anything so ridiculous. The Mexican people would rise up in rebellion, just as they had against Spain and a host of others.

"I can tell by your expression that you think it's as stupid as I do. Nevertheless, there was a lot of criticism from those who regard it as America's Manifest Destiny to take over control of the entire hemisphere. Eventually they want the United States to conquer Canada and South America, too."

"Why stop there?" Fargo said dryly. "What about the rest of the world?"

Blanchard chuckled, then promptly sobered. "There's another aspect to all this. I guess you're aware a number of Southern states have been threatening to secede from the Union over the slavery issue?"

Fargo nodded. It had been going on for half a dozen years now.

"The election of Abraham Lincoln has them fired up worse than ever. If they secede, no one knows what will happen. There could be all-out war between the North and the South. Which is why certain Southern interests wouldn't mind a clash with Mexico right about now. Our government can't fight two wars at the same time. If Lincoln is coerced into invading Mexico, he won't be able to stop the South from breaking away."

Long ago Fargo had decided he wanted nothing whatsoever to do with politics and politicians, who generally were as useless as tits on a bull. "It sounds like you're sitting on top of a powder keg."

"You don't know the half of it." Colonel Blanchard sighed. "I'm under pressure from several of the top brass in Washington to quit sitting on my duff, as one phrased it, and launch a full military campaign against Machetazo. They want me to chase him clear across the border if I have to."

"The Mexican government wouldn't like that."

"With good reason. They'd rightfully regard it as a

57

violation of their national sovereignty, and perhaps declare war on the U.S.—which is precisely what those urging me to invade Mexico want."

Fargo wouldn't care to be in the colonel's shoes. A single misstep could be disastrous—not only for Blanchard's career, but for the entire country.

"I've refused to give in to their demands. I prefer to catch Machetazo on our side of the border and avert a war; which brings us back to your part in this whole mess—the most important part of all." Blanchard was tugging on his sideburn as if fit to rip it off. "I need you to find Machetazo's lair and get word to me so I can take to the field and end this once and for all."

"It might be a while before he strays north of the border again," Fargo noted.

"He's already here." Blanchard grinned slyly. "I've been in secret contact with my counterpart south of the border, and for the past several weeks a Mexican regiment has been nipping at Machetazo's heels, driving him farther and farther north."

"And across the border into your lap." Fargo was impressed. The devious plan was worthy of an Apache.

"The challenge was to time it all out well in advance so when you got here, Machetazo already would be in hiding on U.S. soil."

"I bet you're a wizard at poker."

Blanchard seemed not to hear. "I can't stress the gravity of the situation enough. You'll not only be helping to stop Machetazo's slaughter of innocents, you'll be averting another war between our country and our neighbor to the south. And possibly preserving the Union, to boot."

"I'm happy to oblige," Fargo reiterated. "In return, I need a favor."

"Anything."

"It's the two Pimas. I'd like Lieta and Culazol to stay at the fort until this is over. The boy can use medical attention, and they'll be safe here until I'm free to take them back to their own people."

Colonel Blanchard smiled. "Is that all? Consider it done. I'll have them assigned to our guest quarters. They can eat at the mess and have the run of the post."

Fargo finished off the biscuit with one last bite, gulped the rest of the coffee, and set the china plate and cup on a small table next to the settee. "That's settled then. I'll head out at first light."

"I know it'll be like looking for a needle in a haystack. Those mountains are vast. And there's more than one range: the Peloncillos, the Hatchets, the Mongollons. Machetazo could be lying low in any of them."

"I'll find him. Now, if you'll point me to the infirmary?"

"Better yet, I'll walk you there."

It was at the northwest corner of the square, a long room lined with cots, the majority empty. The doctor, a Captain Hartman, took Fargo and Blanchard aside as soon as they entered. "I've completed my examination of the boy, and there's really not much I can do. Head wounds of the sort he sustained often result in trauma. Memory loss, either short or long term, is common."

Colonel Blanchard winked at Fargo. "You'll have to excuse the good doctor. He attended one of those elite Eastern schools and he never uses words of one syllable when words of four or more will do."

Hartman took the ribbing good-naturedly. "You're fortunate to have me, and you damn well know it, sir." He nodded at the cot where Culazol lay. Lieta was on a stool beside it, holding her brother's hand. "From what the girl has told me, the boy is showing marked improvement since he was struck. That's encouraging. I expect that, given time, he'll fully recover the use of his faculties."

"Have you told her yet?" Fargo asked.

"I was just about to when you arrived. You can do the honors, if you want. I have a corporal with a boil that needs lancing. So if you'll excuse me. . . ." Hartman hustled down the aisle to a soldier on another cot.

Fargo walked over to the Pimas. Lieta rose expectantly, while her brother studied him as if seeing him for the first time. "The doctor says Culazol will be his old self with time. All you have to do is be patient."

Beaming, Lieta impulsively hugged him, then quickly stepped back. "I cannot thank you enough for all you have done for us."

"Thank the colonel. He's putting us up until I can get you home."

Blanchard made light of his generosity. "Fighting hostiles is only part of my job. I'm also supposed to do what I can to foster relations with friendly tribes and there are none friendlier than the Pimas. Now, come. The three of you must be hungry. I'll have the cook rustle up some food and then show you to your quarters."

The mess hall was a surprise, and helped explain Blanchard's popularity with his men.

It was no secret Army food at frontier posts was notoriously bad. Army policy was in large part to blame, since it was standard practice to have the enlisted men take turns serving as cooks. Most, though, couldn't boil water, let alone prepare a decent meal. And it didn't help that all they had to work with was hardtack, beans, bacon, and flour. Occasionally low-grade beef was shipped in, but usually it arrived partly spoiled. So on most posts the meals were poor.

But not at Fort Fillmore. Colonel Blanchard had found a couple of enlisted men who worked as cooks before they joined up, and he assigned them to permanent mess duty. Then he arranged for a regular supply of game, courtesy of several local men who loved to hunt; and for regular shipments of vegetables and fruits, courtesy of the sutler; turning the Army's bland fare into meals fit to eat.

The enlisted men loved him for it. But Blanchard told Fargo he was doing only what any good officer would do. "Sickly, miserable soldiers can't perform well in combat. When I go up against the Apaches and Navajos, I want my men in top condition."

Lieta said little during supper. Several times Fargo caught her staring at him, and she always looked away. He ate his fill of venison, bread, potatoes, and pie. It might be a while before he enjoyed another such meal.

In an adobe building near Blanchard's house were four rooms set aside for visitors. They weren't much to boast of. Each had a bed, dresser and chair, wash basin, and spittoon. That was it. Colonel Blanchard offered to put the Pimas up in separate rooms but Lieta refused.

"I must be with my brother in case he needs me."

Fargo was given a room next to theirs. He tossed his saddlebags on the dresser, propped his Henry in a corner, and lay on his back, fully clothed. Dawn would arrive all too soon and he had a hard day in the saddle ahead. A forearm over his eyes, he drifted into dreamland. About an hour had gone by when light scratching at his door roused him from slumber. "Is someone there?" he demanded.

"Just me," Lieta whispered. "May I come in?"

Springing up, Fargo threw the bolt. "Is something wrong?"

"Not at all." Lieta brushed on by. She wouldn't meet his gaze and was wringing her hands together. "Thanks to you everything is fine. My brother has finally fallen asleep and shouldn't wake up until morning."

"I was catching some shut-eye myself." Fargo wasn't quite certain why she was there.

"I'm sorry. I wanted to see you before you leave."
Lieta stepped to the window and drew the plain
curtains.

"About what?"

Marching up to him, Lieta placed her hands on his
shoulders and molded her mouth to his in a kiss that
lingered for minutes. When she drew back, she was
smiling seductively, her eyes aglow with the kind of
look that a man who had just crossed a burning desert
would give a canteen.

"Oh." Fargo closed and bolted the door.

"I have been thinking of you a lot," Lieta revealed.
"Of how handsome you are, and how kind you have
been."

Fargo liked the direction their conversation was
leading. "What have you decided to do about it?"

"This."

The next kiss lasted longer than the first. Lieta
pressed flush against him, her fingers in his hair, her
breasts like ripe melons against his corded chest.
When Fargo eased her soft lips apart with the tip of
his tongue, she moaned deep in her throat and ground
her hips against him in simmering desire.

"Well, now," Fargo said huskily when she broke for
breath. "Keep this up and we're liable to get carried
away." He thought it would spark a grin but Lieta
had grown solemn.

"Were my mother still alive she would not agree
with what I am about to do. She taught me a woman
must give herself only to the man she takes as her
husband, and no other."

"Some people feel that way—" Fargo began, only
to have her place a finger to his lips.

"Hear me out. I do not think what I am about to
do is wrong even though I know we will never be
husband and wife. I do this because of the great fondness I have for you. I have never felt about a man as

I do about you. But it is not love. It is something different."

"I don't quite savvy," Fargo admitted, glad she hadn't fallen in love with him. He had meant what he said earlier about moving on once his job was done.

Lieta snuggled against him, nuzzling his neck. "I am not sure I understand, either. It is a new feeling, one hard to describe." She grinned self-consciously. "I have an urge to kiss you all over your body."

"There are worse urges," Fargo quipped.

Gripping him by the chin, Lieta said, "Listen to me. No one must ever hear of what we do here tonight. Promise me you will never tell another living soul as long as you live."

"Can I tell my horse?"

"I am serious." Lieta gave him a rough shake. "What we share must be our secret, and only ours. Agreed?"

Fargo had never been the gabby sort. A lot of people had a habit of chattering like chipmunks about every aspect of their lives but he wasn't one of them. His personal affairs were his own and no one else's. Taking her in his arms, he kissed her cheek and whispered in her ear, "Agreed."

Lieta melted like hot wax, hungrily fastening her mouth to his. Fargo cupped her pert bottom and kneaded her nether cheeks as if they were freshly rolled dough. Her hands were all over him, exploring his head, his shoulders, his chest, his back. Unbidden, the comment she had made about giving herself only to her husband intruded and he wondered if she was still a virgin. If so, she was making up for lost time. She sucked on his tongue, on his upper lip. She nibbled a path down over his jaw and around to his left ear. Inhaling his earlobe, she flicked and teased it with her moist tongue, her breath growing hotter by the second. It was she, not Fargo, who steered them to the bed, and she, not Fargo, who sank down, pulling him with her.

The hem of Lieta's dress slid up and Fargo helped it along, raising it above her knees. She had superbly muscled legs and incredibly smooth inner thighs. When he stroked them, she shivered deliciously and, pulling him closer, whispered, "Something tells me you have had a lot of experience with women."

"A little," Fargo allowed, unsure what she was fishing for.

Lieta inhaled him, her knees rising on either side of his hips. Her lips were wonderfully soft, her tongue liquid honey. Fargo slid his right hand up over her hip to her flat stomach and from there cupped a breast. Her nipple was as hard as a tack. When he pinched it she squirmed and panted.

Fargo eased onto his side and pried at her dress. He intended to hike it clear over her head but he had it only as high as her upper thighs when there was a loud thump on the wall that separated his room from the room she shared with her brother.

"Culazol!" Lieta exclaimed, sitting bolt upright. The thump was repeated, and she was off the bed in a flash. "Something must be wrong."

Fargo raced out after her, adjusting his shirt so it hid the bulge in his pants. Lieta barreled into the other room, and over her shoulder Fargo saw her brother curled against the wall, clutching a pillow in fright. He had woken up, found her gone, and panicked.

Lieta wrapped an arm around her sibling and soothed him. After a while he lowered his head to her lap and closed his eyes, as content as a kitten. "It hurts me terribly to see him like this," she remarked.

"Remember what the doctor said." Fargo leaned against the jamb.

"He cannot recover fast enough to suit me. I want my old brother back. The one who laughed all the time and liked to tease me." Lieta tenderly ran a hand over Culazol's temple. "When we are back to our village I will never leave it again. I have seen enough of the white man's world to last until I am an old woman."

It was obvious they weren't going to get to finish what she had started, so Fargo backed on out, saying, "I'll be gone before you wake up. If you need anything while I'm away, see Colonel Blanchard. He'll take good care of you."

"Skye?" Lieta called.

Fargo paused in the act of closing the door. "Yes?"

"I am sorry."

"So am I."

5

Skye Fargo rode out of Fort Fillmore before first light. He nodded at a yawning sentry, reined west, and applied his spurs. The cool morning air was refreshing but it wouldn't last. By noon the temperature would hover at the one hundred degree mark. In Fargo's saddlebags were some extra provisions, hardtack and bread provided by the cook. From his saddle horn hung not one but two canteens. Where he was bound he would need every drop.

Fargo had given a lot of thought to which direction to take. General Machetazo might be anywhere, and he had to narrow it down or give up any hope of success.

To the southwest were three mountain ranges, one after the other: the Hatchet Mountains, the Animas Mountains, and the Peloncillo Mountains. To the northwest reared the formidable Mongollon Range. North of the post lay the Mimbres Mountains. All made good hiding places; thousands of square miles of rugged, untamed wilderness, home to the scorpion and the rattlesnake, and to roving bands of marauding Apaches.

Fargo discounted the Mimbres right from the start. They were too near the fort and were routinely patrolled. He dropped the Hatchet Mountains from consideration for essentially the same reason. That left the Animas, Peloncillo, and Mongollon ranges. The first two extended down into Mexico. The Mongollons did not. And the way he saw it, anyone who wanted to sneak across the border without being spotted would choose a range that did.

The Animas range was smaller than the Peloncillo, so there was less area in which to hide. And much of it was on the near side of the Continental Divide rather than the far side, where troops were less likely to venture.

After working it all out in his head, Fargo had decided the Peloncillo Mountains were the likeliest. He rode all day with only brief stops to rest the Ovaro, and camped in an arroyo so his fire wouldn't attract hostile eyes.

Days two and three were more of the same. On the third, while crossing a desert basin, Fargo came upon some tracks. They were a month old and had been made by unshod horses. Apaches, Fargo guessed.

By the fifth day Fargo was in the Peloncillos. The vegetation had gone from cactus and yucca to mesquite and grama grass. He had his right hand on his Colt at all times and made it a point to frequently check behind him.

The key to finding Machetazo was water. Fargo had been through the Peloncillos before and knew the location of a few springs and tanks. None was large enough to indefinitely supply the needs of a hundred men—which was how many Colonel Blanchard estimated were in General Machetazo's self-styled army—not to mention all their mounts and pack animals.

Fargo had a hunch Machetazo must know of a special spot well back in the Peloncillos. Maybe one of the hidden valleys rumored to exist. To find it, first he had to find the trail Machetazo's army left. It shouldn't be difficult; more than a hundred horses would leave a lot of sign.

Three whole days of searching, though, turned up only a lot of game trails and a small spring. Fargo filed the location away in his memory in case he was ever back in that neck of the woods again. That night, having watered the stallion and picketed it, he lay under a multitude of stars and reflected on how best to continue his hunt. At the rate he was going, it could take weeks. He wondered if Colonel Blanchard were mistaken. Maybe General Machetazo was still south of the border.

The next day began no differently than the others. By noon Fargo and the Ovaro were caked with dust and sweating profusely. He drew rein on a ridge in the shade of an isolated stand of trees. Munching on jerky, he paced back and forth, his mind racing faster than an antelope. There had to be a way to find Machetazo without scouring every square inch of the Peloncillos. There just had to be.

Fargo had barely entertained the thought when thin columns of dust rose a quarter of a mile to the southwest. A string of riders was heading north. Ten men, all wearing sombreros. Even at that distance Fargo saw that every man had something long and black dangling from his hip: a machete sheath.

As the riders came abreast of the ridge, Fargo noticed something else. Their horses were dragging bushes tied to ropes, effectively erasing their own tracks as soon as they were made. That accounted for the columns of dust. And might account for why Machetazo's army was so hard to find.

Fargo put a hand over the Ovaro's muzzle to keep it from nickering. The Black Sheaths didn't spot him, and as soon as they were out of sight, he forked leather and shadowed them, staying far back.

At last Lady Luck had smiled on him. Fargo expected to find Machetazo's encampment by nightfall. A quick ride to the fort, and he would bring Blanchard and the Third Cavalry to mop things up. Then a week to escort the Pimas home, and he'd be free to do as he pleased.

The plumes of dust were easy to keep in sight. Fargo pulled his hat brim low against the sun and held the pinto to a walk. He had traveled about a mile when a troubling feeling came over him, a feeling he himself was being followed. Twisting, he saw nothing out of the ordinary.

Fargo rode on but couldn't shake the feeling. Half a dozen times he scoured the country behind him. Half a dozen times its emptiness mocked him. He tried to chalk it up to his imagination but he was fooling only himself. Living in the wild had instilled in him a heightened sense of danger. A sense he dared not disregard.

Whoever was stalking him was good. Extremely good. Fargo couldn't see it being more Black Sheaths. They were run-of-the-mill bandits posing as revolutionaries. Only someone with as much wilderness savvy as he possessed could avoid being seen. Someone as stealthy and elusive as a mountain lion.

It had to be Indians, but not just any old kind. It had to be Apaches. Fargo hadn't come across fresh sign but that didn't mean Apaches weren't around. They were masters at stealth, of moving like the wind. He speculated that maybe an Apache war party had been trailing the Black Sheaths all along, and he had blundered between them.

Fargo decided to put his idea to the test. Reining eastward, he skirted a hill. Once on the other side, he rode to within ten feet of the top, slid off, and crawled the rest of the way. Minutes dragged by but no one appeared. In the meantime the dust plumes grew smaller and smaller. The Black Sheaths were getting farther and farther away. He waited as long as he could, then climbed back on the Ovaro and held to a trot to make up for lost time and distance.

Fargo looked behind him again and again but the only signs of life were a rabbit that skittered off into the mesquite and a large hawk soaring high in the sky. "I must be getting skittish," he said to the stallion.

The afternoon waxed and waned. Fargo hung a mile

back from the Black Sheaths, who were making for a series of high peaks. They were deep in the Peloncillos, deeper than Fargo had ever gone. Trees took the place of grama grass. Wooded slopes became common.

The dust plumes vanished. Fargo learned why when he came to where the bushes the Black Sheaths had been dragging were strewn about. From then on he tracked them. Their hoofprints wound into the heart of the rocky fastness, into a part of the Peloncillos Fargo was positive no white man had ever set foot in before.

And all the while, Fargo was plagued by the feeling someone was dogging his steps. He debated whether to try to trick them into revealing themselves and elected not to. If gunfire broke out the Black Sheaths were bound to hear.

Little by little the shadows lengthened. Fargo reduced the distance by a quarter of a mile, on the watch for lookouts. The trail climbed along a shelf no wider than the Ovaro. On the right was a sheer drop of hundreds of feet with jagged boulders at the bottom.

In the distance a tableland appeared. By then the sun was almost gone. Fargo sought in vain for the glow of campfires, but if they were there, they were well hid. Rounding a bend, he drew rein.

More minutes dragged on tortoise feet. Fargo spotted the Black Sheaths. He waited for the last of them to ride over the rim before he committed himself. Resting a hand on the pommel of his saddle, he pushed his hat back on his head, and froze. From behind him, past the last bend, came the scrape of a sole on stone. He was sure of it. Palming the Colt, he swiveled, his thumb on the hammer.

A shadow appeared, rippling around the bend like a thing alive. It resembled a giant caterpillar but that was a trick of the fading sunlight. The "head" of the caterpillar was only a yard from the Ovaro's tail when the distorted apparition abruptly halted.

Whoever it was had sensed Fargo was there. Since he couldn't turn the stallion around on the narrow shelf, he did the next best thing. Easing his left boot from the stirrup, he swung his leg over the saddle and slid off. There wasn't much space, barely a foot to the edge, but by placing his boots with care, Fargo made it past the Ovaro. Another few steps and he would find out who was back there. Then one of his spurs jingled.

Like a bolt of ebony lightning, the shadow streaked around the bend.

Fargo threw caution aside. He reached the bend within seconds but no one was there. The next stretch of shelf was as bare as a miser's cupboard. No one could have reached the next turn in that short a span, yet he couldn't deny the proof his eyes offered. Baffled, he glanced high and low. "It's just not possible," he said under his breath.

Not possible for most men, Fargo answered himself. But for an Apache it was a different story. They were human mountain goats. Their uncanny reflexes and ability to camouflage themselves enabled them to do things others couldn't. It was no wonder many Mexicans credited them with supernatural abilities.

Fargo was strongly tempted to keep going but common sense won out. Fighting Apaches on their own terms was as foolhardy as baiting a grizzly in its den. Climbing back onto the Ovaro, he glimpsed the last few Black Sheaths ride onto the tableland. Somewhere up there must be General Machetazo's lair.

The shelf narrowed from there on. Several times the Ovaro's hooves were partway past the brink but they never went over the side. At length they reached the final slope. Imprinted in the dirt were the tracks not only of the eight men who had preceded him, but of countless others, overlaid in a jumble.

General Machetazo was a crafty butcher. A large military force seeking to bring him to bay would be severely handicapped. Bringing in heavy ordnance was out of the question. And if Machetazo had advance warning, he could block the trail and hold off attackers for as long as his ammunition and provisions held out.

Fargo started up. The absence of sentries surprised him. Either the Beast was careless or overconfident—or both. When he was near enough to the top, he stopped and rose in the stirrups to see what lay ahead.

The tableland was vast, stretching to a ring of stark mountains so high their summits brushed the clouds. A well-defined trail led to a gap or pass, and through it, as Fargo looked on, filed the Black Sheaths he had been following.

Machetazo's stronghold was farther on, in those mountains.

The sun had relinquished its reign, and the final rays of light faded. Night rapidly claimed the land. There was no cover between the rim and the distant gap, so Fargo stayed where he was until it was dark enough to be safe for him to go on. Something about the trail bothered him. Its width and depth hinted at regular use over a long span of time, but according to Colonel Blanchard, Machetazo seldom strayed north of the border.

Fargo was at a loss to explain it; nor could he explain why the ring of peaks seemed unusual. He had noticed how different they were from the surrounding mountains. Their size, their shape, the color of the soil; nothing was the same.

Another mystery was how Machetazo came to find the place. The odds of stumbling on it by mere chance were a million to one. Someone had told him. But who had cause to penetrate so deep into the mountains?

The answer was the same as before.

The Mescalero Apaches had explored the entire region. From north to south and east to west, they literally knew the mountains like they did the backs of their bronzed hands.

Was there a link between Machetazo and the Apaches? Fargo wondered. Could it be they were working together? On the face of it the notion was preposterous. Apaches regarded everyone else as enemies. Whites, Mexicans, other Indians—it was all the same to them. Still, the possibility was worth keeping in mind. Should General Machetazo and just one Apache band join forces, the consequences for the United States and Mexico could be dire.

Alert for the slightest noise, Fargo reined up when he heard faint voices. He also smelled the acrid scent of cigarette smoke. A red pinpoint flared high on the right side of the pass, giving the sentry's position away.

Reining to the left, Fargo hugged his saddle and hoped the sentry didn't spot him. When the stallion was out of sight beyond a bluff, he halted again and took stock of the situation.

Fargo was willing to bet all the money he had that Machetazo's army was on the other side of those peaks. But unless he saw the troops with his own eyes, he couldn't justify flying back to Fort Fillmore to tell Colonel Blanchard.

Dismounting, Fargo let the reins dangle, yanked the Henry free, and climbed. The slope was steep but there was no talus to contend with, and inside of half an hour he was high enough to work his way around into the pass without being noticed.

The red dot was still there, lower down on the facing slope, burning bright with every puff the sentry took.

Fargo glided from boulder to boulder until he was through the pass. Before his marveling gaze unfolded the Beast's lair.

The peaks formed a natural palisade. At the center, its surface glistening like an emerald, was a pear-shaped lake. Woodland framed the north shore; grass, everywhere else—enough to feed a thousand horses for a thousand years. It had to be a mile, as best Fargo could gauge, from one side to the other. Tents had been set up along the south shoreline. At least twenty campfires were burning. Around them sat scores of Black Sheaths. Their mounts and pack animals were grazing undisturbed.

Fargo could not have been more amazed if he had stumbled on a white buffalo. To call this a lair did not do it justice. It was a haven, a sanctuary; the last place on earth anyone would think to find Machetazo, and an ideal spot to hole up in for a month—a year—ten years.

Blanchard had to be told without delay. Fargo turned to retrace his steps and suddenly sensed he wasn't alone. It was the same feeling he'd had earlier, only now ten times stronger. A heartbeat before they struck he saw them; three sinewy forms who were on him in a blur. The rifle was torn from his grasp as iron arms wrapped around his legs and a shoulder slammed into his sternum.

They moved as one mind, one body, but from three directions at once.

Fargo crashed onto his back and kicked out. He sent one tumbling but the other two pounced as he heaved to his knees. The Henry's stock arced at his head. That was when he realized they wanted him alive.

Dodging, Fargo landed a solid uppercut that staggered the one who had his rifle, but the third attacker kicked him in the stomach. And although his gut resembled a washboard, it doubled him in agony. Again the moccasin-shod foot swept at his head but this time he grabbed it and wrenched.

Surging upright, Fargo clawed for his Colt. He almost had it clear when a pair of calloused hands seized his wrist, preventing him from leveling it. He whipped his left fist in a tight jab that buckled the man's knees, but the other two were on him before he could capitalize. One slammed into his ribs, the other grabbed a leg and upended him.

Not once did the three apparitions utter a sound. They were as silent as ghosts and as savage as wolverines.

Fargo lashed out with his other boot. His heel opened up a cheek. Another of the silent ones dived from the right, a fist-sized rock raised to strike. Rolling, Fargo saved himself, then delivered a sweeping kick that gained him the breathing space he needed to regain his feet.

But so did they.

Fargo wanted to see whom he was fighting but they were vague shapes against the black of night—shapes that sprang as one, seeking to overwhelm him by numbers. He slugged one, staggered a second, and was tackled by the third. Steely fingers clamped onto his throat, choking off his breath. With a powerful heave, he broke loose and flung the man off. But as soon as he did, the other two were there, taking their companion's place. They sought to pin his arms and legs.

Fargo resisted with a ferocity born of desperation. His knuckles scraped a chin. His knee found a groin. Pushing up, he barely set himself when the third one was on him once more. He swung a looping right but the phantom ducked and snapped both legs out, catching him about the ankles in a scissorslike grip. His own legs were wrenched out from under him. As he fell the other two piled on. His wrists were seized, and the razor edge of a knife was pressed against his throat.

"You move, I cut!" a guttural voice hissed.

Fargo held himself still. They had him. Further resistance would only get him killed. He was rolled onto his stomach and his arms were twisted behind his back, then bound with whangs cut from his buckskins.

When they had him good and secure, they roughly pulled him to his feet. One stepped up, grinning, and shoved his hat back on his head.

"You fight good, white-eye. What be your name?"

Fargo didn't answer. Another was gathering up his Colt and the Henry. The third was rubbing his chin.

The knife flashed again, the tip gouging Fargo's cheek. "I ask question, white-eye. You tell or I mark you, eh?"

Now that they were standing still, Fargo could see them better. They were dressed as Apaches, in headbands, plain shirts and pants, long breechcloths, and knee-high boots. Cartridge belts were around their waists. They had the swarthy aspect of Apaches, and dark hair that fell to their shoulders. But peering closely, Fargo saw that they weren't Apaches after all. They were mixed-bloods—part Apache, part Mexican—half-breeds, most called their kind; or simply " 'breeds." They looked enough alike to be related.

"My name is Fargo. What's yours?"

Lowering the knife, the 'breed slid it into a sheath. "In which tongue, eh? My mother gave one name. Father another. Whites call me a third name." He tapped his chest. "I be Antonio."

One of the others had gone into the rocks and was returning with three Sharps rifles they had set aside when they jumped him.

"These are your brothers, aren't they?" Fargo said.

Antonio showed his teeth again. "You have eyes like eagle. Most whites not tell us apart." He pointed at the one with the rifles. "That be Manuelito. Him oldest." Antonio pointed at the last one. "Amarillo. Him quiet one."

Spanish names, Fargo noted. It was customary among Apaches, even those of mixed descent, not to reveal their Apache name to anyone outside their band. He noticed, too, that Antonio's eyebrows and eyelashes had been plucked, a distinctly Apache trait.

76

"You hard man catch," Antonio commented. "Hard man sneak up on."

Manuelito grunted. "You talk all time, like woman. He our enemy. We get horse and go."

Gripped by both arms, Fargo was ushered around the mountain and down to the Ovaro. The brothers did not have mounts of their own. They had been following him on foot. Like true Apaches, they could go all day without tiring if they had to.

Fargo expected them to take him to their band. He assumed they had been shadowing the Black Sheaths with an eye to stealing horses or guns and then decided to jump him instead. But rather than quietly sneak off, the trio boldly hauled him into the pass.

It took the sentry only a few moments to spot them. *"Quien es?"* he demanded.

"Demonios!" Antonio shouted up, and they were allowed to proceed unchallenged.

It was a long walk to the lake, and Fargo wanted to learn more before he got there. Glancing at Antonio, he prompted, "You call yourselves demons?"

All three brothers laughed as if it were a private joke. "We do not," Antonio said, and motioned toward the Black Sheaths. "They do. They be afraid of us. We have Apache blood, eh?"

Fargo was well aware of the widespread terror in which Apaches were held. For hundreds of years the Mescaleros, Chiricahuas, Jicarillas, Mimbres, and other bands had preyed upon the people of northern Mexico. Striking when and where they liked with lightning speed and unmatched savagery, the Apaches were considered inhuman devils capable of feats beyond those of ordinary men. "Your mother is Mexican?"

"Sí." Antonio did not say more.

Fargo tried another tack. "You speak English, Spanish, and the Apache tongue, I bet. Not many know all three."

"Three worlds, three tongues. Father was Mescalero. Taught us Mescalero ways. We be Apache more than Mexican."

Manuelito grunted again. "Maybe cut tongue out will stop talk," he told his brother, and from then until they reached the camp silence reigned.

There were no sentries. Evidently Machetazo felt the one at the pass was enough. Black Sheaths stopped whatever they were doing to turn and stare as the three 'breeds led Fargo toward the largest tent on the lakeshore. Everyone in their path hastily moved out of their way. Fear and loathing was on many a face but Antonio and his brothers did not seem to notice. Heads high, they marched Fargo to the flap and Manuelito called out in Spanish.

"General! We have gift for you!"

The flap parted. Out strolled General Machetazo, his hands clasped behind his back, his hawkish face fixed in predatory interest. "What have we here, my demons?"

"This *americano* followed Sergeant Gonzales here," Manuelito reported. His grasp of Spanish far exceeded his fluency in English. "We caught him spying on your camp. His name is Fargo, and he fights like ten men."

"Indeed." Machetazo said, switching to English and facing Fargo. "That is high praise, *gringo*. My demons are renowned for their fighting prowess."

Fargo hesitated. He saw nothing to be gained by pretending he didn't know Spanish, so he responded, "*Your* demons?"

"These three were nothing before they met me—outcasts, shunned by Mexicans and Apaches alike. I made them my personal bodyguards, men of importance. They also scout for me, they hunt down deserters, and do much more. And they do it all extremely well." The general clapped Manuelito on the shoulder. "I could not be prouder if they were my own flesh and blood."

78

The brothers glowed at the praise, like kittens lapping up warm milk.

"Are they the ones who told you about this place?" Fargo bobbed his head at the encircling peaks.

General Machetazo's dark eyes narrowed. "Very perceptive of you. *Sí*. They learned about it from their Apache father and were kind enough to share the secret with me. Magnificent, is it not?"

"But isolated. You must plan to head back south of the border before too long." The more Fargo could learn before he made his bid to escape, the more help he could be to Colonel Blanchard.

"Enough of your fishing for information, *gringo*." Machetazo took the Henry from Amarillo. "Now it is my turn. Who sent you?"

"No one. I was passing through and saw some of your men heading into the mountains. It made me curious, so I followed."

"Is that so?"

The Beast drove the Henry's stock into Fargo's stomach with such force, it was a miracle Fargo's spine didn't snap. He pitched to his knees, his gut churning, the world spinning madly, and barely felt the Henry's muzzle gouge his temple.

"My second question, *gringo*, is simpler: How do you want to die?"

6

Skye Fargo heard a round being levered into the Henry's chamber and braced for the blast that would kill him. He tried to throw himself to one side but his legs were mush. The blow had not only knocked the breath out of him, it had left him momentarily as weak as a newborn foal.

"I think not," said General Machetazo, cradling the rifle in his left arm. "It would be too quick, too merciful. And I have many more questions for you to answer, whether you want to or not."

Fargo gulped in air and felt strength seep back into his limbs. His hands were inches from the top of his right boot and the Arkansas toothpick, but he couldn't draw it with Machetazo and the 'breeds standing over him.

"We will try this again later," the general said. "After I have finished my supper, which your arrival interrupted." He turned to a bullnecked Black Sheath. "Captain Ruiz, you will confine him under guard in the main supply tent until I send for him."

"At once, my general."

The captain clapped his hands and bawled orders, and other Black Sheaths gripped Fargo on both sides. As they were about to cart him off, General Machetazo touched the Henry's barrel to his chest.

"A word to the wise: If you do not supply the information I want, you will suffer like few ever have. My demons are masters of torture, and I have some small skill in that regard myself." Machetazo's grin was masterly. "Something for you to think over while you wait for me to finish my meal."

The supply tent was crammed with packs and crates except for a narrow center aisle. After dumping Fargo on his side, one of the Black Sheaths sneered in contempt and kicked him in the leg.

"I only wish the general would let me torture you, *americano* pig. I hate all you sons of whores."

Fargo had an urge to return the favor but he resisted it and they trudged out. The instant the flap closed, he tucked his feet up to his buttocks, bent backward, and slipped his fingers into his right boot. Palming the slender hilt of the Arkansas toothpick, he slid the double-edged blade free, carefully reversed his grip, and began sawing at the whangs binding his wrists.

The toothpick was razor sharp. Fargo honed it regularly with a whetstone he kept in his saddlebags. In short order the whangs parted, and he sat up and rubbed his wrists to help restore circulation.

Outside, things had quieted down.

Rising, Fargo examined the supplies. Most of it was clothes and food. No guns anywhere, and precious little ammunition. He was disappointed. He'd hoped to find a revolver, at least. He did come across several black-handled machetes and helped himself to one.

Squatting at the back of the tent, Fargo placed an ear to the canvas. All he heard was the gentle lapping of water on the shore. He used the toothpick to poke a hole so he could confirm the way was clear. Inserting the toothpick again, he sliced down to the ground. Then, poking his head out, he looked right and left, and forced himself on through.

After taking a moment to replace the toothpick, Fargo crawled to the corner. The supply tent was only a stone's throw from the general's but the open ground between was lit by the glow of a campfire. And Captain Ruiz and others were loitering near where he had seen them last.

Fargo crawled to his left, down to the lake, and then along the water's edge until he was a dozen yards to the rear of Machetazo's tent. The sand was damp and clung to his buckskins but he didn't care. With a little luck, in just a bit he would slit the Beast's throat, reclaim the Ovaro, and get the hell out of there. Without Machetazo to lead them, the so-called army might break apart. If not, the Third Cavalry would soon make them wish they had stayed south of the border.

Fargo snaked toward the Beast's tent. Movement near it froze him in place. Several shadows had flowed out of the darkness, and he did not need to see them clearly to know who they were. The demons were leaving. When he could no longer see them, he mentally counted to a hundred for safety's sake, then resumed crawling.

Of all the tents, the general's was the most brightly lit. Fargo drew the toothpick again and cut an inch-long slit. Placing an eye to the opening, he discovered the interior was divided into compartments. In front of him was a small bed, an oak stand with a lit lamp resting on it, and a large trunk. Past the bed, blankets had been hung to afford some small measure of privacy.

Fargo's second surprise came when he heard the tinkle of feminine laughter. None of the Black Sheaths had been female, so it was a good guess Machetazo had brought a woman along to satisfy his physical needs.

Enlarging the cut, Fargo eased inside and crouched. He looked for a firearm but there was none. Inching around the bed, he heard a pop, and then the sound of liquid being poured, followed by a loud sip and a contented sigh.

"This wine is most excellent, Juanita. That last *haci-*

enda we raided had a well-stocked cellar. It is unfortunate I could not have brought it all with me."

"I would rather have stayed there than here, Vicente. All those fine rooms, with all that furniture and those other nice things. Why did you have to burn it down?" By her voice, the woman was quite young.

"I have explained it to you before. In order to instill fear into the elite who rule our land, I must destroy them in their nests. The owner of that *hacienda* was an important man, highly respected in Mexico City."

"And now he is piles of dung in a hog pen. Why did you have to chop him up and feed him to those swine?"

The Beast did not answer her right away. When he did, he did not hide his irritation. "Three months you have been with me. Longer than any girl, ever. I keep you on because you amuse me—except at times like this, when you remind me why women should be seen and not heard."

"I am sorry, Vicente." Juanita was frightened. "But I am a lowly *peón*. A farmer's daughter. How can you expect my mind to be the equal of yours? If I ask questions that annoy you, I am only trying to understand so you will not think me so stupid."

Fargo was searching for a break in the blankets. He thought it was to the left but he couldn't find a seam.

"You cannot help being born a peasant," Machetazo told her. "Any more than I can help having greatness thrust on me. So listen closely." A glass scraped on wood. "It is my destiny to one day rule all Mexico. I know it, as surely as Santa Anna did when he was my age. To achieve my destiny, I must sweep all my enemies before me. I must slay them or send them fleeing our country."

"So you burn *haciendas*? You kill women and children?"

"As a lesson to those who oppose me, Juanita. I want them to fear me—to tremble at the mention of my name. Fear is more potent a weapon than all the rifles in the world. It wins more battles than cannons. When my enemies are afraid, I have beaten them before they lift a finger against me." Machetazo took another noisy sip. "Do you understand now?"

"I think so." Juanita did not sound entirely convinced.

Fargo still couldn't find where the blankets overlapped. But he had learned something important. The U.S. government thought the Beast was nothing more than a petty bandit interested solely in murder and plunder. That wasn't the case. Machetazo sincerely intended to take over all of Mexico. Not that it mattered—either way, he must be stopped.

"Finish your supper, my dear. I have pressing business to attend to."

"The *gringo* your *demonios* brought in? I peeked out at him. He is most handsome, Vicente, for a *gringo*."

A chair was slid back. "Take care, damn you! I will tolerate many things, but hearing another man praised is not one of them." Boots tramped, and a hand struck a cheek with a sharp smack. "Have you forgotten that once you no longer please me, I will cast you aside as I have all the others? Anger me, and maybe I will give you to my men so they can amuse themselves. Or perhaps to my demons, which would be far worse."

"*Por favor,* Vicente! I am sorry!" Juanita wailed.

Fargo found the seam at last and parted the blankets a fraction. The rest of the tent was furnished in lavish style with plunder—furniture, rugs, lamps, and more. A maple table occupied the center, and at one end, cowering in her chair, sat Juanita, her hands upraised to ward off a second blow.

Machetazo had her by the hair, his arm was over his head, his hand poised, but instead of slapping her, he stepped back and glowered. "I have warned you about my temper. Never provoke me, woman, or I cannot be responsible for the consequences.''

Juanita placed a palm to her red cheek. She was a beauty. Lustrous brown hair with reddish tints cascaded past shapely shoulders clothed in an elegant dress fit for a lady. Her oval face harbored exquisite green eyes, a button nose, and lips as red and full as the petals of a rose in bloom. Her bosom was more than ample. Breasts as large as melons strained against the silken fabric. A marvelously small waist completed the portrait. "I will be sure never to make that mistake again," she declared.

"See that you don't." Pivoting on a boot heel, General Machetazo stepped to an upright rack by the front flap to don his hat, a revolver, and a machete. "I have lost my appetite. But I expect it to return after I've finished interrogating the prisoner. So keep some food hot for me."

"*Sí*, Vicente.''

The Beast pushed the flap open. "And take a bath while I am gone. Torture also fuels my other appetite, and I like you clean and smelling of lilacs."

"*Sí*, Vicente," Juanita repeated with little enthusiasm, but if it bothered Machetazo, he gave no sign of it and departed.

For a few moments Juanita stared at the swaying flap. Then she covered her face with her hands and her shoulders shook to a convulsive shudder. Almost immediately she straightened again, composed herself, and smoothed her dress. She nibbled on a *tortilla* but dropped it on her plate and said aloud, "What did I ever do to deserve this?"

Fargo was debating whether to show himself when someone just outside coughed.

"Your pardon, *señorita*. The general has ordered us to fill the tub."

"Do what you must, Sergeant Gonzales," Juanita responded.

A bearded Black Sheath entered at the head of a four-man detail. Gonzales walked to a blanket strung across the other end of the tent and moved it aside, revealing a large wooden tub. "Here are the buckets!" he snapped at the others. "Fill them at the lake. It shouldn't take more than ten to twelve trips."

Juanita pushed her plate away and watched the quartet scurry out. "What is the latest news, Sergeant?"

"I would imagine you know more than I do, *señorita*," Sergeant Gonzales said. "We are still waiting for Colonel Fraco to send word from Fort Fillmore."

Fargo perked his ears. He would very much like to learn what the Beast was up to, but bellows from the direction of the supply tents brought Gonzales to the front flap in a rush.

"It is the prisoner, *señorita*! He has escaped! I must go. The men will finish filling your tub."

"*Muchas gracias,* Sergeant." Juanita stepped to the opening, her countenance, her bearing, that of someone in great despair. Without warning she turned and came briskly toward the nook containing the bed.

Fargo had only seconds to hide. Dashing around it, he slid onto his stomach in the narrow space between the bed and the canvas wall. The blanket was jerked wide and a shadow flitted across him. He heard her sigh, then the hinges on the trunk lid creaked.

"God forgive me, but I cannot take any more of this nightmare. I would rather die than go on."

Silently rising on an elbow, Fargo saw her on her knees, rummaging through the trunk.

Her back was to him, and she didn't hear him rise and cat-foot up behind her. She stiffened when he laid the flat of the machete across her right shoulder, but she didn't cry out. "*Habla* English?" he asked.

"*Sí, señor.*"

"Do not make me harm you. Get up and turn

around. Slowly, if you please." Fargo kept the machete where it was.

"You!" Juanita gasped on seeing him. "How did you get in here?" Her gaze drifted to the cut and a slow smile curled her enticing lips. "Clever, American. Most clever. But you cannot stay. The demons will be after you, and they can track a man anywhere, any time of the day or night."

"I'll be gone before they can find me." Fargo sidled to the blanket to watch for the return of the water detail. "I need some information first. Why did Machetazo send men to Fort Fillmore?"

"To spy on the soldiers," Juanita disclosed. "They have been gone several days and are not due back for several more."

"What is Machetazo up to?"

"I do not know. He never confides in me. I learn only what I hear him tell his officers." Juanita's eye danced with spite. "To him I am a plaything, nothing more. His army was passing our farm and he stopped to demand food. One look at me and he could not keep his hands to himself. When my father objected, Vicente had him staked out to die but spared him on the condition I become his consort."

"If you want out, I'll take you with me."

Hope lit Juanita like a flame. "Would that I could, *señor*! But his men are under orders to keep me confined to this tent. I cannot take ten steps outside without being surrounded." Her features softened. "I thank you, though, most warmly, for your gracious offer."

"I'll come back for you then, when the time is right." Fargo hurried to the slit he had made.

"Wait!" Juanita urged, and ran out. Within seconds she was back, carrying the Henry and his Colt. "He brought these in a while ago. I assume they are yours?"

Tossing the machete onto the bed, Fargo twirled the revolver into his holster and accepted the rifle. Now he had a fighting chance. "Any idea what they did with my horse?"

"I saw it tied to a tree not fifty paces north of this tent."

Again Fargo bent to the slit, and again he paused. "Thanks for your help. I meant what I said. I'll be back for you."

"But you don't even know me, *señor*."

"I'd like to," Fargo said. Grinning, he winked, then parted the canvas as far as it would stretch. He established that no one was lying in wait, and slipped on out. From the sound of things, the Beast was giving someone in the supply tent a tongue-lashing. They had yet to find the opening he had made, but it wouldn't be long before it occurred to Machetazo to have his men go over the tent from end to end.

Keeping low, Fargo hastened northward. Most of the Black Sheaths had rushed to the supply tent and many of the fires were unattended. He wasn't challenged as he crossed toward the tree.

The Ovaro saw him and nickered.

A heartbeat later a Black Sheath yelled, and Fargo glanced back to see a man at the fringe of those near the supply tent pointing at him. He broke for the pinto. More shouts rose as the alarm spread. A rifle cracked, then another. Both missed, and someone roared for them to stop firing; the general wanted him alive.

Not all the Black Sheaths were by the supply tent, though. From out of the darkness rushed two others, armed with machetes. They must not have heard the order to take him alive because they hefted their weapons as they closed in.

As lethal as machetes were, they were no match for firearms. Fargo shot them and leaped over their twitching bodies. He was ten feet from the pinto when

88

the night disgorged another Black Sheath who launched himself in a flying tackle. Dodging, Fargo smashed the Henry's stock against the man's skull. Two more bounds, and he was undoing the reins and hauling himself into the saddle.

A raging torrent of Black Sheaths poured toward him. In their midst, vainly trying to be heard above the uproar, stormed General Machetazo.

Wheeling the Ovaro, Fargo galloped toward the pass. It was three-quarters of a mile off but the sentry was bound to hear the din and be on guard. He spied other horses but none with riders. Some Black Sheaths were snatching up saddles and saddle blankets but it would be a bit before they caught their mounts and saddled up.

Fargo was almost clear of the camp when he spied three pantherish shapes streaking toward him from the east. They were spread across the trail, blocking it, and the very moment he laid eyes on them, one whipped a rifle to a shoulder and squeezed off a shot. The boom of a Sharps confirmed what he had already deduced: The demons were racing back to lend a hand. He couldn't say whether Antonio, Manuelito, or Amarillo had fired, but whoever had, rushed his shot. The heavy slug missed his head by the width of his hat brim.

Reining north, Fargo sped across the grassland, his intention to swing wide and continue on to the pass before the Black Sheaths could reach it and box him in. He rode low over the saddle to make it harder for the 'breeds to hit him, but they didn't try. They did turn and come after him, running with incredible swiftness—which he thought pointless, since on flat, open ground, they had no hope of overtaking a horse.

In another minute Fargo felt safe enough to sit up and shove the Henry into its scabbard. Riders were streaming from the encampment but he had a large enough lead to ensure they wouldn't catch him.

The only problem now was the sentry. Fargo peered

hard but the Black Sheath was invisible against the inky night. He expected the man to open fire well before he reached the pass yet he drew within a hundred yards and no shots rang out. Fifty yards, and Fargo thought he saw movement at the bottom of the pass, not up where the sentry had been perched. He also saw something else.

The pass was only twelve feet wide. From inside, a small unit could hold off a much larger force with very little effort. It could be barricaded with ease—an idea that had already occurred to General Machetazo. For now, to Fargo's considerable consternation, he discovered a barrier had been dragged across it—a crude latticework of tree limbs and thorny brush. Lightweight, but sturdy enough that a rider would have to be a fool to try to bust through. The only recourse was to dismount and move it aside, but the sentry had other notions.

A rifle cracked, and only the fact that Fargo had reined northward saved him. The sentry was on the right side of the pass, a dozen feet up among boulders. Racing out of range, Fargo drew rein. He could sneak back on foot and try to remove the barrier before the demons and Black Sheaths caught up, but unless he disposed of the sentry first he'd be shot dead. And there wasn't time to pinpoint the man's exact position and pick him off. In a couple of minutes the Black Sheaths would be there.

There was nothing else to do but look for another way out.

Fargo counted nine peaks encircling the hidden valley. Nine stark mountains towering to the sky. Surely, he reasoned, there was another pass somewhere. Trotting to the base of the nearest, he began his search. There had to be game trails, and if he could find one used by deer and bear and other large game, it might lead out.

In a flurry of hooves, Black Sheaths galloped toward

the barrier, with many more not far behind. Soon they would fan out, and they wouldn't rest until they brought Fargo to bay. He didn't hurry, though. In the dark he might miss indications of a trail if he wasn't careful. Half an hour elapsed—an hour. Clusters of Black Sheaths were doing exactly as he predicted. Ten or twelve to a group, they were ranging across the valley. Whenever any came near him, he hid in the deepest shadows he could find until they had gone by.

The Big Dipper shifted on its axis. It had to be close to two o'clock in the morning when at last Fargo came on a game trail winding toward the craggy heights. He started up but soon the going became so steep, he climbed down from his mount and walked. He made steady progress until he had to cross a slope covered with treacherous talus. Loose rocks slid out from under him with every step. The same with the stallion. A turtle could have beaten them across but eventually they reached firm footing, and Fargo paused.

The valley floor was hundreds of feet below. Here and there were knots of riders. A dozen campfires still blazed by the lake and a lot of Black Sheaths were moving about, although what they were up to at that late an hour, Fargo couldn't begin to guess. He stared at the brightly lit tent that constituted Juanita's prison and hoped she was all right.

Somewhere to the west a coyote yipped.

Fargo craned his neck to scan the upper elevations. The trail continued on high until it was lost among the ramparts. The pass, if there was one, couldn't be seen from where he was. "Time's a wasting," he said aloud, and tugged on the reins.

The climb became steeper. So steep, Fargo had grave doubts they would make it to the top. His legs ached from the constant strain of standing at an angle, and it was all he could do to keep his balance.

Then another coyote yipped. This one was below them, about midway up the same mountain. It was answered from lower down. But there was a difference between these coyotes and the coyote that yipped earlier. The other had been four-legged; these had two legs.

The demons were after him.

Fargo pushed on. He had no choice now. He must find a way over or the 'breeds would catch him. And this time they wouldn't bother taking him alive. They would try their best to kill him, and being part Apache, they were ten times as deadly as most anyone else.

The next slope leveled slightly and Fargo made better time. At a point where the game trail meandered between boulders the size of wagons, he stopped and raked the gloom below. Within seconds he saw them, climbing a lot faster than he could, one well in front of the others. A swarthy face was fixed on him, and despite the night, despite the distance, he swore it was Antonio, and that Antonio saw him and smiled a mocking smile.

Fargo passed between the boulders, then drew up short. More boulders loomed in the darkness—dozens upon dozens—a virtual maze into which the trail disappeared. It would take time to wend through it, time he could ill afford to spare. But it was too late to turn back. He had to follow the trail to wherever it led, come what may.

Many of the boulders were so large they blotted out the stars. Fargo moved deeper in among them, in a nether realm of shades of black and gray. Several times there was barely enough space for the Ovaro to make it through. Once he heard a faint sound out near where the boulder field began. Antonio, possibly, although the brothers were too savvy to make mistakes like that.

A sigh of relief escaped Fargo when the boulders ended. He was near the crest. The trail wound around an earthen knob, and beyond, he hoped, was the pass.

But when he stepped past it, he saw another talus slope, so steep it was impassable. And that was all—the game trail ended.

There was no way over the mountain.

Releasing the reins, Fargo dashed right and left, vainly seeking a safe route. But there was none.

From out of the boulder field rose the yip of a human coyote on the scent of blood. Antonio was close. His brothers answered, and they weren't far behind. They would be coming on fast now.

Fargo stepped to the pinto and gripped the Henry. He was trapped. He was outnumbered. But he wasn't giving up without a fight.

7

Skye Fargo had the Henry halfway out of its saddle scabbard when his gaze fell on the exact spot where the game trail ended and the talus began. Something he should have realized sooner now struck him, and shoving the Henry back, he grabbed the saddle horn and swung into the stirrups.

Game trails didn't just *end*. Deer and bears didn't wander aimlessly. They went where food was. They went where water was. The trail didn't stop at the talus. The animals using it had gone up and over.

And if they could, Fargo could. Reining the Ovaro around, he rode about twenty-five feet, then reined around again, facing the talus. It wasn't much but it was all the space there was, and it had to do. He waited a few seconds, girding himself. Then he lashed the reins and slapped his legs, and the stallion exploded into motion, hurtling toward the near-vertical slope at a full gallop.

When they were almost on top of it, Fargo reined again so the Ovaro took the talus at an angle instead of head-on. Hooves flying, it pounded five feet. Eight feet. Ten. Another yard and they would reach the top. But suddenly the Ovaro stumbled. Rocks and earth were streaming from under its hooves. Fargo lashed the reins again and used his spurs but the Ovaro started to slide. Behind them a Sharps boomed and Fargo felt the slug nudge his hat. He applied his spurs hard, raking the rowels—something he rarely did.

It had the desired effect. Regaining its balance, the pinto scrambled over the top and down the other side.

Fargo barely had time to absorb the sight of slope after benighted slope rolling away under them like an unending series of waves, and then they were hurtling down at breakneck speed. The slope on this side was also covered with talus, but this one seemed to stretch on forever.

The Ovaro locked its front legs, dropped onto its haunches, and slid.

Levering his boots against the stirrups, Fargo leaned as far back as he could. They gained momentum rapidly. There was a very real danger that by the time they reached the end of the talus, they would be moving so fast the Ovaro couldn't stop.

Dust spewed out from under them in great billowing clouds, choking Fargo's nose and mouth and getting into his eyes. He could hardly see. He had lost track of how far they slid when in the blink of an eye a jagged boulder materialized dead ahead. He reined to the right—or tried to—and the stallion responded as best it could, averting a collision. But then there was another, and yet a third.

From up on the crest wafted a feral screech of thwarted bloodlust.

Shifting his weight, Fargo reined to the left and the Ovaro slewed past several boulders in a row. On the alert for more, Fargo saw small pines instead. And where there were trees, there had to be solid ground. He tried to bring the stallion to a stop but he was asking the impossible. They shot from the talus like a stone from a slingshot.

The Ovaro whinnied, and was catapulted mane over tail. Fargo couldn't stay in the saddle. He was pitched forward and tumbled like a leaf caught in a gale. His hat went flying. The sky and the earth swapped positions a dozen times, and suddenly he slammed into a pine tree hard enough to snap some of its limbs like kindling but not hard enough to do the same to his bones.

Dazed, Fargo lay on his back, sucking air into his lungs. He was battered and bruised and his cheek was bleeding but otherwise he was unhurt. Slowly sitting up, he saw the Ovaro down. Fear spiked through him, and he shook off the momentary weakness and lurched to the stallion's side.

The Ovaro was wheezing like a bellows. Caked with dust and grime, cut and torn, it lifted its head when Fargo patted its neck, and nuzzled him.

"There, there, boy," Fargo said softly. He ran his fingers from shoulder to flank, probing for severe injuries or broken bones, and found neither. He checked all four legs with the same result. The pinto was impatient to stand, and when he stepped back, it lunged upright, torn and worn but unbowed.

Placing his forehead against the Ovaro's, Fargo closed his eyes. It had been close—so very close. He would rather lose an arm or leg than have anything happen to the stallion. "We've got eight lives left," he joked.

The rattle of stones up above reminded Fargo of their pursuers. Shucking the Henry, he stalked to the edge of the talus but didn't see Antonio or the other two. It could be they had turned around and gone back, but he wasn't taking anything for granted. He hurried down, and along the way stumbled on his hat, crumpled and dirty but wearable.

It was a long ride to the bottom of the mountain but Fargo didn't stop until they were there. Only then did he feel safe enough to find a spot to rest up. Dawn was breaking when he halted beside a spring, stripped the Ovaro, and plopped down without bothering to spread out his blankets. He was bone-tired. The second he closed his eyes he was out to the world, sleeping like one dead until the sensation of heat on his face roused him from a dreamless slumber.

The sun was at its apex. Yawning, Fargo sluggishly rose and shuffled to the spring. He splashed some water on his face and felt awake enough to check on the Ovaro. It was dozing in the shade. Daylight revealed it was scraped up a lot worse than Fargo had thought. One thigh had a furrow a quarter inch deep and several inches long.

Fargo's own nicks and cuts could wait. He took a strip of rawhide he sometimes wrapped jerky in from his saddlebags, wetted it until it was soaked, and cleaned every wound the stallion had. Afterward, he let it graze while he chewed some pemmican and pondered. He had to get to Fort Fillmore quickly. Machetazo might pack up and head south now that his secret sanctuary had been discovered.

Fargo had two routes he could take. One was the roundabout route that had brought him there. It was safer but a lot longer. The direct route would take him through prime Mescalero country. It would also shave two whole days off the ride.

Fargo wanted the stallion good and rested when he started out because he intended to push on until well after sunset, so it was another half an hour before he saddled up. He had only gone a short way when the crack of a pistol to the northeast drew him to a hill overlooking an arid plain, and a bewildering sight.

Two people were a little distance off, standing over a dead horse. One was a man dressed in a new suit and a short-brimmed silk hat, both dusty from long travel. That alone was remarkable. Even more so was the man's companion, a young woman attired in the height of fashion and holding a pink parasol over her head to ward off the sun. Behind them stood another horse that appeared about done in.

Fargo scanned the plain but saw no one else. Just

those two, looking as if they were out for a Sunday ride in a big city. They were as out of place as two Apaches would be in the heart of Chicago or New Orleans, and for a moment Fargo wondered if maybe his tumble the night before had done more to his head than leave a few bumps. But then the man started cursing and stamping back and forth like a five-year-old throwing a fit, and he decided they were too real to be figments of his imagination.

Nudging the Ovaro, Fargo draped his right hand over the Colt.

The woman spotted him and said something to the pilgrim in the silk hat, who stepped in front of her to shield her with his own body and extended a nickel-plated pistol. "Hold up there, suh!" he bawled.

Fargo did so. "If you want to be left alone that's fine by me!" he called out. He couldn't afford to be delayed.

Astonishment gripped Silk Hat. "I declare! You're white!" Lowering his hardware, he grinned from ear to ear and dashed forward, hollering, "Don't go, suh! Please! Forgive my rudeness! We'd very much like to talk to you!"

The man's accent came from below the Mason-Dixon line. Tennessee, Fargo guessed, or maybe Georgia. For some reason that made him think of the emigrants he had tangled with, the Owensbys.

Winded from the short run, the man shoved the pistol into a holster, doffed his hat, and gave a slight bow. "I trust you won't hold my deplorable manners against me, suh. Fatigue and hunger have dulled my wits, I'm afraid. My sister and I are about done in."

The woman was leading her horse over. Fargo liked the sway of her hips and the swish of her thighs against her dress. She had an hourglass figure crowned by a mane of gorgeous blond hair, eyes that were sky blue, and a mouth cherries would envy. "Pleased to meet you." He touched his hat brim.

"Likewise." Her eyes twinkled as she said it.

The man removed his hat and mopped at his brow with a white handkerchief he pulled from an inner pocket. "If you don't mind my asking, what on earth are you doing out in this wretched wilderness? In my humble estimation it's fit for neither man nor beast."

The blonde cast a look of irritation at him. "Where *are* your manners, Tarleton?" She offered her slender hand. "Pay no attention to him, sir. A little discomfort and he becomes as uncouth as common riffraff. I'm Susannah Wilkes."

Fargo noticed that her accent was different from her brother's. It was a lot less pronounced. She said "sir" while the brother drawled it out into a "suh." He thought it strange but he made no comment. Introducing himself, he added, "If this were a desert, I'd have took the two of you for a mirage."

Susannah laughed gaily. "Fiddledeedee. I'm as flesh and blood as the next person." She gave her parasol a playful spin.

"I can see that," Fargo agreed, and was treated to another twinkle.

Tarleton replaced his hat and squared his shoulders. "We would be extremely grateful if you would consent to lending us aid. I just had to shoot my horse after it had the misfortune to step on a rattlesnake."

"They're all over out here," Fargo said. But most men had the good sense to watch out for them.

"We've also lost our guides, Rodrigo and Lorenzo. They went off to hunt for game and never came back."

"When was this?"

"Two nights ago," Tarleton said and pointed northeast, toward the heart of Mescalero country. "They were bringing us from Mesilla for a very important meeting."

Fargo wondered whom they were supposed to meet in the middle of the Peloncillos. "I can guide you back to civilization if you want." He would take them to the fort, and from there they could go wherever they desired.

"We'd rather push on. We can't be far from the man we're supposed to meet, and it's imperative we reach him. You could say the fate of entire nations hangs in the balance."

Susannah gave him the same sharp look as before. "Tarleton!" she said sternly, then smiled sweetly up at Fargo. "Please forgive him. He has a tendency to exaggerate. But we truly must keep our appointment. And we're willing to pay extremely well for your assistance."

Fargo couldn't spare the time, not with the urgent information he had to convey to Colonel Blanchard.

"Extremely well," Tarleton stressed. "Upon our return to Mesilla, of course. We don't have much money with us at the moment."

"I can't," Fargo told them.

Tarleton bristled and took a step but Susannah placed a hand on his arm, restraining him, and shook her head. To Fargo she said, "You must be quite familiar with this region. So perhaps instead of leading us where we need you go, you would be courteous enough to provide directions on how to get there?"

"I can try," Fargo said, "but you'd be smart to let me lead you back. These mountains are full of Apaches and—" He was going to say "renegades from south of the border," but Tarleton interrupted.

"We're trying to find a valley surrounded by high mountains. It has a lake, the only one within hundreds of miles, we were told. Are you familiar with it, by any chance?"

Fargo hid his surprise, but not without effort. Never in a hundred years would he have suspected the pair were on their way to meet General Machetazo. "I can't say that I know the place," he fibbed. "I've only been through this area a few times myself." He would get them to Colonel Blanchard and let Blanchard sort it out.

"How terribly disappointing." Tarleton shifted toward Susannah, and when he shifted around again he had the nickel-plated Remington in his right hand. "I'm afraid, suh, you leave us no choice. We must relieve you of your mount."

"You're stealing my horse?" Fargo almost went for his Colt. But the Southerner might get off a shot, and he wouldn't risk the Ovaro taking a stray bullet.

"I prefer to think of it as borrowing. In a week or so you'll find it at the stable in Mesilla, along with some money for your time and trouble."

"Stranding a man on foot out here is considered the same as trying to murder him," Fargo mentioned.

"I can understand why. But I assure you it's a matter of utmost importance or I wouldn't be so desperate. Kindly step down. And please don't try anything foolish. I am a crack shot or they wouldn't have sent me on this mission."

"*Tarleton.*" Susannah vented her displeasure again. "Must I sew your mouth shut? Simply take his damn animal and let's get on with it, shall we?"

"Has anyone ever informed you that for a lady your language is deplorable?"

Fargo kept hoping Tarleton would turn toward her or lower the Remington. Sliding his left boot from the stirrups, he tensed his leg to kick the pistol out of the other's hand.

"Watch out!" Susannah cried.

Tarleton sprang back, elevating his revolver so it was aimed at Fargo's head. "I warned you, suh! Now do as I told you or this will get ugly. And be sure to keep your back to your pinto and your hands where I can see them at all times."

Fargo slowly eased to the ground. The Southerner

motioned for him to step away and he reluctantly complied. "I suppose you're stealing my rifle, saddle, and saddlebags, too?"

"I haven't the time nor the inclination to switch with the rig on the dead horse," Tarleton said. "But have no fear. I will leave your belongings at the stable when I drop off your horse."

"If you live that long," Fargo said.

"Was that a threat, suh? If so, I must warn you. So far I have been civil, but if you continue in this vein I will be forced to deal most harshly with you." Tarleton paused. "Susannah, prepare to ride. I would help you climb on but at the moment I'm occupied."

"Aren't you forgetting something?" the blond belle asked.

Tarleton finally glanced at her, but only for the briefest of instants. "We have what we need. What else is there?"

"His revolver, unless you prefer he shoot us as we ride off. In that case let him keep it." Susannah oozed sarcasm.

"You heard her," Tarleton snapped truculently. "Take it out using two fingers and only two fingers, and toss it over here."

In Fargo's opinion, the three most skittish creatures anywhere were rabbits, whitetail bucks, and Easterners with guns. He watched the other man's trigger finger closely as he inched the Colt out and did as he had been instructed.

"Thank you." Tarleton picked it up and wedged it under his belt. "I'll leave this with the rest of your belongings."

Susannah was boosting herself up. She sat sidesaddle and arranged her dress so it accented the sweep of her legs, then held the pink parasol overhead. "I'll be so glad when I am back at the plantation. What I wouldn't give to be sitting in the shade of the verandah right this minute, sipping a mint julep while watching the darkies work in the fields."

"Why would you want to watch a bunch of sweaty Negroes?" Tarleton commented offhandedly. Covering Fargo, he swung stiffly astride the stallion. "I can hardly tolerate being on the same planet with them."

Fargo would have loved dearly to throw himself at the bigoted horse thief, haul him down, and pound him within an inch of his life. He keenly regretted playing the Good Samaritan, but how was he to have known what they were like?

Amazingly, Tarleton said, "No hard feelings, I trust, suh?"

The man's gall was limitless, Fargo reflected. Here they were, leaving him with nothing except the clothes on his back and the Arkansas toothpick, and Tarleton acted like they were merely borrowing a set of silverware. A sharp retort was on the tip of Fargo's tongue but he held his anger in and said simply, "I hope we meet again real soon."

"I wouldn't suggest following us." Tarleton bent and patted the saddle scabbard.

"With this Henry of yours I can drop you at two hundred yards."

Susannah's eyes were twinkling again. "It's a shame we didn't meet under different circumstances. My intuition tells me getting to know you would be well worth my while." She slapped her feet against her horse and said over her shoulder, "Thanks for the loan of your horse. It was sweet of you."

Fargo watched until the haze and the dust swallowed them. Then he squinted up at the sun, frowned, and hiked after them. Unless a storm obliterated their tracks, which was unlikely at that time of the year, he would stick to their trail until either he caught up to them or hell froze over.

With nothing better to do, Fargo reviewed the encounter for a clue as to why the pair had traveled halfway across the country and were risking life and limb to find General Machetazo. He was stumped until he recollected a few comments Colonel Blanchard had made. Then the meeting took on a whole new importance, with sinister implications for the United States.

Ahead reared the mountain range Fargo had crossed the night before, the pass a tiny niche near the summit. It would take too long to climb that high on foot. He was better off doing as the Southerners were doing and follow the mountains around to the other pass.

For hours Fargo trudged under the blistering sun, the only other sign of life a lizard that slithered under a rock. By sunset he had over a mile to go. His lips were parched, his throat dry. He thought of the lake, and continued on until he came within sight of the pass.

Stars were sparkling in the firmament, and coyotes—the four-legged variety—were in full chorus.

Fargo had figured the People's Army for the Liberation of Mexico would be long gone but the tents were still there, awash in the light of new campfires. Hunched low to the ground, he stayed close to the right side where it was darkest. A cough from high up gave him some idea of where the sentry was posted. The man never spotted him, and presently he was through to the other side and jogging toward the encampment.

Some people might consider Fargo *loco* for baiting the Beast's jaws unarmed, but the way he saw it, he would be more *loco* to attempt to reach Fort Fillmore on foot and armed with no other weapon than a knife. He needed the Ovaro. He needed his Colt and the Henry. And he aimed to do whatever it took to get them back.

Black Sheaths were once again clustered around the fires or moving about the camp engaged in various tasks. Machetazo's tent was not only lit up brighter than a whorehouse on a Saturday night, but the front flap was open and chairs had been set up in front to take advantage of the cool evening breeze.

Fargo paced himself so he wouldn't be tuckered out when he got there. He spied the pinto tied to the same tree as on the night before, its white patches standing out like the white slats of a picket fence.

Soon Fargo was close enough to hear the murmur of conversation punctuated by occasional laughter. Most of it came from the big tent where Machetazo was entertaining his guests. The Black Sheaths, Fargo noticed, were giving those in the chairs a wide berth. He also noticed there were fewer fires along the north shore of the lake than the south shore. Fewer Black Sheaths and fewer horses, too. So it was to the north he circled, until he was near enough to the lake to skip a stone. Hunkering, he looked for sentries, and for any sign of three swarthy figures who posed more of a danger to him than all the Black Sheaths combined.

Satisfied it was safe enough, Fargo sank to the ground. The scent of the water was so tantalizing it made his throat hurt just to think of how delicious it would taste. Moving only a few inches at a time and then stopping to scan the camp and cock his ears, Fargo crawled to the lake. He removed his hat, set it aside, and dipped his face in the water. Waves of relief rippled through his body, invigorating him with new-found energy. He drank slowly so as not to make himself sick, and he didn't drink half as much as he would like to spare himself the bellyache that sometimes resulted from guzzling too much.

Fargo raised his head. His chin and beard were dripping wet and water was running down the inside of his buckskin shirt. It felt good. None of the Black Sheaths had drifted anywhere near, so he gave in and drank a little more, then willed himself to slide back into the brush, his hat in hand. Putting it on, he crabbed toward the rear of the big tent.

By rights Fargo shouldn't have even thought about eavesdropping on Machetazo and the Southerners. He was asking for trouble. But he was determined to learn what Susannah and Tarleton were doing there, and he would wager all the gold in Colorado that Colonel Blanchard would like to know, as well. How close he could get depended on whether the general had found the slit he made last night, and whether it had been sewn up.

Fargo moved from bush to bush, tree to tree, until all that blocked his view of the section of canvas he had slit were some weeds. Warily rising on his hands and knees, he saw the slit was still there.

Out in front of the tent, General Machetazo made a statement too low to hear and Susannah Wilkes laughed heartily. It sounded like they were having a grand old time.

Fargo vaulted over the weeds. Lying on his right shoulder, he removed his hat and poked his head inside. Everything was exactly as he remembered it: the bed, the trunk, the oak stand, the lit bronze lamp. The blankets were pulled shut. He slid all the way in, jammed his hat back on, and stalked to the seam to listen.

"—why, Vicente, you do pay a lady the most flattering compliments," Susannah was gushing. "There is a lot more to you than I suspected. I'm afraid our superiors gave us the wrong impression entirely."

"Yes, indeed, suh," Tarleton agreed. "Our supper was excellent. After two days without food, I'd have settled for raw horsemeat. But you, suh, served a meal my cook in Georgia would be proud of."

"*Muchas gracias.*" Machetazo acknowledged their praise. "But you should direct your thanks at Juanita. She oversaw its preparation. In addition to her more obvious charms, she has many hidden talents."

"It was nothing," Juanita said.

"A word to the wise," Susannah said. "Never belittle your accomplishments, my dear. Men are naturally stingy with compliments, so when they give you one, milk it for all it is worth."

"What were those exquisite eggs we were served?" Tarleton inquired. "I've never tasted any quite like them."

"Hawk's eggs," General Machetazo said. "Some of my men found a nest up in the mountains."

Susannah said something, but Fargo didn't hear what it was because just then the muzzle of a rifle was jammed against the base of his skull and he heard a hammer thumbed back. He didn't look around—he knew who it was. "*Buenas noches,* Antonio."

"Again we meet, eh, *gringo*? It be mistake you come back. This time you not leave alive."

8

Antonio stepped back and told Fargo to walk out the front of the tent. Glancing over his shoulder, Fargo found all three of the demons behind him, their Sharps trained on his back. He was glad he hadn't tried anything. Manuelito and Amàrillo were as somber as hangmen; Manuelito in particular looking as if all he needed was the slightest excuse to shoot.

Fargo pushed through the hanging blankets. Being taken by surprise rattled him a bit. The brothers were good—damn good, maybe even be better than he was—and he rarely met anyone he could say that about. "You were waiting for me, weren't you?" he asked. It couldn't be mere coincidence.

"Since sundown," Antonio confirmed. "We knew you cut tent. We hide. We see you come, see you drink."

"I never saw you," Fargo admitted, upset with himself. He emerged into a wreath of cigar smoke, and halted.

Six chairs were arranged in a semicircle, placed so Machetazo and his guests could admire the adjoining peaks. In addition to the general, Juanita, the Southerners, and Captain Ruiz were also present. The sixth chair was empty. When he stepped out, they twisted in their seats.

"So, my last guest finally arrives," the Beast declared, and nodded approval at his demons. "We have been expecting you, *gringo*. Have a seat, *por favor*." He pointed at the empty chair. "I saved one for you."

Tarleton Wilkes laughed.

Burning with anger, Fargo sat down. He was mad at himself more than at them. For the second time that day he had been made a fool of, and it rankled. The half-breeds fanned out behind him, their Sharps leveled. Adopting a grin, he remarked, "I hope you saved me some food, too."

General Machetazo snorted. "I am afraid I must plead negligence. I could not be certain when you would arrive."

Susannah Wilkes was resplendent. She had bathed and done up her hair, and her dress and shoes had been brushed clean. "Our host was most interested to hear about our little run-in with you," she relayed. "You lied to us, sir, when you claimed you had never heard of this place."

"And a true gentleman never lies," Tarleton threw in.

"But they steal horses?" was Fargo's rebuttal. He relished the flush of resentment that darkened the Georgian's features.

Machetazo was wearing a uniform cobbled together from those of slain *Federale* officers. The insignia were those of a major, not a general, but a general's would be extremely hard to come by. Medals he never earned adorned his chest, and his boots had been polished to a sheen. "I knew you would come, *gringo*," he said. "So I prepared a suitable welcome."

Captain Ruiz coughed and nervously asked, "Do you want me to have him taken away and put under guard, my general? I swear to you, on my own life, that he will not escape us this time."

Machetazo dismissed the suggestion with a wave. "My demons are more than competent in that regard. And my new friends and I want to have some fun with him."

"I'll say we do," Susannah purred, that twinkle back in her eyes. "It isn't every day we get to have our way with a government man. That is what you are, isn't it, Mr. Fargo? Somehow the government learned of what we were up to and sent you to stop us."

Tarleton still had Fargo's Colt tucked under his belt. Placing a hand on it, he said scornfully, "If that darkie-loving excuse for a president thinks he can keep the South from seceding, then Abe Lincoln is more deluded than I thought."

So there it was. Fargo had suspected their purpose in meeting the Beast was linked to the impending break between the North and the South. But he was puzzled as to the part General Machetazo was to play. Since they weren't likely to tell him if he came right out and asked, he had to prod them. "You're the one who is deluded if you think Machetazo can help your cause."

"That shows how much you know!" Tarleton predictably took offense. "The good general is our invaluable ally. He is going to see to it that the United States is kept so busy waging war with Mexico, Lincoln will have no troops to spare to send against the South."

Susannah spun. "Tell him everything, why don't you? Have you forgotten our mission is secret?"

Tarleton switched his indignation to her. "I haven't forgotten anything, you Kentucky tart. He's not going anywhere. The general will see to it that our secret dies with him, won't you, General Machetazo?"

Before their host could answer, Susannah was out of her chair, her face a mask of icy fury. "What did you just call me?" She held her right hand close to her left wrist, her fingertips brushing the end of her long sleeve.

Genuine fear gripped the Georgian, and Tarleton snapped back as if she were about to slap him. "My apologies, my dear. In the heat of the moment I forgot my manners. We were instructed to work together, and work together we will, although why we had to pretend to be brother and sister is beyond me."

Susannah wasn't pacified. "So much is beyond you that I can't help but question the wisdom of our superiors in saddling me with a buffoon."

Now it was Tarleton who forgot himself and leaped to his feet. "Buffoon, am I? I got us here, didn't I? And the others have arrived with the gold, precisely according to my plan, haven't they? So where do you get off—"

General Machetazo suddenly clapped his hands and bellowed, "Enough! All this petty bickering is childish. This is a time to celebrate, not to squabble among ourselves."

Tarleton bowed. "You are right, of course, suh. Thanks to you, we are about to strike a blow for liberty and the preservation of a whole way of life. On behalf of Southern sympathizers everywhere, I can't thank you enough for your dedication to our cause."

"Do not delude yourself, *señor*," Machetazo said harshly. "Were it not for the wagonload of gold, I would spit on you and your ridiculous cause."

While they were bickering Fargo had been watching Juanita. She was in a different dress than last time. This one had gold trim, lace at the throat, and clung to her as if molded to her body. He caught her eye, and she frowned and gave a tiny shake of her head.

General Machetazo rose with the air of a predator about to pounce. "I warn you. Understand this, and understand it well: Should anything go wrong—should the gold not be there as promised—neither of you will set foot in your beloved South ever again. I am not one to be trifled with."

"But the gold is here!" Tarleton declared. "In bars, as you requested."

"It was not a request," Machetazo corrected him. "It was a *demand*. Either we do this on my terms or we do not do it at all. I am taking all the risks. I am the one who will have two governments after my head."

Susannah wasn't intimidated in the least. "And you are the one who will be wealthier than you ever dreamed if you pull it off." She stepped close to him, again holding her right hand strangely close to her left wrist. "Now let me warn *you*. Should you try to keep our gold without doing as we've asked of you, those who sent us will place a bounty on your head. A bounty so high killers from both sides of the border won't rest until it is claimed. You'll never be safe, never get any rest, never stop looking over your shoulders."

Fargo thought her comments would incite the Beast's notorious temper, but Machetazo only nodded.

"Just so we understand each other, *señorita*."

Juanita broke her long silence to say, "All this talk of gold and intrigue bores me, Vicente. I would rather talk about something else. Or perhaps we can go inside and play cards."

"There will be time for such silliness later, woman. Right now I have a different amusement planned." Machetazo rotated toward Fargo. "I have neglected you long enough, *hombre*. My demons and I have been looking forward to paying you back for making fools of us the other night."

"How did he do that?" Tarleton asked.

"By getting away," Machetazo answered. "No one has ever eluded my demons before. To my *soldados* these three are invincible." He swept an arm at the 'breeds. "Or they were, until this Fargo did what no one else ever has. When my demons came back empty-handed, I saw many of my men whispering among themselves."

Captain Ruiz stood. "Only the conscripts, General. The rest, like myself, are with you because we want to be. Whether the *demonios* fail or not is of no consequence to us."

"*Idiota!*" the Beast spat. "You miss the whole point. It is fear of the demons that keeps the conscripts here.

Until the other night, they believed that anyone who deserted would be brought back to share the fate of Esteban and those before him. But now Fargo has given them a ray of hope: They think that if he can get away, they can, too."

"Every time one has tried it has ended the same," Captain Ruiz said. "They know whoever runs will be caught."

Machetazo balled his fists. "Can it be you still do not comprehend? Yes, if one conscript deserts, Antonio and his brothers can hunt the *bastardo* down— even if two or three go at the same time. But what if it's five or six? Or if all the conscripts sneak away in the middle of the night?"

"They would not dare defy you."

"Can it be you know nothing of human nature?" Machetazo asked in exasperation. "Our conscripts are sheep pretending to be *soldados*. The glue that holds them here—that keeps them wearing a Black Sheath—is fear. Without it, our hold on them is broken. They will flee like the mice they are, and with them goes half my army."

Captain Ruiz glanced at Fargo. "What can we do now that the harm has been done?"

"We can instill new fear. We will tie the *gringo* and gather everyone around. Then we will—" Machetazo stopped. "But why tell you, when I can show you? Stand up, *gringo*. Let us get this under way."

Fargo hadn't heard the brothers come up behind him. But he felt a sharp pang when Antonio jabbed him with the Sharps, and he slowly rose.

The only one still seated was Juanita, but she did not stay there long. "More torture, Vicente?" she said bitterly. "Hasn't there been enough?" Rising, she started toward the tent. "Unlike you, I do not have an appetite for seeing men hacked to bits. I will pass on the festivities, if you don't mind."

Machetazo grabbed her arm. "But I *do* mind, my

dear. In fact, I insist you stay since one of the questions I will put to *Señor* Fargo has to do with you."

"Me?"

"I find it strange that he was able to enter our tent and take his revolver and rifle without you seeing him." Machetazo suddenly wrenched her arm, and Juanita cried out. "Strange, because only you and I knew where they were. Strange, because nothing else in the tent was disturbed except the *sarape* the guns were under." He raised a hand to slap her and she cringed. "Almost as if he knew right where to look."

"I did." Fargo came to her rescue.

The Beast's head swung around like the head of a sidewinder about to strike. "What is that you say, *gringo*?"

"I told her I'd kill her if she didn't tell me where they were." Fargo would no more harm a woman than he would the Ovaro, unless in self-defense, but Machetazo didn't know that. "Don't blame her for what I did."

Machetazo leaned over Juanita, his gaze boring into hers with feral intensity. "Why didn't you tell me he had threatened your life when I discovered the weapons were missing and questioned you?"

"Because I was scared!" Juanita shrilly exclaimed. "I thought you would punish me anyway, just as you punish your men for the slightest of infractions."

Straightening, Machetazo released her and ran his palm down her arm. "There, there, my dear," he soothed her, and she shivered as if cold. "The error in judgment is mine. I have been too hard on you. I tend to forget that women are weaker and more emotional than men."

Susannah Wilkes, or whatever her real name was, made a sound reminiscent of someone gagging. "We are? That's news to me, General. I've always believed women can do anything men can do—and sometimes do it better."

114

"*Americano* women are cats," Machetazo said, and didn't elaborate. "As for you"—he turned back to Fargo—"for threatening Juanita your punishment will be twice as severe." He snapped his fingers. "Manuelito, Amarillo, if you please!"

Fargo sure as hell wouldn't submit to torture without resisting, but as he pivoted toward the brothers, the barrel of a Sharps barrel was jammed against his spine.

"I would not, white-eye, were I you." Antonio was so eager to shoot, he was lightly stroking the trigger.

Fargo submitted to being seized and hauled midway between two cottonwoods that were about eight feet apart. His hat was tossed into the grass. His shirt was stripped off. Manuelito and Amarillo tied ropes to his wrists, stretched the ropes tight, and secured the other ends to the trees.

General Machetazo strutted over. "I have heard it claimed a man can last for a week under the most brutal torture if it is done skillfully enough."

"And I've heard that if pigs had wings, they could fly."

That stopped the Beast midstride. "Is that what is called a 'figure of speech'? I do not understand. Why would pigs want wings?"

"Go look in a mirror and maybe it will come to you." Fargo's one regret was that he couldn't rid the world of Machetazo before he cashed in his chips. He would give anything for the chance.

"Ah. An insult."

Nodding to himself, General Machetazo made as if to walk off, then abruptly whirled and slammed his fist into Fargo's unprotected stomach. Fargo felt his throat burn with rising bile and swallowed it back down, only to be punched again and again and again—in the gut, in the ribs, in the chest. Machetazo had gone berserk and was snarling in a manner fitting one called the Beast. He landed blow after blow, his thick knuckles thudding like hammers. Only when he was breathing so heavily he couldn't continue did he stop and step back.

Fargo was on the verge of passing out. Pain ravaged his rib cage and abdomen. A groan welled up within him but he smothered it. He refused to show weakness, refused to give his tormentor the satisfaction of knowing how bad off he was.

Susannah and Tarleton and Captain Ruiz had drifted over, but Juanita hung back, her face averted.

"My, my," the blonde said breathlessly. "For a moment there I thought you would beat him to death."

"The thought crossed my mind, *señorita*, but depriving him of life is not enough. Before I am through he will beg a God that does not exist for help that will not come. He will scream and cry and plead." The Beast drew himself up to his full height. "He might even go insane. I have had that happen."

"I hope you'll let me watch, General," Susannah requested. "I find it highly entertaining."

Machetazo grinned. "You are a woman after my own heart, even if you are a *gringo*. It is unfortunate we must leave for Mesilla tomorrow to get the gold or you could stay and see it through to the finish."

Had Fargo heard correctly? He forced himself to concentrate.

"What about your prisoner?" Susannah asked.

"He is not going anywhere. I will let him hang here, with five of my Black Sheaths on guard every hour of the day and night to prevent his escape. He cannot help but dwell on the suffering to come, and it will be that much worse when it does." Machetazo took a dozen steps straight back, then barked at Ruiz: "Captain, bring my bullwhip from my tent. And have the men fall in. Their fear will now be rekindled."

Fargo glanced at the Ovaro. If only he could break free and reach the stallion! But he might as well yearn to walk on the moon. No one bucks the odds forever.

He had played his cards, now he must accept the consequences.

Tarleton scrunched up his face as if he had sucked on a lemon. "Far be it from me to interfere in your personal affairs, General Machetazo, but I can't help but think that what you are doing is hardly conduct becoming a gentleman."

"What is this obsession you have with that word?" Machetazo demanded. "I am engaged in a war. It is kill or be killed. And I do not intend to be a casualty." His chest expanded like a peacock's. "I intend to be the president of all Mexico. That is why I need your gold: to finance a bigger, better army. More Black Sheaths, more guns, more ammunition. Enough to assure victory."

"War is for those who aren't smart enough to achieve their goals any other way," Tarleton said. "Take the gold and go off somewhere and live the rest of your life in ease and luxury. That's what I'd do."

"I am not you." Machetazo made the statement a scathing insult. "I believe a man must make his own destiny. I could never have others do my work for me and then live off the sweat of their brow."

Tarleton scowled. "I fail to see any difference, suh, between the slaves on my plantation and these miserable wretches you've forced into joining your army."

"The difference, *gringo,* is that I lead them into battle and fight at their side when the need arises. I do not sit in the shade and comfort of my plantation while they break their backs toiling in a cotton field."

"A fine distinction, if you ask me, and an unjust one."

Machetazo's scar flamed red. Tarleton didn't seem to notice but Susannah did, and quickly stepped between them. "Please, gentlemen, we are allies, remember? Our enemy is this government man."

But the Beast did not stop glaring until Captain Ruiz dashed back with the bullwhip. Without a word the general grabbed the handle and uncoiled the whip at his feet, then snapped his arm forward.

The lash snaked through the air almost faster than the eye could follow. There was a loud *crack* inches from Fargo's face, and he involuntarily flinched. He had been on the receiving end of a bullwhip before, and it was not an experience he cared to repeat. When wielded skillfully, a bullwhip could peel skin and flesh the way a knife peeled an apple or a pear. And the pain! He would rather run naked through a cactus patch than endure what was in store.

The Beast, though, had turned toward the Southerners.

Susannah and Tarleton glanced uncertainly at each other, and Susannah asked, "Is something wrong, General?"

"Wrong? What could be wrong?" Machetazo flicked the whip lightly so it wriggled in the grass like a snake. "A short while ago, woman, you threatened me. And now this milksop sees fit to argue with me. Both of you need to be reminded of something."

Black Sheaths were gathering, but they hung back, sensing their lord and master's displeasure. Fargo used the distraction to test the ropes by pulling against them. There was no slack. The demons had done their work well.

"I have a certain nickname," Machetazo was saying. "Perhaps you have heard of it. Some think it highly unflattering but I regard it with pride." He snaked the whip again, harder. "For, you see, unlike the two of you, I answer to no one but myself. I bow to no man, to no woman. My will is supreme because I make it supreme, as those who oppose me find out to their sorrow."

The Southerners had their eyes glued to the whip.

"The only reason I have endured your insults until now is because I do not yet have the gold. But no more. My pride means more to me than your gold bars, for without pride a man is nothing." Machetazo sent the lash sizzling at Tarleton's face, but expertly stopped it a hair's width before it struck. Tarleton jerked back at the *crack,* and turned as pale as a sheet of paper. "The next time either of you tries my patience will be the last. Is that understood?"

"Yes, suh," Tarleton responded.

Susannah had more grit. "It's understood, sure enough. But like you, General, I bow to no one. Not even you."

Fargo saw Machetazo's hand tighten on the whip's handle. He expected the general to swing again, and Machetazo did—but not at Susannah. Machetazo pivoted toward *him,* and the next instant searing agony ripped through Fargo's chest. Gritting his teeth, he glanced down at his rent flesh and the blood seeping from it.

The Beast wasn't done.

Fargo tried to draw back but the ropes held him fast. He almost cried out as the lash bit deeper than previous time. More blood flowed. Forgetting himself, he surged toward Machetazo, straining for all he was worth.

A mocking sneer greeted his effort. "Are you so worked up already, *gringo*? I have just begun." The Beast glanced at Susannah. "This could well be you, woman. Talk back to me ever again and it will be."

The gauntlet had been thrown down. Susannah opened her mouth to speak but bit off whatever she was going to say. Whirling, she stormed off, Tarleton trailing after her like a kicked puppy.

Machetazo threw back his head and laughed in pure sadistic glee. "Did you see, *gringo*? They have learned the airs they put on mean nothing to me. The woman still has fire in her but I will quench it in my own good time."

A small part of Fargo wondered what the Beast meant, but he was more concerned with the bullwhip, and when it would strike. Clamping his teeth, he steeled himself.

"Now, then. Where were we?" Machetazo faced him and raised his right arm. By now almost all the Black Sheaths in camp were watching in stony silence. "I think I will start with your ears and work my way down."

The whip rose. Simultaneously, from out of the night came the drumming of hooves. The Black Sheaths parted as two more on lathered mounts trotted up to the general and drew rein. Both were covered with the dust of many miles. One saluted crisply and reported in Spanish, "Colonel Fraco sends his regards, sir! He says to tell you the American troops have taken the bait. Only a handful remain at Fort Fillmore. The rest have left and are heading south."

Machetazo lowered the bullwhip. "They are more gullible than I dared hope. Very well, Lieutenant. Get new mounts and inform Colonel Fraco we are on our way."

"You want us to head back immediately, sir?"

"I'm sorry. Would you rather take a *siesta* first? And maybe have a hot bath?" Machetazo took a step toward his subordinate and roared, *"Of course I want you to head back immediately, simpleton!"* He spun toward Captain Ruiz. "Assemble the men! Full packs, full rations! We march within the hour!"

The camp dissolved into a whirlwind of activity. Oblivious to the storm he had created, the Beast calmly walked up to Fargo and rapped the bullwhip handle against his chin. "You are the luckiest *hombre* alive, do you know that? I regret we must cut this short. Pressing matters demand my presence elsewhere."

There might never be a better opportunity. Fargo arced his knee at Machetazo's groin but the general sprang out of reach.

"For that affront, when I return I will cut yours off

and have it crammed down your throat." The Beast headed for the big tent, throwing back one last taunt. "It will give both of us something to look forward to. Me, more than you, but no one ever said life was fair." And he cackled anew.

9

Twenty-four hours: an entire day without water, without food. That was how long Skye Fargo had been tied between the two trees. His mouth and throat were as dry as the Sonora desert, and the thought of food caused his stomach to growl and rumble like a hibernation-starved bear's. So he shut his mind to the idea of both, and stared sullenly at the five guards assigned to keep watch over him.

A dozen Black Sheaths had been left behind. The rest were long gone, filing out of the valley the night before: General Machetazo at their head; half on horseback, the rest on foot. A small supply column had brought up the rear.

Since then, Fargo had only one thing on his mind: escape. Whenever the guards weren't looking, he twisted his wrists back and forth, trying to loosen the ropes enough to free himself. His wrists hurt abominably. He had rubbed them raw, searing deep into his flesh, and they were both bleeding. But he didn't stop. He had to keep at it while he still had the strength. Another day or two and he would be too weak.

The Black Sheaths did not pay much attention to him. With the officers gone, discipline was lax. Sergeant Gonzales had been left in charge but he spent most of his time relaxing in a chair and sipping from a flask. So long as the guards stayed nearby, he didn't care if they talked or smoked or indulged in a game of dice or cards.

The only other person in camp was Juanita, and she

kept to herself. Twice she had gone for short strolls, and the Black Sheaths always avoided her as if she had the plague. Fargo had heard Machetazo warn Sergeant Gonzales that no one was to go near her or the big tent under penalty of death. Only Gonzales was allowed to talk to her, and then only if she addressed him first.

Fargo could tell something was bothering her. On her walks she repeatedly glanced at him, inner turmoil written large on her lovely face. He always smiled but she never smiled back. To the contrary, she always turned her back to him as if offended.

Exactly twenty-four hours had gone by since the People's Army for the Liberation of Mexico had marched off, and Fargo was having a hard time keeping his eyes open. He was tired, so terribly tired. Several times that day he had dozed off, but his legs always gave way and the pain in his arms jolted him awake again.

The flap to the big tent opened and out came Juanita, carrying a chair. She set it down and sat, a book in her lap. Thirty paces to the south, Sergeant Gonzales raised his flask in salute and grinned. She ignored him. Opening the book, she began to read, but Fargo noticed she had no real interest in it. She kept glancing at him and at the five guards. Four were involved in a card game. The fifth was leaning against a tree, his arms across his chest, looking as bored as it was possible for a human being to look.

A quarter-moon had risen. With the bulk of the army gone, along with almost all the horses—including the Ovaro—the valley was disturbingly quiet and empty.

The pain in Fargo's wrists had become almost unbearable. Every time he twisted one or the other, agony racked him. He would end up rubbing clear down to the bone before he freed himself. There had to be a better way, but for the life of him, he couldn't think of one. He couldn't bend far enough to use his teeth, and the ropes were too strong to break.

Then a coyote yipped—probably the same one Fargo had heard up on the mountain. At the sound he had a brainstorm that brought a quick grin—a grin he promptly wiped off his countenance before the Black Sheaths noticed. Biding his time, he waited for the coyote to yip again, and when it did, he put on a show of straightening and staring into the night as if he were worried. He had to try twice to speak, his mouth was so dry. "It can't be," he said aloud, his voice sounding strange even to him.

The Black Sheaths playing cards failed to notice but the one leaning against the tree did. "What is wrong, *gringo*?"

Fargo licked his lips, trying to moisten them. "Didn't you hear that?"

"The coyote? *Sí.*"

"Listen closer next time. Hasn't anyone taught you how to tell the difference between coyotes and Apaches?"

At his mention of the Southwest's most feared denizens, the cardplayers stopped their game. One addressed the man by the tree in Spanish, asking what Fargo had said.

"He says there are Apaches close by."

That brought the other four to their feet, their hands on their machetes. Only the tallest had a gun, an old rifle slung across his back. "Sergeant Gonzales!" he hollered. *"Venga pronto, por favor!"*

But the stocky sergeant took his sweet time. Capping his flask, he slowly rose and lumbered over.

The remaining five Black Sheaths were scattered about the camp; two lounging on their blankets, two others drinking coffee, and the fifth sewing his shirt. They all looked up to see what was going on.

"What is the matter?" Sergeant Gonzales growled. "The first peace and quiet I have in weeks and you want to spoil it." When several tried to answer him at once, he raised a hand. "*Silencio!* One at a time."

Fargo hoped the coyote would yip again, and it didn't disappoint him. Tugging at the ropes as if in a panic, he feigned no interest in the Black Sheaths until thick fingers wrapped around his left arm and squeezed.

"What is this game you play with my men, *gringo*?" Sergeant Gonzales was not pleased. "Scaring them with talk of Apaches."

"Don't you have ears?" Fargo rejoined.

"*Sí*. I heard a coyote."

"You go on believing that if you want. But I'm a scout for the U.S. army, and I know a Mescalero out for my hide when I hear one. There's a war party out there, I tell you."

Gonzales gazed at the darkling ring of mountains, his indecision as plain as his bulbous nose. "We have been here almost a month. Why would Apaches come around now?"

"Because they aren't stupid. There were too many of you before but now they have the advantage." Fargo did his best to sound sufficiently scared. "Cut me down and give me a weapon so I have a fighting chance."

"Ah. So that's what this is. You think I am dumb enough to free you."

Another coyote yipped from a different direction, and Fargo tugged even harder, wincing at the pain. "What more proof do you need?" He played his part to the hilt. "Damn you, I don't want to die trussed up like this."

The five Black Sheaths nervously edged closer to Sergeant Gonzales, who again scanned the valley from end to end while gnawing on his thick lower lip.

"What if the *norteamericano* is right, Sergeant?" a particularly timid Black Sheath asked. "The eleven of us are not enough to hold off Apaches."

"I know those devils, I know how they fight," said a second. "They will wait until most of us are asleep, then take as many of us alive as they can to torture us."

"*Sí,*" agreed a third. "They love torture even more than General Machetazo."

"Still your tongue!" Sergeant Gonzales ordered, but their fears were having an effect. When a coyote yipped from across the lake, he whirled and started to draw his machete. "Maybe they really are Apaches. If so, we cannot stay in the open. Roberto, get everyone into the big tent."

"But Sergeant, the general said no one is to step foot in it."

"I take full responsibility. And the *señorita* will not mind, I am sure." Gonzales looked toward the chair where Juanita had been sitting but it was empty. "Where is she? Did anyone see where she went?"

Several of the Black Sheaths shook their heads or mumbled that they hadn't.

Fargo hadn't seen her get up, either. He figured she was in the big tent, and he was as shocked as everyone else when a scream shattered the stillness from somewhere near the supply tents south of it.

"The Apaches have her!" Sergeant Gonzales exclaimed. "Follow me!"

There was a moment's hesitation on the part of the other Black Sheaths. Then all ten rushed after the burly sergeant. Shouting to bolster their courage, they waved their machetes overhead and raced into the darkness.

Fargo was left alone, but not for long. Hardly had the Black Sheaths disappeared than Juanita came running around the north end of Machetazo's tent. She no longer had the book. In one hand she held a revolver; in the other, a machete. She came straight toward him, wearing the frightened look of a doe afraid a pack of wolves would catch its scent. But the Black Sheaths were over near the lake, making enough noise to be heard in Mesilla. "Watch out!" she said, and swung.

The blade narrowly missed Fargo's left hand. Without the rope to keep it taut, his arm dropped to his side, his shoulder spiked by torment. When she cut the other rope, he tried to take a step and tottered like a toddler. He thought his knees would give way but he steadied himself and said, "Thanks."

"We must flee!" Juanita urged, shoving the revolver at him. "They won't be gone long. I have prepared a pack with food, enough to last us until we are out of the mountains." Gripping his right arm, she started to pull him toward the big tent.

Fargo almost pitched onto his face. His legs were tingling and half numb, his arms so wooden that straightening them required every ounce of concentration he could muster. "We're not leaving."

"But the Black Sheaths! They will be back any moment."

"Give me the machete." Fargo was in no shape to go anywhere. Shuffling to a particularly dark spot under one of the trees, he cocked the revolver. It was an old Walker Colt, so big and heavy it would be hard to aim. He gave the machete a few light swings and realized he didn't have the strength to beat a soggy potato. He gave it back to her.

Juanita's fingernails dug into his biceps. "What has gotten into you? You are in no condition to fight. This will only get us killed."

Not if Fargo could help it. They had one chance. It all depended on how careless the Black Sheaths were.

Into the firelight came Sergeant Gonzales, leading the others. They hadn't liked being out there in the dark where Mescaleros might be lurking about, and they were bunched up like sheep frightened of wolves.

The man with the rifle, which he now gripped nervously, turned toward the trees. "Look! The *gringo* is gone! The Apaches took him, too!"

They fell for the ruse and barreled forward. Fargo let them. In the shape he was, he needed them close. Gonazles picked up one of the severed ropes and announced it had been cut. Before they could spread out to start a searching, Fargo dug deep into the wellspring of his stamina and hollered, "Don't any of you move! I have a gun!"

The Black Sheaths froze except for the man with the rifle, who jammed it to his shoulder. Fargo fired first, and nearly wished he hadn't. The big Walker boomed like a cannon and kicked like a Missouri mule. His arm whipped back, his wrist and shoulder spiked with agony, and he almost lost his grip.

The slug slammed into the Black Sheath's sternum, smashing him off his feet. He hit with a thud and never so much as twitched.

"I warned you! Now drop your machetes!"

Sergeant Gonzales raised his empty hands, but not all that high. "*Señorita* Tarasco? Is that you I see?"

Juanita didn't reply.

"Very clever of you, *señorita*, to lure us off. The general, though, will not appreciate it very much. I would not want to be in your shoes when he finds out."

Fargo thumbed back the hammer. "Who is going to tell him?"

Gonzales smiled thinly. "You have five shots left and there are ten of us. If we rush you, you might get two or three at most. All I need do is say the word."

"Say it," Fargo goaded, "and you'll be the first one I shoot." He played his wild card: "But there's no need for anyone else to die. The rest of you can go if you want. Take all the food and water you can carry and head home to your wives and families." There was no way of telling how many were conscripts who would leap at the chance, but he was banking there had to be some.

"No one is going anywhere," Sergeant Gonzales flatly declared.

Some of the Black Sheaths swapped glances behind his back or gazed longingly to the south.

"What is to stop them?" Fargo fed their fledgling hopes. "The Beast is gone. The officers are gone." He paused so that would sink in. "You're the only thing keeping them here, Sergeant."

Gonzales shifted so he could see the others, and he didn't like what he saw. "Don't listen to this *americano*! He is thinking only of his own skin. If you run off, General Machetazo will send his demons after you to drag you back. And you know the punishment for desertion."

"It could be weeks before the general returns," Fargo pointed out. "By then all of you will be long gone. There won't be enough sign left for the half-breeds to track you."

"Do we dare?" one said.

"No, you do not!" Sergeant Gonzales snarled. "You forget that I know where each of you lives. As surely as I stand here, I will show up on your doorstep one day and you and your loved ones will pay for your treachery."

Fear eclipsed their hope, and several visibly withered like plants too long in the sun. "I would rather go on being miserable than let anything happen to my family," one summed up the sentiments of them all.

"Do you hear, *gringo*?" Gonzales gloated. "I have won!"

Fargo refused to give up, not with his life hanging in the balance. He had to convince the downcast Black Sheaths that desertion was in their own best interests. "Look at you! You finally have a chance to return to your loved ones and you stand there like bumps on a log. What would your wives and children say?"

Juanita broke her silence to interject, "Think of it! To hold your women in your arms! To bounce your children on your knees! To live as you please!"

Murmuring broke out but Sergeant Gonzales nipped it in the bud by thundering, "Silence! The *gringo* and the girl won't suffer if you desert. *You* will!" He motioned at Fargo. "Help me subdue this pig and there will be extra rations for all of you—and maybe a promotion or two."

"More food on your plate will not restore your freedom to you," Juanita countered. "It is a poor substitute for once again living under the same roof as those you most care for in this world."

Fargo edged closer. The debate had gone on long enough. His limbs were growing leaden and he had to act before he was too weak. "If you want me, Gonzales, here I am. That is, if you're man enough to do it by yourself."

The sergeant's nostrils dilated and his thick neck and shoulders swelled like those of a mad bull. "Brave talk when you are holding a gun. Put it down and try me man to man, machete to machete."

In his condition Fargo wouldn't last two minutes, and Gonzales knew it. He would just as soon gun Gonzales down, but if he killed an unarmed man he wasn't any better than Machetazo. So, tucking the Walker under his belt, he responded, "I'll give you more of a chance than you'd ever give me. Grab a machete. Or that rifle. I won't draw until you touch it." He lowered his arms.

Sergeant Gonzales glanced at the machetes scattered in the grass, then at the rifle beside the dead Black Sheath. He was calculating his prospects for success, and he must have rated them high because he scornfully responded, "*Gringos* are always so noble, so *fair*. I spit on you and your country. You can measure your life in seconds."

"General Machetazo wants him alive!" Juanita protested.

"As your friend keeps pointing out, the general isn't here. I was left in charge, to take whatever steps I see fit. And I think it necessary the *gringo* die." And just like that, Gonzales whirled and dived for the rifle. He was as stout as a wall but he was no turtle. His outflung fingers wrapped around it and he rolled up onto a knee, the stock against his side. It was an older percussion model but that didn't make it any less lethal. The slug would leave an exit hole as large as a pie plate.

Fargo's hand flew to the big revolver. Trying to bring it to bear, though, was like trying to pluck a tree stump from the ground. The Walker was one of the earliest models Colt made, and one of the bulkiest. It weighed four pounds. Under the best of circumstances, unlimbering one swiftly took great skill—and Fargo wasn't in the best of shape. He jerked it out but he couldn't straighten his arm.

Gonzales was grinning. He thought he had Fargo dead to rights; thought he had the fraction of a second he needed to aim and be sure. So instead of firing from the hip he fixed a quick bead down the barrel, centering the muzzle for a heart shot.

Fargo's wrist was throbbing, his right arm next to useless. Given a minute, he might be able to lift the Walker one-handed. But he didn't have a minute. He had to defend himself right then or he was buzzard bait. And since one arm wasn't enough, he grasped the Walker with both hands and thrust it forward while simultaneously sidestepping to the right.

The rifle boomed, belching a cloud of smoke that wreathed Sergeant Gonzales like fog. All Fargo could see was a dark outline, but it was enough. He fired at where the shape was widest. Using both thumbs to pull back the hammer, he fired once more just as Gonzales lurched out of the smoke wielding the rifle like a club.

Fargo tried to spring aside but his legs, like his arms, weren't equal to the occasion. He stumbled and fell. Something brushed his hair—the rifle stock, he suspected. Then he was on his side, struggling to lift the Walker. He felt what he took to be a heavy blow to his hip but it wasn't the rifle, it was Gonzales. The sergeant had keeled over on top of him.

Pinned to the ground, Fargo saw a Black Sheath scoop up a machete and spring. He banged off a shot as the glittering blade descended. The impact knocked the Black Sheath off balance, and the machete thudded into the dirt beside his head. Again he forced back the hammer.

Gushing scarlet from his mouth, the Black Sheath reeled as if drunk. He managed to take four or five erratic steps, then melted like so much hot wax.

"Anyone else?" Fargo demanded, training the big revolver on the others. They were statues, their mouths agape. He kicked at Gonzales and the heavy body rolled off, leaving a dark smear on his buckskins. Slowly sitting up, he marshaled his energy to rise. No one tried to stop him. Juanita reached out to help but withdrew her hand when he gave an almost imperceptible shake of his head. He didn't want the Black Sheaths to learn how truly weak he was.

"We are still free to go?" one asked.

"I meant what I said," Fargo confirmed.

"What about the Apaches?" another inquired.

"Idiot," said a third. "Haven't you been paying attention? It was all a trick." He headed toward the supply tents and the others barreled after him, a few giggling like schoolchildren let out after a long day of school.

Juanita tossed her machete down. "How about us? I can have mounts saddled in five minutes."

An important fact had almost slipped Fargo's mind.

Only four mules and two horses were left in camp; the mules because they hadn't been needed, the horses because one had a sore leg and the other had lost a shoe. "Bring two of the mules over to the big tent. I won't be able to leave for a while yet but we don't want anyone else to claim them."

Fargo would have done it himself if he hadn't been at the point of near-total exhaustion. The best he could do was cover her and ensure none of the Black Sheaths interfered. He had her picket the animals near the flap and left it open so he could keep an eye on them. Sinking into a chair, he placed the Walker on the table. "I need food. And whiskey, if there's any to be had."

Gently squeezing his shoulder, Juanita said, "Leave everything to me. I will also find bandages." She ran her fingers along his collarbone. "Do not feel obligated to hurry off on my account. It is important you are fit enough to ride."

"A good night's sleep would help."

Juanita was staring out the tent. "Take as much time to rest up as you want. When they leave, we will have the whole valley to ourselves."

Fargo had no intention of leaving before noon, at the earliest. He watched her bustle to a corner, the contours of her pert backside accented by her clinging dress. On her return she brought a half-empty whiskey bottle, which he upended and chugged. It wasn't the smartest thing he'd ever done. He had gone so long without anything to eat or drink that his stomach rebelled. It felt as if a keg of black powder had exploded in his gut, and the whiskey began to come back up. Refusing to be sick, he swallowed it down again.

"Are you all right?" Juanita asked, her warm fingers on his back.

"Never better," Fargo answered between coughing fits. His eyes were watering and his insides were churning but that didn't stop him from upending the bottle again and downing even more. This time it stayed where it should.

Juanita went into the corner and brought back a fresh haunch of venison on an ornate silver tray, along with a fork, knife, and cloth napkin.

Fargo was too famished to care about proper etiquette. Taking the haunch in both hands, he tore into it like a starved wolf into a moose. Biting deep, he ripped off great chunks and chewed lustily.

"You are all male, *señor*," Juanita said, grinning.

Wondering what that was supposed to mean, Fargo responded with his mouth full to bursting, "And you're all woman." He imagined himself running his hands over her ripe young body, and his manhood twitched. But had to admit he was getting ahead of himself. "Didn't you say something about bandages?"

"*Sí*. My apologies."

A commotion outside brought Fargo to his feet. Snatching up the Walker, he strode to the flap. The conscripts weren't wasting any time. Laden with waterskins and packs, they had laid claim to the other mules and horses and were hurrying eastward, eager to get out of there. Several looked back and cheerfully waved.

"They are the happiest men alive," Juanita commented. "When they get home they will tell everyone about you."

Fargo hoped they would make it. Ahead was a long, arduous trek across some of the most hellish country on the continent. "There's not much to tell."

"On the contrary, *señor*. You were magnificent."

"If you say so." Retaking his seat, Fargo renewed his assault on the haunch. There was enough meat on the bone for three people but he was hungry enough for five. It had to be twenty minutes later that he dropped it on the silver tray, sat back, and patted his stomach.

Juanita, meanwhile, had filled a basin with water

and cut a towel into strips. Depositing them next to him, along with a pair of scissors, she pulled up a chair. "You look like a new man."

"I feel like one." The whiskey and food had invigorated him, and Fargo felt as if he could leap over the tent in a single bound.

"Lay your arms on the table," Juanita directed.

Fargo expected it to hurt but she exercised such delicate care he felt little pain except when she was prying the ropes from his raw flesh. Dry blood had fastened to them like glue, and she had to soak them before they would peel off. When she was done, he sat back and lightly rubbed each bandage. "You'd make a fine nurse."

Juanita's eyes met his and she asked in a low voice, "Is there anything else I can do for you?"

10

Skye Fargo knew women as well as any man could. Juanita Tarasco had more in mind than fetching another bottle of whiskey. Normally, he would be on her faster than a bear on honey, but although new vitality was pumping through his veins, he still felt as if he had tangled with a grizzly. He also smelled like one.

Fargo wasn't one of those people who believed bathing was harmful to the health. A lot of frontier folk never formed the habit of taking regular baths because they believed it made them susceptible to colds and disease. A bath every few months was more than enough for them. Some took one only once a year—if that—and didn't seem to mind that they smelled rank enough to gag a skunk.

Fargo liked to bathe more frequently. To him, few pastimes were more pleasurable than diving into a cold mountain lake or clear flowing river to wash off the dust and grime of the trail. Hot baths were another matter. They were a luxury in which he rarely indulged. But if ever he needed one, it was now. Sweat was plastered to his skin from head to toe, and his chest was a patchwork of dried blood from the lash wounds.

So now, smiling at Juanita, Fargo replied, "You can help me fill the tub."

"Is that all you want?"

Fargo almost laughed at the disappointment in her voice. "For now. But there's more you can do later."

He said it in a way that left no doubt as to his true meaning, and she perked up like a little girl promised a batch of hard candy.

The camp lay unnaturally quiet under the stars. Two fires still burned, and putting down his buckets, Fargo took a burning brand and scoured the area near the trees. He found his buckskin shirt right away but had to search awhile for his hat.

Juanita helped. They crisscrossed the area, and every now and again as she passed him she would brush against his shoulder, or her hand would touch his.

Some women, Fargo reflected, *were as subtle as an avalanche.* Not that he minded. Give him a female who liked to be intimate over a female who didn't, any day of the week. Some never learned to accept their own desires, and making love to them was like making love to a block of ice. He preferred passionate women.

It took repeated trips to the lake to fill the tub. While Juanita heated the water, Fargo ransacked Machetazo's tent. He left no drawer unopened, no chest overturned. He found uniforms and other clothes. He found three pairs of boots. He found several machetes and a sword. There was a solid silver snuffbox and a silver-trimmed cigar box. There were china dishes and bowls, fine blankets and sheets, a rolled-up tapestry, and much more—but not what he wanted to find the most. There were not any revolvers or rifles, and he found only half a box of ammunition for the Walker.

"I could have told you there were no others guns," Juanita said when he mentioned what he was after. "Machetazo owns a set of pistols and a rifle but he took them with him. Tarleton Wilkes has your weapons."

Fargo had last seen the sham brother and sister at the head of the Beast's army, riding on either side of

General Machetazo. Both were quiet and subdued, as well they should be now that their ally had revealed himself for the sadistic butcher he truly was.

Watching Tarleton ride off on the Ovaro had seared Fargo like a Comanche lance. No matter what else, he would hunt the Southerner down and recover his stallion, even if he had to travel all the way to Georgia to do it.

At last the bath was ready. Fargo pulled the blanket to give himself some privacy, stripped off the rest of his clothes, and eased down into the tub. Leaning his head back, he closed his eyes and let the tension drain from his body. He didn't mean to doze off but he did. The next thing he knew, he awoke to Juanita's softly calling his name and was baffled to discover the water had gone from scalding hot to lukewarm.

"Skye? Are you all right in there?"

Cobwebs of weariness shrouded Fargo's mind, and before he could answer, the blanket slid back.

"Why didn't you answer me?" Juanita demanded, coming over. "I was worried something had happened."

"I fell asleep." Fargo gave his head a vigorous shake to clear it. "How long have I been in here?"

"Three and a half hours." Juanita stepped over to a stack of towels. "I was reading and hadn't realized how long it had been until a little while ago." She brought the top towel over and unfolded it. "I've put new sheets and pillowcases on the bed. Let's get you out of there before you shrivel like a prune."

Fargo looked down at himself. "I already have," he said, and chuckled. Thankfully his arms had been draped over the side, so the bandages, were still dry.

"I will leave you to dry yourself off." Juanita draped the towel over the rim. "Call me if you need anything."

"You can dry my back," Fargo suggested, and deliberately stood up.

Juanita made no attempt to avert her eyes. On the

138

contrary, her gaze lingered on his muscular form, drifting to a point at the junction of his thighs. *"Magnifico,"* she breathed.

Climbing out, Fargo held out his hand for the towel. The next move was up to her. She could throw it to him or do what she did, namely, wrap it around him herself.

Her breath warm on his chest, her cheeks the color of strawberries, Juanita grinned self-consciously and said, "Has anyone ever told you that you are terribly naughty? You make it hard for a woman to control herself."

"Letting you dry me isn't naughty." Taking hold of one of her hands, Fargo slid it below his waist onto his hardening manhood. *"This* is naughty."

Juanita's entire face flushed bright red but she didn't take her hand away. "You are feeling a lot better now, I see." She cupped him, her throat bobbing. "Do not ask me why, but I have wanted you since first I set eyes on you."

"Do tell." Fargo removed the towel and threw it to the ground. Her dress was getting wet but she didn't seem to care and he sure didn't. Clasping her chin, he tilted it and molded his mouth to hers. At the contact Juanita uttered a tiny mew and pressed against him. Her lips were as soft as twin feathers, her tongue as smooth as silk. It met his midway and he sucked on it while gently massaging her shoulders. Soon her breaths became volcanic fire and her fingers were everywhere, exploring.

Fargo's weariness had evaporated like morning dew under a blistering sun. His pole was now as hard as iron and jutting like a redwood. Although his chest was sore and his wrists hurt when he moved his arms, the pain wasn't bad enough to lessen his pleasure. Sliding his right hand to her chest, he cupped her left breast. It was so huge it dwarfed his fingers. He squeezed, eliciting a moan, and probed for the nipple.

"You make me weak inside," Juanita cooed.

Were it not for his wrists, Fargo would have swept her into his arms and carried her across the tent to the bed. Instead, he began undoing a row of tiny buttons at the front of her dress and was surprised when she gripped his forearm to stop him. "Is something wrong?"

"The flap. It is still open."

"So? We're the only ones here." Fargo hadn't pegged her as overly modest but with women there was no predicting. Some were shy about intimate matters but turned into sexual tigresses in bed. Others were frisky in public but as lively as lumps of coal when it counted the most.

"I would rather it were closed," Juanita insisted, and hurried to do so.

Fargo left his clothes where they had fallen and walked buck naked over to the table.

When she turned, her lovely features were alight with wanton desire. Sashaying toward him, she undid some of the buttons and stays herself. "Satisfied?" he asked.

Juanita's smile was ripe with lust. "I will tell you in the morning."

Pulling her close, Fargo locked his lips to hers. Her nails raked the back of his neck as he covered both glorious mounds with his hands and moved his palms in small circles. The heat she gave off was enough to set kindling ablaze. Delving his left hand down over her thigh, he gripped her firm bottom.

"You are a man with much experience, I think," Juanita playfully commented.

"I've done this once or twice," Fargo said, rimming her lips with his tongue.

Juanita took hold of his elbows and began to back toward the bed. Her eyelids were hooded, her huge breasts rising and falling rhythmically. When he suddenly slid a hand between her legs, she stiffened and cried out softly, *"Oh! Oh!"*

Fargo's craving was as great as hers. He nearly exploded prematurely when she enfolded his pole in a velvet grip and stroked him up and down. Fastening his mouth to an earlobe, he lathered it, then nibbled the edge of her ear. She was sensitive there, arching her back and purring like a she-cat in heat.

"I am going to eat you alive, *señor*."

"Promises, promises." They had reached the hanging blankets at the other end and, grabbing one, Fargo pulled so hard it came partway off. Heedless of the discomfort, he bent and picked her up.

"Your wrists!" Juanita objected.

"Are holding up just fine, thank you, ma'am." Fargo placed her in the middle of the bed. Sliding next to her, he finished unfastening her dress and slid it over her head. Underneath she had on a chemise, three petticoats, long cotton drawers, and thigh-high stockings—but no corset, thank goodness, or it would have taken him another fifteen minutes.

Fargo's mouth wasn't idle as he worked. He kissed her lips, her eyelids. He licked her throat and dipped his tongue between the swell of her cleavage. Hiking her chemise to her shoulders, he bent to suck on a nipple. Since her breasts were enormous, he had imagined her nipples would be larger than average, too. But they were the smallest nipples he ever saw, baby peas with tan aureolas a small coin could cover. They were also as sensitive as her ears, if not more so. When he inhaled one and flicked it, she nearly bit a chunk out of him.

"Yesssss, señor! Like that! Do that again!"

Fargo obliged her. Juanita squirmed deliciously, her body giving off a musky scent that fueled his hunger. Her thighs were opening and closing in invitation. She gripped his right hand and tried to lower it between them but he massaged her hip instead. They had all night and he wanted to make it last as long as he could.

Juanita gave up trying to rush him and devoted herself to kissing every square inch of his face, neck, and shoulders. Tiny kisses that sent tingly sparks shooting through his body and prickled his skin like a heat rash.

Rolling her onto her stomach, Fargo kissed her shoulders and her shoulder blades while sliding his hands around in front to squeeze her melons. Taking his sweet time, he licked a path down her spine from her neck to her buttocks, and liked how she wriggled and breathed harder than ever.

"You make me so hot!"

It was mutual. Fargo nipped at her bottom, then rolled her over again and nuzzled her nether mound with his nose and chin.

Juanita gasped, then placed her hands on the back of his head and pushed his face harder against her. *"Ah! Ah!* Deeper, *por favor!"*

Not yet, Fargo decided. He trailed his tongue along her smooth inner thigh down to her knee, shifted to her other leg, and licked a path back up to her waist.

"Please!" Juanita pleaded, sliding her ankles over his shoulders and scooting her backside higher to grant him better access.

His mouth watering, Fargo pressed it to her drenched slit.

Juanita bucked upward. Her eyes were closed, her cheeks crimson, her breasts twin mountains caught in the upheaval of an earthquake.

Extending his tongue as far as it would go, Fargo tasted her sugary essence. He moved it in and out a few times, then shaped his mouth to her swollen knob and sucked. Her thighs became a vise against his temples, and her fingers mashed his head into her with a fervor born of the need for release. A few more licks and she crested, heaving against him like an untamed mustang. A long, low moan escaped her, filling the tent and drifting out into the night.

The lower half of Fargo's face became drenched with her nectar. When she went momentarily limp and her legs parted, he rose onto his knees and gripped his member.

A vixenish grin curled Juanita's luscious lips. She watched as he rubbed his tip along her slit, the pink tip of her tongue protruding from her mouth. When he inserted himself, she threw her head back and let out a long sigh of contentment. "I wish I could have you inside me forever."

Fargo lay still for as long as he could, delighting in the feel of her inner walls. Ages-old instinct would not be denied, however, and he commenced rocking back and forth on his knees, thrusting himself up into her again and again. He did it slowly so as to prolong their ecstasy. She pumped her hips at the same pace, her nails daggers in his back.

"I am close again," Juanita sighed. "So very close." Her lips inflamed his neck and chest.

Sliding his right hand lower, Fargo tweaked her. That was all it took. Clinging to his shoulders, Juanita wrapped her legs tight and spurted. Her whole body shook and a wail of release tore from her throat—a wail she stifled by biting him. For his part, he continued stroking but held himself back from the brink.

Gradually Juanita slowed and was still except for the quivering of her flat belly and the fluttering of her lips.

Fargo lay quiet, too, which was hard to do with his pole throbbing like it was.

"You were marvelous," Juanita whispered languidly. "We must do this again sometime."

"How about now?" Fargo said, and rammed up into her again.

Juanita looked up at him in wonderment. At his next thrust, her mouth yawned wide but no sound came out.

Fargo began moving faster and faster, harder and harder. She hugged herself to him, her face buried in his chest. He prolonged the inevitable as long as he could. His hands on her waist, he rode her with feverish intensity. The combined weight of their bodies bent the mattress and caused the bedposts to thump the ground like sledgehammers. The bed was making so much noise that when she called out his name, he barely heard her.

"Oh! Again! Again!"

Her inner walls contracted, and Fargo felt a torrent wash over him. His own release came seconds later.

Afterward, once their hearts had stopped hammering, Juanita nestled against him and toyed with his hair. "And to think, a week ago we did not even know each other." She kissed his chin. *"Muchas gracias."*

Hoping she wasn't going to bend his ear, Fargo hovered between wakefulness and sleep. He had fulfilled one craving; now he had another: hours of uninterrupted slumber.

"You have reminded me there is more to lovemaking than the pain the Beast delights in," Juanita commented.

Fargo had noticed a lot of bruises on her arms and shoulders but thought it best not to ask how she came by them.

"My greatest fear now is that he will come after me. His pride will not let him accept I have left."

"I won't let him lay a hand on you." Fargo had already made up his mind that Vicente Machetazo's days of brutal bloodletting were about to end. The man was a rabid dog in human guise, and there was only one thing to do with rabid dogs.

"I believe you, *señor*." Juanita rubbed her cheek across his chest. "There is something about you. I feel safe in your arms."

Fargo patted her shoulder. He could no longer stay awake and the world around them receded into an inky haze—but only for a few moments. Pain in his right wrist snapped him back.

"Did you hear that?" Juanita whispered. She had grabbed him without thinking and was staring apprehensively toward the front flap.

"I didn't hear a thing." Fargo tried to roll onto his side but she held on to him.

"Someone is out there, I tell you. I heard footsteps."

"The Black Sheaths are miles away by now. All you heard was the mules." But even as Fargo said it, he realized he was wrong. He had forgotten someone. There was one Black Sheath unaccounted for: the sentry out at the pass.

"There! I heard it again!"

Sitting up, Fargo swung his legs over the bed. He had heard it, too—the stealthy rustle of grass and the rasp of a gun hammer being cocked. He slowly rose, mad at himself for leaving the Walker Colt and his clothes clear at the other end of the tent. Suddenly Juanita clamped onto his arm and pointed at the front of the tent.

A hand had gripped the flap and was slowly pulling it open. The muzzle of a rifle poked through and moved from side to side.

As yet the man hadn't spotted them. Crouching, Fargo crept to the mahogany table, which was between the flap and the bed. His bare feet made no noise. Taking a firm hold on a chair, he sidestepped over to the canvas and raised the chair over his shoulder. His wrists spiked with pain, but it couldn't be helped.

The flap parted wide enough to reveal a ferret-faced Black Sheath in dirt-stained clothes and a straw sombrero. He peered toward the tub, then at the table, then toward the bed. Astonishment registered, and he blinked a few times.

Fargo had seen Juanita step brazenly into sight wearing nothing but the skin she was born in. She did it to help him by distracting the Black Sheath, and he didn't disappoint her. Lunging, he swung the chair.

The Black Sheath tried to pivot but he hadn't quite completed his turn when the chair smashed into him, shattering on impact and sending him tottering into the darkness. The rifle went off but all the slug did was dig a furrow in the ground. Then the flap swung shut.

Without breaking stride, Fargo ran to the Walker and scooped it up. He thought the Black Sheath would come barging back in but the man was too smart for that. Across the tent, Juanita was hurriedly dressing.

Tense seconds passed. To the northeast rose an angry shout in Spanish. "Damn you, *gringo,* and the whore who bore· you! I, Paco, will kill you for that! Do you hear me?"

Fargo wasn't about to advertise where he was. Grabbing his pants, he tugged them on one-handed.

Again Paco yelled, only now he was north of the tent. "I am not a dirt farmer like those who ran off! I have been with the general from the start, and he will reward me well if I keep you from getting away!"

Jamming his hat onto his head, Fargo sat down and pulled on his socks and boots. Instead of strapping the Arkansas toothpick around his ankle, he tucked it under his belt for the time being. The spare ammunition for the Walker went into a pocket. That left his shirt, which he slung over a shoulder as he glided toward the flap.

"Nothing to say for yourself, *gringo*?" Paco taunted, now from west of the tent. "Very well. Let us get this over with."

The rifle boomed. Instinctively, Fargo ducked, then realized the shot wasn't intended for him. A hole had appeared in the canvas near one of the lamps. It dawned on him what the Black Sheath was up to and, dashing over, he blew out the flame, shrouding part of the tent into shadow.

There were two others lamps, though—one by the bed, another by the tub. Fargo chose to extinguish the former, first.

Juanita was almost dressed but paused to stare in bewilderment. "What are you up to? she whispered.

Another blast of the rifle answered her for him. The lamp near the tub exploded, showering fingers of flame every which way. Within seconds the canvas had caught fire, and flames spread with startling rapidity.

"He intends to burn us out!" Juanita declared.

Fargo raced to the tub. Already tendrils of smoke were sinuously intertwining, and a hole as big as the silver tray had been eaten away by the flames. Snatching up a bucket, he plunged it into the tub. When it was almost full, he yanked it out, spun, and flung the water at the burning canvas. Some of the flames were snuffed out, but nowhere near enough. The tent was burning too rapidly, and the fire had now spread to the top.

Again Fargo dipped the bucket into the tub. Again he dashed water on the blaze, but he was fighting a lost cause.

Juanita ran to help. Her back to the hole the fire had made, she sank a bucket into the bathtub.

Only Fargo saw the sombrero-crowned figure materialize out of the night. Only he saw the firelight glint off a gun barrel. Throwing himself at Juanita, he bore her to the ground a split instant before the rifle spat lead. He heard the slug strike the tub, heard the gleeful laughter of the Black Sheath.

"What do we do?" Juanita cried. "We can't let the tent burn to the ground. All these nice things!"

Fargo would be damned if he would risk being shot to try to save the Beast's plunder. They *were* going to let it burn. But they had to get out while they still could. Not by the front, since Paco would expect that and be ready to pick them off. And not by the slit near the bed, either. Paco might know it was there.

Grasping Juanita's hand, Fargo pulled her toward the back to a spot a dozen feet from the roaring flames. The smoke was swiftly spreading. Juanita had a hand over her mouth and nose but could not keep from coughing.

Holding his breath, Fargo made a new slit. If Paco was still on that side of the tent, he'd make a perfect target. He cocked the Walker, dug in his heels, and burst on through like a cannonball exploding from a cannon. He thought he saw the Black Sheath at the southwest corner but it was a trick of light and shadow.

Juanita slid out after him. His shirt had fallen and she scooped it up. Her eyebrows arched quizzically, asking a silent question.

Putting a finger to his lips, Fargo backed toward the lake. Crackling flames leaped skyward above the new slit. The whole south end was now engulfed. Paco, though, was nowhere to be seen, confirming Fargo's notion he had gone around to the front.

Once among the bushes lining the shore, Fargo squatted and motioned Juanita down beside him. "I have to go find him. Wait here until I come back."

"But what if something happens to you?"

Without any hesitation Fargo placed the big Colt in front of her. "Keep this handy. I'll use my knife." He started to rise but she clutched his arm.

"Let me come with you. I can—" Juanita abruptly stopped, riveted in fear.

Paco was slinking around the north end of the tent, confusion rampant on his countenance. He couldn't understand why they hadn't made a break yet.

Picking the Walker back up, Fargo rose and adopted a two-handed grip. The distance was about twenty yards. With his own Colt he could make the shot without half trying, but he wasn't accustomed to the Walker. He centered on the Black Sheath's chest, then elevated the barrel a hair. "Over here!" he hollered.

Paco whirled, bringing up the rifle. It wasn't quite to his shoulder when the Walker thundered. The first shot rocked him; the second felled him like a poled ox.

Fargo wasted no time hastening around to the mules. Half the tent had been consumed, the heat so intense the animals were on the verge of panic. Yanking the picket pins, he led them toward the supply tents.

Juanita hovered at his side, wringing her fingers in his shirt. "Do you think the fire will spread across the valley?" she anxiously asked.

In Fargo's estimation, no. Most of the ground near the tent had been worn bare by the tread of countless feet, and none of the trees were close enough for the flames to reach. He told her as much, adding, "We might as well get some shut-eye. Dawn will be here before we know it."

"I couldn't sleep if I tried." Juanita's ripe lips curled in an impish pout. "Have any idea what we can do to pass the time?"

11

"This is interesting." Skye Fargo reined his mule to a halt and leaned down to study the tracks they had been following.

"What is?" Juanita's windblown hair was disheveled but otherwise she showed little evidence of having pushed hard the past two and a half days in an attempt to catch up to the People's Army for the Liberation of Mexico. It was all the more remarkable since she was riding bareback. Not once had she complained or asked him to slow down.

"Twelve riders split off from the main group and headed due east. The Beast, the Southerners, and some others."

"How do you know it was them? To me all hoof-prints look pretty much the same."

Not to Fargo. He had spent years honing his talents as a tracker, and to him every print was as individual as the person or animal that made it. Machetazo's chestnut; the Ovaro; Susannah's dun; each had different characteristics that set them apart one from another. "The rest continued south with Captain Ruiz," he mentioned. Most likely to meet up with Colonel Fraco.

"What way do we go?"

Fargo pondered that very question. Warning Colonel Blanchard took precedence over all else. But whatever Machetazo was planning, Fargo couldn't see the Black Sheaths attacking the U.S. Army until the general was there to lead them. For a while Blanchard and the Third Cavalry should be safe.

"We head east," Fargo announced, enticed by the idea of killing two birds with one stone. Apparently the Beast was on his way to claim the gold promised by the Southerners. If the transfer could be thwarted, or, better yet, a bullet put through Machetazo's brain, the plot to instigate war between the United States and Mexico would collapse.

"How far behind them are we?" Juanita inquired.

Fargo glanced at the tracks again. "They have better than half a day on us."

"Then we have very little chance of catching up."

"Maybe. Maybe not." Fargo had the impression a lot of gold was involved, too much for a dozen horses to carry. Machetazo would need a wagon, and wagons moved exceedingly slowly.

"What can you hope to do if we do overtake them? All you have is that horse pistol and your knife."

"Don't forget my teeth." Fargo tried to make light of her anxiety but she didn't crack a grin.

"Were it up to me I would head straight for Fort Fillmore or Mesilla," Juanita commented. "I think you are making a mistake."

"It won't be the first time." Fargo had made more than his share but he refused to harp on them as some were prone to do. Life was for living, not fretting.

Hour after hour they pressed on. The mules held up well even without water. By nightfall that was remedied by a tank Fargo found in a rocky outcropping. A large stone cavity shielded from the sun, it was used by wild animals for miles around. Their tracks led Fargo to it, and after the mules had drunk and been tethered, he spread a blanket and stretched out on his back.

Juanita had grown pensive. Seated beside the pool, she swirled the water with her foot. "Do you still plan to do to General Machetazo as he deserves? As he has done to so many others?"

Fargo looked at her. She had posed the same question half a dozen times. She seemed to need to be constantly reassured he hadn't changed his mind. A large part of her worry had to do with her parents. She was afraid of what might happen to them should anything go wrong.

As if Juanita read his thoughts, she said, "I am sorry to keep bringing it up. But men sometimes say things in the heat of anger they do not mean."

Fargo wasn't one of them. Especially not where the Beast was concerned. Machetazo had taken a bullwhip to him. His mission for the army notwithstanding, it was personal now. He wasn't leaving New Mexico Territory until Machetazo answered for what he had done.

Juanita came over and sat beside him. Opening one of the packs they had brought, she held out strips of jerked venison. "I take it no fire again tonight?"

"Not unless you want Apaches to pay us a visit."

"What I wouldn't give for a hot meal."

Fargo bit off a piece and chewed hungrily. Jerked meat and pemmican were staples of his diet. In parts of the country where game was scarce they often meant the difference between breathing air and breathing dirt.

Taking a few nibbles, Juanita casually asked, "How much longer do you think we will be together?"

"No way of telling," Fargo answered honestly. "It could be a couple of days, it could be a week. Why?"

"I was thinking how much I enjoyed the other night before Paco interrupted us. And I wonder why it is you haven't touched me since."

If Fargo lived to be a hundred, women would continue to perplex him. The past two nights they had slept with her head cradled on his shoulder—the first night on a shelf high in the Peloncillos, then in an arroyo in the foothills. She had been tired and sore from riding all day, and it never entered his mind she might want to do anything except sleep.

"Was I so bad you do not want a second helping?" Juanita inquired, pouting like a small girl denied her favorite plaything.

Fargo looked around. It should be safe enough. Slabs of rock hemmed them on three sides, boulders on the fourth, and he had not seen evidence of Apaches.

"I've always considered myself pretty." Juanita wasn't done sulking. "Not beautiful like all those gorgeous *señoritas* in their big *haciendas*, but pretty enough to keep a man's interest. I guess you have proven me wrong."

"The man who wins your heart will never lose interest," Fargo stated to cheer her. "If I'd known you wanted more, I'd have done this sooner."

"Done what?"

Grabbing her hair, Fargo pulled her down on top of him and ground his mouth into hers. He wasn't gentle, like in the tent. He kissed her roughly, probed roughly with his tongue. The suddenness of it caused Juanita to gasp and then to groan as he covered her left breast and squeezed it as if it were a gourd he was trying to crush. A shudder passed through her. When he broke the kiss, she looked into the depths of his eyes and said softly, "Take me hard. But take me."

Fargo slid his left hand between her thighs and kneaded them as a baker kneads dough. Again he was none too gentle, and she was soon panting as if she had run a mile, her mouth formed into a delectable oval. Kissing her, he bit her lower lip. Not hard enough to draw blood but enough to tantalize her with what was in store.

Juanita wasn't idle. She tugged at his belt, and once she had it unbuckled, she thrust a hand into his pants. The feel of her fingers on his manhood aroused

Fargo to new heights. Sliding her legs over his so she straddled him, he buried his right arm up her dress. The drawstring to her cotton drawers wasn't easy to reach but he managed. Dispensing with foreplay, he shoved his hand underneath and stroked her core. She was already wet. He plunged his forefinger up into her and she bent her body back like a bow, and moaned.

Pumping his finger in and out, Fargo hitched at his buckskin pants to free his member.

She didn't notice. Her eyes were closed and she was adrift in the delirium of undiluted rapture. It was the work of a moment for him to pull her drawers down around her knees and raise her a foot into the air.

"What are you—?" Juanita began.

Fargo had his pole aligned just right. Bucking upward, he simultaneously pulled on her hips and impaled himself to the hilt. The whites of her eyes expanded and a feral cry was torn from her throat. For a few seconds she was completely still. Then she pumped against him in an urgent frenzy of total abandon.

The soles of his boots flat on the ground, Fargo levered up into her—times without number, always hard, always burying his sword in her silken scabbard. His hands were on her breasts, squeezing, pinching.

Juanita's hands were on his chest, her eyes were closed. She was intent on one thing and one thing only. Her loud breaths sounded like the hiss of a steam engine climbing a grade.

Fargo had learned long ago that sometimes women liked it rough. They became excited more quickly, and when they reached the summit, experienced a shattering release that left them completely spent. Juanita Tarasco did exactly that. When she spurted, she bucked like a bronc and barely stifled a screech that would have been heard in Mesilla. She pumped against him so fiercely it felt as if she would snap his spine.

Fargo's turn came a few minutes later. Juanita had sagged against him, her dress up around her hips, barely able to stay awake. Gripping her shoulders, he bent his legs to gain more penetration and drove his manhood into her with unrestrained relish. His own explosion came out of nowhere. He tried to mentally contain it but it was like trying to contain the raging waters of a breached dam. For a while he was conscious only of the purest physical thrill a man could know. Of ambrosia pumping through his veins.

As always, it didn't last. Fargo reluctantly coasted down from the lofty heights of bliss to the real world of sweat and fatigue, and of Juanita slumped on his chest, sound asleep, her hair covering his face. Some strands were in his mouth and he pulled them out, then eased her onto her side.

Fargo lay awake as long as he could, listening to the sounds of the night. He heard nothing to indicate they were in any danger, and at length, his eyelids as heavy as anvils, he sank into a dreamless sleep that lasted until the first pink rays of light dappled the eastern sky.

Fargo almost always woke up at the crack of dawn. He had trained himself to be up and ready to ride by sunrise. When a man spent as much time on the go as he did, daylight was too valuable to waste.

Rousing Juanita from sleep took some doing. All she would do when Fargo shook her was mumble incoherently, feebly swat at his hand, and go right on sleeping. He tried seven or eight times. Finally, cupping cold water from the tank in both hands, he held it inches above her face and announced, "This is your last chance."

Juanita began snoring.

Fargo parted his palms, then jumped back. It was well he did because she came up sputtering and swearing and flailing her arms like a wildcat. He laughed at her antics, which didn't improve her mood any.

"How *could* you?" Juanita fumed. She made an un-flattering comment in Spanish, comparing him to the hind end of a horse, then switched to English. "I would have thought you would show a little more consideration."

Fargo didn't help himself any by responding, "It's not my fault you were sleeping like a log."

Juanita's glare could melt stone. The rest of the morning she was unusually quiet, but by noon she was more like her old self and apologized for her outburst. That night she snuggled against him, content merely to sleep. The night after, too.

It was about ten in the morning the next day when Fargo drew rein and squinted into the distance. A couple of miles ahead smoke from a campfire was curling toward the azure sky.

"Is it them, do you think?" Juanita asked.

It had to be. Nodding, Fargo reined to the left, to a series of low hills, and on around to the far side. Keeping the hills between them and the smoke, every sense alert, he covered the next two miles at a trot. Midway up a hill due north of the campfire he reined up and slid down. "Stay with the mules."

"Not on your life!" Juanita attached herself to his elbow. "As you keep reminding me, this is Apache country."

She had a point, Fargo conceded. Mescaleros might have spotted the smoke, too. "All right. But do exactly as I say."

Juanita grinned. "My body is yours to command."

The slope was virtually bare except for small boulders near the top. Twenty-five feet from the crest Fargo dropped onto his belly and crawled the rest of the way. Removing his hat, he raised his head high enough to see what lay below.

General Machetazo had made camp at a spring that gave life to a handful of trees and some scrub brush. The Beast and the Southerners were lounging in the shade. Several Black Sheaths were by the fire; four more were near the spring; the last two had been posted as sentries, one fifty yards to the east, the other to the west. Fifteen horses were tied in a string at the center of the camp, a precaution against their being stolen by Apaches.

All but three of the horses, Fargo saw, were saddled for quick use. The rest must be pack animals. His gaze was drawn to the Ovaro. The stallion seemed none the worse for wear, and was dozing in the heat.

"Why have they stopped?" Juanita whispered.

"They're waiting for someone," was Fargo's guess.

"I gather we'll wait, too?"

Without a rifle there was nothing else Fargo could do—not in broad daylight. Sliding back below the rim, he sat up. Beyond the hills lay broken country slashed by gullies and ravines, home to snakes and lizards and little else. Nothing moved for as far as the eye could see. "This is as good a spot as any." Food and water wouldn't be a problem. They still had plenty of jerky left, and since they had refilled their waterskin at the tank, they had enough water to last four or five days.

"Here in the open?"

Fargo understood her concern but he needed to keep an eye on the camp. And it would be hard for anyone, including Apaches, to get near them without being spotted. "You can always go hide in one of those gullies."

"By myself?" Juanita shook her head. "I'm not *loco*, thank you very much. Here will do just fine."

The rest of the day passed uneventfully. Along about sunset, though, General Machetazo had a heated argument with Tarleton and Susannah. What it was about, Fargo couldn't say. Their voices didn't carry far enough. Afterward, the Southerners moved off by themselves and kindled their own fire.

Presently evening spread its welcome cool relief across the land, and Fargo's stomach was set to growling by the fragrant aroma of percolating coffee and the appetizing odor of *frijoles* and other food.

Juanita sniffed the air and groaned. "Do you smell that? It is almost enough to make me want to walk down there and let them take me prisoner."

Even to Fargo their jerky tasted bland that night. So did their lukewarm water. When Juanita was ready to turn in, he bundled her in the blanket and had her curl up between a couple of boulders where she was out of the worst of the wind. He slept sitting up, his back against another one. The slightest sounds from below snapped him awake, so his rest was fitful at best. By morning he felt as if he hadn't had any rest whatsoever.

Juanita didn't stir until the sun was several hours high. Sitting up, she cast off the blanket and scowled. "Every muscle in my body aches! My hair is a mess! I need a bath and my dress smells like dirt! What a wonderful way to start the day."

"Nice to see you holding up so well," Fargo said dryly.

"I am a woman, *señor*. I like my 'creature comforts,' as you *americanos* call them. Clean hair, clean skin, clean clothes. Little things like that." Juanita arched her spine and winced. "Another night like this and I will be a ruin."

"You have forty good years on you yet before you'll start falling apart," Fargo said.

"Was that supposed to cheer me up?"

"It should. Most men would give anything to be with a fine filly like you."

"How nice. Now you compare me to a horse."

Arguing with a woman in a bad mood was like baiting a bear in its den. Only a simpleton did either. Fargo turned to check on those below. General Machetazo and Tarleton were talking and the Georgian did not appear any pleased. Susannah joined them. Soon all three of them were gesturing in anger and raising their voices but he still couldn't hear what they said.

Suddenly the Black Sheath on sentry duty to the east gave a shout and pointed.

A pair of wagons were approaching, dust swirling in their wake. Prairie schooners, with riders in front and behind. Although they were a long way off Fargo recognized those in the lead. There was no mistaking the husky form of Tyrel Owensby. Beside him was Elwin. In Mesilla they hadn't been armed but they sure were now. Each had a brace of pistols and a rifle. The same with those in the wagons, men and women alike.

Tarleton Wilkes whooped for joy and waved his arms in greeting.

Tyrel lifted one of his in acknowledgment.

"The gold is in those wagons, isn't it?" Juanita whispered.

Fargo nodded. To think that he had been a few feet from small fortune and not had any idea. The Owensbys weren't settlers; they were agitators like the Wilkeses, part of the plot to instigate war with Mexico—a crucial part. For to them had been entrusted the task of transporting the gold needed to buy the Beast's cooperation.

General Machetazo yelled orders. The sentries came running, and all the Black Sheaths formed into a long row facing the newcomers.

Something interesting struck Fargo. The People's Army was short on guns. Only about half had any, as he recollected. Yet every last one of the Black Sheaths down there had a rifle, plus a full bandoleer. It couldn't be coincidence.

Tarleton and Susannah started to walk out to meet the wagons but stopped at a sharp word from General Machetazo. Their mutual distrust was thick enough to cut with a butter knife.

Fargo turned to Juanita. "I need to hear what

they're saying. For once do as I say and stay put."
Sliding past her, he crawled down the east side of the
hill. An erosion-worn notch hid him most of the way,
and from there he crawled from boulder to boulder
until he was as close as he dared go.

The wagons were only a few hundred yards out and
Tyrel Owensby spurred his dun on ahead. Dismounting, the big Georgian threw his arms wide and
wrapped Susannah in a bear hug. "We've done it,
cousin! It took some doing, fordin' rivers and such,
but we've brought the gold! I'm as happy as a pig in
mud to get this over with."

The blonde disengaged herself and said testily,
"We're pleased, Tyrel, but try to control yourself.
There are others present."

"You mean the Mexicans?" Owensby laughed.
"Who in hell cares what a bunch of bean-eaters
think?"

Tarleton shook Tyrel's hand and said something in
the larger man's ear. By the wary look Owensby then
gave General Machetazo, the seed of distrust had
spread.

Soon the wagons arrived and were wheeled close to
the spring. Five more men and two more women were
added to the Southerners' ranks, and now that both
sides were about evenly matched, Fargo noticed a
change come over Tarleton Wilkes. He snapped com-
mands like a born officer, forming the Southerners
into an uneven row of their own, and together they
advanced on the Black Sheaths, who stood at attention
with the stocks of their rifles resting on the ground.

The Beast did not appear the least bit concerned.
That alone should have given Tarleton pause but he
swaggered up and said much too loudly, "Before we
hand over your gold, General, I want to set you
straight on a few things."

"It would be best for all concerned if you do not
let your immaturity run away with your intellect,"

General Machetazo said with an iciness that was ample warning in itself, but Tarleton was too full of himself to realize it.

"For days now Susannah and I have had to abide your rude manners and insults. Your conduct has been contemptible, and I demand an apology."

General Machetazo's brow knit and he ran a hand across his chin as if he were seriously considering it. But Fargo knew better. The Beast was signaling someone.

Out of a dry wash to the southwest galloped fifteen more Black Sheaths, Captain Ruiz at the forefront. They bore wide of the trees and brush and came up on the Southerners from behind, forming into a skirmish line with their rifles leveled. At the same time, the Black Sheaths by the spring snapped their own rifles to their shoulders and cocked them.

Tyrel, Elwin, and some of the others started to raise their guns but stopped at an order from Tarleton, who was red as a beet. "What is the meaning of this newest outrage?" he blustered. "Ruiz is supposed to be on his way to join Colonel Fraco."

"That is what I wanted you to think, *gringo*," the Beast rasped. "His real orders were to shadow us and remain concealed until I needed him."

Susannah tried to reason with him. "We've held up our end of the bargain. Don't you intend to hold up yours?"

"Let me see," Machetazo said. "You want me to wipe out a detachment of United States cavalry, confiscate their uniforms and arms, then pose as *americanos* and attack a few towns in northern Mexico. Is that right?"

"You know damn well it is," Tarleton replied. "How else are you going to stir things up so the two countries go to war? Each side will blame the other, just as we want."

"Just as *you* want, *gringo*."

It finally sank in. Tarleton and Susannah glanced at each other, and to Fargo it was clear they had divined their fate.

Not Tyrel Owensby. "I don't savvy any of this," the big Georgian stated. "What the hell is this two-bit greaser going on about, anyhow?"

General Vicente Machetazo drew a nickel-plated revolver from a holster on his left hip and shot Tyrel through the forehead. It happened so fast that it took the rest of the Southerners by surprise. They gaped at the sprawled figure in the dust, then at his killer. Several looked mad enough to kill Machetazo where he stood, but the two dozens rifles trained on them dampened their thirst for vengeance.

Machetazo returned the revolver to its holster. "Where was I? Oh, yes. Your pathetic plan for pitting my country against yours in another war." His features hardened. "Did you honestly believe I would let that happen? I want to rule Mexico myself, not have the United States conquer her and set up a puppet government under Washington's control."

Tarleton was a pasty shade of gray. "You misled us from the very start. The only reason you agreed to help was to get your hands on the gold."

"I used you as you tried to use me." Machetazo began moving to his left, past the row of Black Sheaths. "You made the mistake of underestimating me, *gringo*. You assumed that because I was once a *bandido*, I must be stupid. You assumed that because I plunder and steal, I must hunger after riches. But your biggest mistake was to think you could bend my iron will to your own ends."

"Take the gold if you want," Susannah urged, a note of desperation in her tone. "Just let us go. We'll promise never to say a word to anyone."

Machetazo paused. "This from the woman who threatened my life if I dared to lift a finger against

162

any of you? What about the bounty your masters will put on my head?"

"There won't be any. I'll see to that."

The Beast glared in simmering hatred. "You are right, woman. There won't. But not because of you. I am going to send them a message—a token, if you will, to demonstrate what will happen if they presume to send someone after me."

Susannah shivered even though the day was sweltering hot. "What kind of token, might I ask?"

"Of course you may, my dear," Machetazo said, patronizing her. "I plan to send them your head."

12

Skye Fargo faced a dilemma. He wasn't obligated to help the Southerners. They had brought this on themselves, and in a sense it was fitting. Had their plan succeeded, thousands of innocent people on both sides of the border would have died. But he couldn't bring himself to lie there and do nothing, not when three of the agitators were women. That might not make a difference to some people, but west of the Mississippi women were held in high regard. Harming one was considered as despicable a deed as horse stealing.

Fargo wanted to do something, but what? All he had was the old Walker Colt and his knife. He didn't stand a prayer against two dozen Black Sheaths armed with rifles. He considered shooting Machetazo but that would only bring Ruiz and the others down on his head, and they weren't conscripts. They *liked* to kill.

The Beast had raised an arm, and now raised his voice. "You have ten seconds to drop your weapons, *gringos*, or I will give the signal to have my men cut you down where you stand."

Some of the Southerners were girded to sell their lives dearly, but not Tarleton Wilkes.

"Do as he says!" he bawled. "Drop your guns and don't resist. We'll live longer that way."

After a brief hesitation all but one man complied. Elwin Owensby screeched like a bobcat and tried to snap off a shot at General Machetazo. Instantly four or five rifles cracked. His chest riddled, Elwin melted into a limp heap next to Tyrel.

"Anyone else?" the Beast demanded.

Their spirit broken, the Southerners meekly submitted to being thrown to the ground and bound hand and foot. All except Tarleton. He was hauled over near the fire, where the Black Sheaths forced him to his knees, jerked his arms behind his back, and tied his wrists.

Like a mountain lion stalking a trapped buck, General Machetazo walked in a slow circle around Tarleton, then halted and placed his hands on his hips. "In which wagon will I find the gold?"

"There are false floors in both. We divided it up to lighten the loads." Tarleton was scared and making no attempt to hide the fact.

"How thoughtful of you." The Beast stepped to the fire and grasped the unlit end of a burning brand.

"What do you intend doing?" Tarleton asked in a mousy squeak.

"Surely you remember my fondness for a diversion most consider perverse?" Machetazo nodded at the Black Sheaths, several of whom grabbed hold of Wilkes to hold him down.

"Please, no!"

"Try to show some courage. You're a true gentleman, remember? A shining example to all us lesser men." Abruptly bending, Machetazo gripped Tarleton by the throat and spat in his face. "*Bah!* You sicken me, *gringo*. You are nothing but a coward with a loud mouth. And it is time someone stilled that yellow tongue of yours."

Other Black Sheaths closed in. Tarleton tried to break free but it was too little effort, much too late. His jaws were savagely pried open and a rock as large as a hen's egg wedged into a corner of his mouth between his upper and lower teeth.

The other Southerners were riveted in horror. Only Susannah broke her paralysis to beg, "In God's name, Machetazo, don't!"

"How many times must I tell you dolts there is no God?" the Beast snarled. Suddenly gripping the back of Tarleton's head, he shoved the burning brand into the terror-struck man's mouth.

Susannah and one of the other women screamed.

Tarleton screamed, too, but it strangled off into a high-pitched wail. Flame and smoke spewed from his mouth, and with them the acrid stench of charred flesh. He thrashed and struggled like a madman but he was powerless against so many hands.

Machetazo did not pull the brand out until it was nearly extinguished. Throwing it down, he motioned at the Black Sheaths and they let go. Mewing pitiably, Tarleton doubled over and retched, his features twisted in acute torment.

"Any clever comments to make, *gringo*?" the Beast mocked his misery. "Any more lectures on what it means to be as perfect as you?"

Tears streaming her cheeks, Susannah had risen to her knees. "Cut me loose, damn you, and I'll do more than lecture you! Give me a knife! A gun! Anything! All I ask is a fighting chance."

General Machetazo regarded her with amusement. "Ironic, is it not?" he said to Captain Ruiz. "These *gringos* like to bluster and brag about how they will rise up and destroy their countrymen to the north. Yet the only one among them with a shred of bravery is this female."

"They are contemptible, these *americano* pigs," Ruiz agreed, then inquired, "Will we stay here a day or two while you dispose of them, Great One? I know how you like to take your time about such things."

"Would that I could." Machetazo sighed, his eyes still on Susannah. "I have urgent business elsewhere, woman, or you would lose your head within the hour. The captain and ten of my men will keep you company until my return."

The Beast's comments mystified Fargo. Since the

madman refused to be duped into instigating a war, what was the nature of the "urgent business" Machetazo had referred to? He wasn't the only one who was curious.

"Where are you off to, butcher?" Susannah asked. "To raid another *hacienda*? To murder more women and children?"

Fargo thought Machetazo would turn on her in fury, but he had to remember how unpredictable the man was.

"No, my dear, not this time. I am on my way to attack the United States Army."

Susannah's surprise mirrored Fargo's own. "I can't be hearing right. I thought you wanted no part of our plan?"

"I don't," General Machetazo affirmed. "I am serving my own interests, not yours." He deigned to explain. "I need weapons—a lot of guns and a lot of ammunition. I could buy them with your gold but the only arms dealers who would sell in quantity to me are overseas, and arranging a shipment could take months. So I have come up with a faster way."

Fargo's mind raced. There was only one place he knew of where Machetazo could get his hands on what he needed.

"So that is why you lured most of the soldiers from Fort Fillmore!" Susannah remarked.

"Precisely. The post armory is well stocked, I am told. So while most of the garrison is away on what you *norteamericanos* call a 'wild goose chase,' I will help myself to enough rifles and revolvers to outfit the rest of my army." He touched his cap. "If you will excuse me, duty calls."

Fargo was thinking of the Pimas. Machetazo wouldn't leave survivors to point the finger of blame. Lieta and Culazol would be slain along with every trooper and civilian still at the fort.

The Beast had a few parting words for Captain

Ruiz. "See to it the gold is not touched. Stress to anyone who is tempted that they will not appreciate the consequences."

"I have proven my loyalty many times over, my general. I will not let you down now." Ruiz gazed toward the hills. "My only worry, sir, is Apaches."

"Then you can put it to rest. The demons say there are no Mescaleros within fifty miles. No harm will come to you while I am gone."

Captain Ruiz saluted. "Slit a *gringo* throat for me, if you would."

"I will slit ten, and bring you an ear for your collection." Returning the salute, the Beast climbed onto his chestnut. Then off he rode, Black Sheaths in a column of twos breathing his dust. In a few minutes they were swallowed by distance and haze.

Fargo glanced at the Ovaro; at his Henry in the saddle scabbard. His Colt was by the spring, one of many weapons taken from the Southerners and dropped in a pile. Somehow he must get his hands on them before the day was done.

Ruiz barked orders of his own. He again sent sentries to the east and west. That left eight, and he put them to work dragging the remaining Southerners close to the fire where they could be easily guarded.

Tarleton was in a bad way. Curled on his side, he wouldn't stop moaning. Blood caked his chin and neck and every so often he convulsed violently. Susannah dragged herself over to help, but with her arms and legs bound, all she could do was speak false words of comfort he paid no heed to.

Practicing the same care he had on his descent, Fargo crawled back up the hill. For once, Juanita was right where he had left her. The tears moistening her face told him she had witnessed the whole thing, and out of the blue she asked him a question.

"What kind of world do we live in, *señor*, where

creatures like the Beast are allowed to do as he just did?"

"You're asking the wrong person," Fargo responded. "I don't claim to have any answers as to why things are the way they are."

Juanita's gaze turned inward. "That devil's cruelty, his wickedness, are an affront to all that is decent in us. If I could, I would kill him with my own hands."

"You'll have to wait your turn." Fargo tried to dispel her gloomy mood. "His days are numbered. He just doesn't know it yet." He smiled, but instead of reciprocating, Juanita rested her cheek on his chest, looped her arms around his neck, and softly wept.

Not knowing what else to do, Fargo held her and let her cry herself out. She had been still awhile when he asked, "Feeling better now?" and glanced down to find she was asleep. He didn't wake her. Why bother, when they had eight hours to kill until nightfall and nothing else to do?

Fargo's own lack of sleep caught up with him and he dozed. He slept only an hour and a half but he was no longer tired when he awoke. Juanita soon stirred and they ate some jerky and drank some water.

Not much was happening below. Captain Ruiz had chosen a spot near the wagons and was sharpening his machete on a whetstone. Most of the Black Sheaths were either taking *siestas* or rolling dice. One tended the coffeepot.

Fargo couldn't remember the last time an afternoon passed so slowly. His patience was stretched to its limit by the time the sun was balanced on the rim of the world like an orange plate on end. Bit by bit the shadows lengthened. Once again the aroma of brewing coffee and food set his mouth to watering.

"I wish you would let me go down there with you," Juanita said.

"Look on the bright side. In a few hours that could

be us eating our fill." Fargo drew the Walker and verified he had six pills in the wheel.

"And if you do not succeed?"

"Head due east. You're bound to come across the Albuquerque-Mesilla road. From there go south to Mesilla. There's a cantina run by a man named Chico and his wife. They'll be happy to help you reach Mexico."

Juanita's hand wrapped around his. "I would rather not have to mourn you, so do your best to stay alive."

Fargo usually did. He marked the sinking sun with increasing eagerness, and as soon as twilight had served as midwife to night, he was in motion, crawling down the right side of the hill this time so he could approach the spring from the northwest where the brush was heaviest.

Ruiz and the Black Sheaths were treating themselves to a large meal whipped up from supplies from the wagons. None of it was offered to the prisoners, though, and as Fargo wound toward the horse string, Susannah Wilkes inadvertently did the best thing she could possibly do. "What about us, Captain?" she shouted, becoming the focus of attention. "Are we to be starved as well as tortured?"

"Shut your mouth, *puta*," Ruiz growled. "General Machetazo said I was to keep you *gringos* alive, not keep your bellies full."

"So you won't even share our own food with us? No wonder you lick Machetazo's boots. You're as big a bastard as he is."

Captain Ruiz came up off the ground as if prodded by a lance. Carrying a tin cup, he walked over to her, smiled thinly, and asked, "Would some coffee do?"

"It's better than nothing," Susannah replied.

"Then drink this, bitch."

Susannah tried to duck but the hot coffee caught her full in the face. She looked primed to scream, and bit her lower lip.

"If you want more let me know," Ruiz said with exaggerated courtesy. "Or perhaps you would like a *tortilla* with the finger of one of your friends inside?"

"You rotten, no good son of a—"

A boot in Susannah's stomach cut her outburst short, and she was knocked onto her back, half across Tarleton.

"Maybe now you will let me eat in peace," Ruiz advised. A little coffee was left in the cup and he poured it over her head. "You better hope a bear does not happen by. It will drag you off before any of us."

One of the Black Sheaths was translating for the benefit of those who did not speak English, and they erupted in glee at their superior's display of wit. Ruiz went back to his spot by the wagons and things quieted down.

Fargo was only a few feet from the horses and rose into a crouch. To reach the Ovaro, which was toward the middle of the string, he had to pass seven others. In the hope they wouldn't whinny, he moved as slow as tree sap. One pricked its ears and bobbed its head but that was all.

Ducking under the picket rope, Fargo sidled to the scabbard and molded his fingers around the Henry's smooth stock. Provided Tarleton hadn't fired it, it should contain fifteen rounds, with one already in the chamber.

Again Fargo ducked under the rope, and moved on down the line. Only a few Black Sheaths were holding rifles. The rest had set theirs aside. Captain Ruiz had a revolver but it was in a military-style holster with a flap and couldn't be drawn quickly. There would never be a better time.

Stepping into the open, Fargo announced his presence by declaring, "Throw up your hands or die!"

Astonishment froze the Black Sheaths, one with a *tortilla* halfway to his mouth.

Then a beefy man with a rifle galvanized to life and and all hell broke loose.

Fargo shot him through the head, shifted, and sent a slug through the eye of a second man. Others scrambled for rifles, and as rapidly as they laid hands on them, Fargo dropped them. Six, seven, eight times he worked the Henry's lever, until only Captain Ruiz was left. Ruiz had his revolver partially drawn but the hammer had caught on the flap and he was tugging madly to free it. He looked up as Fargo swung the Henry toward him, and cursed. Fargo stroked the trigger again.

Two shots echoed his, one from the east, another from the west. The sentries were racing back, firing on the fly. In their reckless haste their aim was atrocious. Fargo's wasn't. As calmly as if he were competing at a turkey shoot, he sighted down the Henry at the man to the west and cored his brain at sixty feet.

The only Black Sheath left had a change of heart. Whirling, he fled on wings of fright, twisting so he could fire from the hip.

Moving to the left for a clearer shot, Fargo fixed a bead on the Black Sheath's spine where it met the skull. Then, taking a breath to steady his aim, he banged off one final shot.

All the Southerners had sat up. All save Tarleton, who hadn't moved. Susannah's expression was one of utter amazement. "You!" she blurted, and gazed at the prone forms littering the ground like so many dead leaves.

"Me," Fargo said. Striding to the pile of confiscated weapons, he fished out the Colt and twirled it into his holster. For the first time in days he felt complete.

"How did you get away from the others?" Susannah quizzed him.

Ignoring her, Fargo cupped a hand to his mouth and yelled up to Juanita. "It's safe to come down!

172

Bring the mules!" Then he poured himself some hot coffee and gulped it with barely a pause.

Susannah turned so her bound wrists were toward him. "Hey, what about us, mister?"

"What about you?" Fargo rejoined. He snatched a *tortilla* from a pan and wolfed half of it in one bite.

"You're not going to leave us tied up like this, are you?"

"I didn't see you offer to cut me down when Machetazo was using me for bullwhip practice." Fargo wolfed the rest. "You and your friends have a lot to answer for, lady."

"I admit I did wrong by you. But surely you can forgive me?" Susannah smiled as sweetly as a choirgirl.

Fargo looked at her—at her beautiful face and hair, at full lips that any man in his right mind would give anything to kiss. No one would suspect that her beauty hid a heart almost as cold and vicious as the Beast's. "Weren't you the one who told Machetazo you think torture is highly entertaining?" he threw her exact words at her.

Susannah didn't bat an eyelash. "I didn't mean that," she said earnestly. "I was just trying to stay on his good side so he wouldn't back out of our agreement."

"Which he did anyway." Fargo poured some more coffee and rose, waiting for Juanita to appear.

"You still haven't answered me," Susannah pressed. "Will you untie me or not?"

"When buffalo fly."

One of the other women rose to her knees. Younger than Susannah and rather plain by comparison, she asked, "Does that apply to the rest of us? We're not like her, mister. I've never treated the darkies on my plantation the way she treats those on hers. There are better ways to keep them in line than beating and scourging."

Susannah bared her teeth like a she-wolf baring its fangs. "Shut up, Violet, you damned fool!"

"Why should the rest of us suffer on your account?" Violet retorted. "The important thing now is that we're allowed to take the wagons and leave."

Fargo took a long sip before dropping the other shoe. "So you can put the gold to some other use in your campaign to split the country?"

Violet recoiled as if he had slapped her. "You know all about that?"

"I know everything," Fargo revealed. "And I don't trust any of you any further than I can throw my horse."

Violet bowed her head in defeat, but not Susannah. "You stinking Yankee-lover! I should have expected as much! What do you care that Lincoln is a tyrant in sheep's clothing? I bet when war breaks out you're one of the first to sign up for the Union cause."

Talk of war had been in the newspapers for months and was a popular topic in saloons and taverns. Fargo had given it a lot of thought, and he answered her honestly. "I've never much cared what happens east of the Mississippi so long as it doesn't affect how I live my own life."

"Spoken like a true frontiersman," Susannah said scornfully. "But you won't be able to hide your head in a prairie dog burrow this time. When war breaks out—and mark my words, it will—blood will flow from the Atlantic to the Pacific. Whether you like it or not, you'll be forced to pick sides."

A beanpole in overalls threw in his two bits. "What if we give you some of the gold to let us go, mister? Enough to last you the rest of your born days? No one ever need know."

"I would," Fargo said, and took a few steps toward the hill. He was tired of their attempts to manipulate him. There were more important things to consider, such as what to do next. He had to get to the fort and warn Blanchard about General Machetazo. But he couldn't just ride off and leave the Southerners there unguarded. Or could he?

Juanita was on her way in, riding one mule and leading the other. Springing down, she ran toward him with her arms open wide as if to embrace him but flew on by to the campfire and clasped a *tortilla* to her bosom as if it were a lover. "At last!" she cried, and stuffed it into her mouth, chomping furiously.

Susannah did not know when to keep her mouth shut. "So the Mexican tart has taken up with you, has she? You're a perfect match. You're both pigs."

Juanita was reaching for more food. Stiffening, she spun and slapped the Southern belle across the face, knocking Susannah onto her back. "Not another word out of you."

Fargo was disappointed Juanita didn't hit her again. He resumed eating, and while they gorged themselves he told her about the Beast's plan to attack Fort Fillmore. "It's up to us to see that he doesn't," he concluded.

"But what can we do?" Juanita said with her mouth full. "He has too much of a head start."

"We can still beat him there if you're willing." Fargo shared his idea.

"*Sí.* It could be done. We rested most of the afternoon, so we are not tired." Juanita wiped a hand on her dress. "Very well. For you, I will do this thing. I only hope I do not let you down."

Susannah had overheard and was sitting back up. "What if General Machetazo was wrong about Apaches being in the area? My friends and I will be as good as dead."

Fargo downed his fourth cup of coffee and slowly rose. His gut hurt, he'd eaten so much, but he didn't mind. He started toward Captain Ruiz, then sprang aside as Susannah swung her legs at his, seeking to sweep his feet out from under him. Wagging a finger, he bent over Ruiz's body and stripped it of weapons.

"Answer me, damn you!" Susannah screeched. "It's our lives that are at stake! We deserve a say in the matter."

"Like hell," Fargo didn't mince words. "Another peep out of you and I'll gag you." That finally shut her up. He spent the next fifteen minutes going from body to body, gathering rifles and machetes and adding them to the pile the Black Sheaths had made.

Juanita, meanwhile, unsaddled all the horses except the Ovaro and five others. She untied the rest, one by one, and made two long strings. Every mount, every pack animal, the teams to the wagons, the mules— they were all soon ready.

Fargo wasn't quite done. He bundled the weapons into blankets, tied the bundles good and tight, and secured them to pack animals. Then he rummaged through the provisions in the wagons and crammed certain items into his saddlebags and those on the other mounts. Giving the camp a once-over, he nodded. "Let's head out."

Susannah Wilkes had kept quiet as long as she could. "What about *us*?" she practically screamed.

Fargo picked up a machete he had left out and dropped it beside her. "Use this to cut yourselves free once we're gone. There's plenty of food left, and you won't want for water."

"That's it? One machete? With us in the middle of Apache country?"

Forking leather, Fargo reined the Ovaro to the head of one of the strings and snagged the lead rope. "If all goes well you won't be here long. In a week or so a detachment of U.S. Cavalry will show up to take you into custody."

"And what if the two of you don't make it to the fort?" Susannah snapped. "No one will know where we are. We'll be stuck here."

"You can always try to walk out," Fargo suggested. "Follow the tracks of your wagons. Who knows? One or two of you might make it." Smiling as sweetly as she had at him a while ago, he touched his spurs to the stallion and headed southeast. On his right trotted Juanita, leading the other string.

From behind them, borne on the wind, keened the cry of an enraged banshee: *"You son of a bitch! May you rot in hell!"*

"I could be wrong, *señor*," Juanita said, smirking, "but something tells me she does not like you very much."

13

Skye Fargo had learned the trick from an old Comanche. Once the bane of Texas, the Comanches ranged far and wide in lightning raids, melting into the wilds again before their pursuers could catch them. A ruse they sometimes used was for each warrior on a raiding party to take several horses, ridden in relays. As soon as one animal tired, the Comanches switched to a fresh mount.

Fargo and Juanita were going to do the same thing. But they needed only three horses apiece, not a dozen. Approximately seven miles from the spring Fargo dismounted and cut the extra animals loose. A few trotted off but the rest milled uncertainly. Moving west of them, he drew his Colt, hollered at the top of his lungs, and banged a couple of shots into the ground.

"I hope they find their way somewhere safe," Juanita commented as the small herd thundered off.

So did Fargo. Unlike people, he had never met a horse he didn't like. If they kept heading east, they would reach ample grass and a stream or two. They might even drift into Mesilla or one of the other settlements.

Instead of swinging back onto the Ovaro, Fargo forked a sorrel and led the pinto and a handsome bay. Hour after hour they pushed on across rough, unforgiving landscape. Other than the occasional yip of coyotes, the rare shriek of a cougar, and once, the throaty growl of a jaguar, the night was deceptively still.

At midnight Fargo called a short halt, not so much for their benefit as for the horses. By pacing themselves they would make much better time.

Juanita was holding up well, all things considered. She stretched, then took a sip from a canteen Fargo had relieved the Southerners of. "Do you still think we can beat the Beast to Fort Fillmore?"

By Fargo's reckoning, General Machetazo wouldn't catch up to the People's Army until sometime the next morning. Odds were the general would spend the rest of the day organizing the attack. Factor in travel time, and the result was: "We'll get there a day or two ahead of him."

In a quarter of an hour they were in the saddle again. Although it was night and there were no landmarks to go by, they were in no danger of becoming lost. Not as long as Fargo could see the Big Dipper, which always pointed at the North Star. Their next stop for rest was at three, and again at six as dawn was breaking.

Uncapping the canteen, Fargo passed it to his companion. "Breakfast," he said.

Swallowing some, Juanita smacked her lips. "All the food we brought and this is all I can have?" She grinned. "Are you keeping the food for yourself? Or is it that you are fond of skinny women?"

Fargo smiled. "We'll eat at midday. Can you hold out that long?"

"After all these months as the Beast's unwilling guest, to go a few more hours without food is a trifle."

For a while the rising temperature was welcome after the crisp chill of late night, but by midday they were parched, hot, and sweaty. True to his word, Fargo kindled a small fire and put on a pot of coffee. Juanita insisted on doing the cooking herself. She sliced strips of bacon from a slab Fargo had taken from one of the wagons, and while the bacon sizzled she mixed cornmeal, water, and a dash of sugar in a pan and made tasty flat cakes. Simple fare, but to them it was a feast.

By one o'clock they were on the move. Fargo was on the Ovaro now. "We should reach Fort Fillmore by sunset," he informed her.

The mountains were behind them. Patches of green sprinkled the perpetual brown, and signs of wildlife were more abundant. At a trickle of a stream they watered their animals. Not long after, they struck the days-old tracks of ten shod horses, formed in a column of twos.

"Troopers from the post," Juanita surmised.

"Maybe," Fargo said. Patrols usually numbered a lot more; twenty to thirty was average. The only other possibility filled him with unease, and from then on he constantly scanned the surrounding country.

Sundown was imminent when Fargo cantered to the top of a rise and spied buildings in the far distance. Drawing rein, he wearily leaned on his saddle horn. "Three guesses what that is."

"At last!" Juanita slapped her legs against her mount to goad it past the Ovaro. "What are you waiting for? In half an hour we can be there."

That they could, but as her dappled mare came alongside, movement in a gully to the northeast caused Fargo to grab her reins. "Not this way!" he directed and, reining around, he hurried back down.

"What in the world has gotten into you, *señor*?" Juanita protested. "We are so close! Where are you taking me?"

Fargo held off answering. At the bottom he slid to the ground, shucked the Henry, and beckoned to her, warning, "Stay low and don't make any noise." They had raised some dust, but not enough to be noticed.

The north end of the rise was choked with cactus. Finding a bare spot, Fargo hunkered. The gully was about a quarter of a mile off, the near side lower than the far side. Ten men in sombreros—each wearing a machete with a dark sheath—were lying near the rim, facing the other way. Picketed close by were their horses.

Forgetting herself, Juanita cried, "Black Sheaths! What are they doing here?"

"Spying on the fort," Fargo responded. The same bunch who'd made the tracks he saw a while ago.

"Fraco and his men." Juanita took the words out of his mouth. "Do you see that big one in the middle wearing a brown sash around his waist and high brown boots? That is the colonel. He claims he is descended from Spanish royalty."

"Another bandit who thinks too highly of himself."

"Oh no, *señor*. General Machetazo often invited Colonel Fraco to eat with us, and I got to know him quite well. He comes from an old family. Once they were rich and powerful but they have fallen on hard times and he wants to restore them to their former glory."

"By overthrowing the Mexican government?"

"Fraco blames those in high places for his family's hardships. He says crooked politicians stripped the Fracos of much of their land and wealth. One day he intends to pay them back by sending them up before a firing squad." Juanita stopped, but she wasn't done. "He is an intelligent man, *señor*. For a while he attended a university in Mexico City. General Machetazo relies greatly on his advice."

"Is that a fact?" The next best thing to disposing of the Beast, Fargo reflected, would be disposing of the Beast's right-hand man.

"*Sí*. It was Colonel Fraco who came up with the idea to plunder the fort's armory. I was curious, naturally, but Machetazo always made me leave whenever military matters were discussed so I did not learn the details." Juanita then asked the question foremost on his mind. "Can we reach Fort Fillmore without them seeing us?"

Fargo had high hopes. Darkness would descend soon. Under cover of its mantle they could swing wide and approach Fort Fillmore by a roundabout route. It would take an extra hour but they were still a full day or more ahead of General Machetazo.

There was only half an hour of daylight left but it seemed a lot longer. On the off chance more Black Sheaths were south of the post, Fargo traveled due south for a mile before swinging east. The sky was moonless, which worked in their favor. They were only a hundred yards from the southeast corner of the square when a youthful voice nervously hailed them.

"Halt! Who goes there?"

Fargo identified himself.

"You're that scout the colonel sent out, aren't you?" From the shadows emerged a soldier barely old enough to shave. "He left orders we were to be on the lookout for you. You can go on in and report to the officer in charge."

"Colonel Blanchard isn't here?" Fargo asked when they were close enough for him to do so without shouting.

"No, sir. He left with most of the command days ago. Lieutenant Jurgenson is in charge."

Fargo would rather it were any officer other than the young cub who was so stuck on himself. "Where is he now, Private?"

"Over at the mess hall, I believe." The trooper stepped aside. "The lady and you are free to go on in, sir."

As Fargo crossed the square he noticed a number of wives and children enjoying a stroll but he saw very few troopers. A couple of sentries, one or two others, and that was it. Lamps lit the windows in the barracks but it was much too still. The same with the mess hall.

Since their horses were too weary to stray off, Fargo merely ground-hitched them. He went to slap dust from his buckskins and realized it was a lost cause.

Juanita was fussing with her hair. "I must look a sight," she complained. "I wish I could wash up and find new clothes."

"I'll see what I can do." Fargo opened the door.

Only seven troopers were in the cavernous mess hall, among them Lieutenant Jurgenson and a certain grizzled sergeant-major over at a corner table.

Sergeant McDermott spotted them first. Jumping up, he bellowed, "Begorra, Lieutenant! It's himself, looking like something the cat dragged in, then threw back out again! And a beautiful woman, too." He chuckled merrily. "But what else should I be expecting from the likes of the bull of the frontier."

Lieutenant Jurgenson rose, all spit and polish, and bowed to Juanita. "Welcome, madam. Perhaps you and the scout would consent to join us? We're just about to partake of a late supper." Stepping quickly around, he politely slid out a chair for her.

"How mannerly you are, Lieutenant," Juanita gushed. "And so handsome in that uniform of yours."

Jurgenson blushed every shade between pink and purple and sat back down as if he were sitting on pins. "Why, thank you," he said civilly. "An officer should always look his best to set an example for the men."

"Indeed, sir," Sergeant McDermott agreed, his weathered face crinkled in silent mirth.

Fargo turned another chair around and straddled it. "I hate to spoil your good moods, gents, but you have a problem—and a bigger one that will show up any day now."

"What sort of problems?" the junior officer absently asked while bestowing his manliest smile on Juanita. "I'm sure I can handle anything that crops up."

"How many troopers are left besides the two of you?"

Jurgenson reluctantly tore his gaze from the brunette. "Fourteen. Colonel Blanchard took the rest with him after he received a reliable tip that the Beast

183

was encamped six days' southwest of here. He couldn't pass up a chance to put an end to Machetazo before that cagey devil slips south of the border again."

"A reliable tip?" Fargo repeated.

"Yes. A Mexican fellow by the name of Garcia showed up here. Said he hated the Beast because Machetazo killed his brother. He wanted to take revenge and had been following Machetazo's army for weeks, waiting his chance. When Machetazo set up camp, Garcia rushed here to let us know." Jurgenson grinned. "So it turns out we didn't need your services after all."

"Where is this Garcia?"

"He went with Colonel Blanchard to act as guide. If all goes well, the colonel will be back here in about two weeks with Machetazo either dead over a saddle or as the colonel's prisoner."

"In two weeks there won't be a post to come back to," Fargo enlightened him. "Garcia is one of the Beast's men sent to lure Blanchard and most of the garrison off. From the looks of things, he did a damn fine job."

Sergeant McDermott stiffened but the young officer failed to fully appreciate the gravity of their situation.

"Is it your contention Machetazo intends to attack Fort Fillmore? Really, now. Even he wouldn't be that stupid. It would bring the entire might of the United States Army down on his head."

Fargo had learned long ago that the only thing worse than a fool was an arrogant fool. "Do you honestly think Machetazo gives a damn? He needs the guns and ammunition in your armory, Lieutenant, and he means to have them if he has to wipe out every man, woman, and child at the fort."

Jurgenson turned a new color, a sickly shade of ash. "Then why are you sitting there so calmly? I must muster the men. We need to strengthen our fortifications, dig trenches, reposition the cannons." He began to rise.

"Hold your horses," Fargo cautioned. "There are a few more things you need to know before you go rushing off."

"Such as?" Jurgenson sank back down and impatiently drummed his fingers on the table. "Speak, man, speak."

Suppressing a frown, Fargo told him, "Black Sheaths have been spying on the post for days. At this moment ten of them are in a gully northwest of here—"

Instantly Jurgenson shot to his feet. "They are? Why didn't you say so sooner! I'll personally lead a detail to rout them."

"It would be the biggest mistake you've ever made."

Sergeant McDermott was a shrewd judge of when to interject his seasoned advice, and he did so now. "Perhaps you should hear Mr. Fargo out, sir. Remember, the colonel thinks highly of him and places great value on his experience."

Indecision rooted the younger man, and Fargo took advantage of it to say, "In two days, maybe less, Machetazo himself will show up with a small army of Black Sheaths. More than enough to overrun the fort and burn it to the ground." He paused. "Unless we set a trap for him."

For a second time Lieutenant Jurgenson sank back down. "I'm listening."

"First off, all the women and children should be sent to Mesilla. Tonight. And it has to be done quietly. The Black Sheaths mustn't know you're on to them or they'll warn Machetazo."

"That makes sense," Jurgenson begrudgingly conceded. "What else?"

Fargo offered half a dozen suggestions, and to the

young officer's credit, he listened intently to each and every one, a slow smile spreading across his baby-smooth face.

"I like how you think, scout. You're as devious as the Beast." Jurgenson smacked the table. "It could work, by God! And what a feather it would be in my career. Why, I'd make Captain in no time."

Both Fargo and Sergeant McDermott glanced sharply at him, and Jurgenson fidgeted like a small boy caught with his hand in a cookie jar. "Don't look at me like that. It's not as if a promotion is all I care about."

"I hope not, for all our sakes," Fargo responded. Or it could well get all of them killed.

Jurgenson consulted a pocket watch. "It's twelve minutes past ten. I'll have word spread quietly to the wives to be ready to leave for Mesilla by, say, one a.m. That should give them ample time to gather up whatever they want to take and get their children ready."

"I'll spread the word myself," Sergeant McDermott volunteered.

"Very well. And I'll discreetly gather up all the men not on sentry duty and apprise them of the situation." Lieutenant Jurgenson looked at Fargo. "Anything I've missed?"

Fargo placed his hand on Juanita's shoulder. "The lady here would like a bath and a change of clothes. It's the least we can do. She's been through hell, and if it wasn't for her I wouldn't be here to warn you about the attack."

"But I don't have any money," Juanita chimed in apologetically.

"Think nothing of it, madam," Jurgenson said gallantly. "I will personally set you up in one of the guest rooms and see to it a tub of hot water is put at your disposal." He rose and offered her his elbow. "As for a dress, the sutler has some fine ones in stock. We'll charge it to my account as my way of thanking you for the invaluable service you have rendered the good people of this post."

Sergeant McDermott rolled his eyes, and as soon as the pair had walked out, he commented, "Saints preserve us, but the boyo sure lays it on thick, doesn't he? Did you see the cow eyes he was making?" He pushed out of his chair. "Well, I have a lot to be doing. What about you?"

"Are the Pimas still here?" Fargo wouldn't be surprised if they had left. Lieta was anxious to return to her people, and once her brother was fit enough, she might take it into her head to go off on their own.

"Last I knew," McDermott said. "They're shy sorts and keep to themselves. I've only seen the lass a few times since you rode out. Seemed to me she was moping about." He smirked and winked. "Maybe pining after a handsome galoot she has a fancy for, eh?"

"Don't trip over your tongue on your way out," Fargo said, making for the guest quarters. In answer to his knock, Lieta opened the door, took one look, and flung herself at him as if he were a long-lost relative.

"You're back safe! I was so worried!"

Over her shoulder Fargo saw Culazol sound asleep on the bed. "How is your brother holding up?"

"He is not quite his old self but he has shown great improvement since you left." Making no attempt to detach herself, Lieta glanced at her sibling. "He sleeps almost all the time, which the doctor says is a good thing. It shows he's mending inside."

"I have some news—" Fargo began, but was silenced by her finger against his mouth. She gently pushed him back a step, then quietly closed the door.

"Can we go to your room? I would rather not disturb him."

Someone had tidied it up since Fargo was there. The bed had been remade, the wash basin had been emptied, and the floor had been swept. He turned from the lamp he had just lit to finish telling Lieta about the impending attack but she had other ideas. Embracing him, she fastened her mouth to his as if she were famished for a kiss.

Fargo let her dictate what happened next. If she changed her mind and left, well and good. If not, that was fine by him, too. They had two and half hours to kill and he could think of no better way.

"I have been thinking about you a lot," Lieta whispered when, after a while, she tilted her head back. "About how much I would like to finish what we started."

"So would I," Fargo admitted, and covered her breasts with both hands. Her only garment was the thin buckskin dress, and the contours of her breasts were as full and firm as if she wore no dress at all. He felt her nipples harden against his palms and a low moan fluttered from her throat.

Stirrings below Fargo's belt pulsed new energy through him. He was tired but not *that* tired. A friend of his, Phinneas T. Boggs, once joked that he had more vinegar in his system than most ten men, and if he could bottle it like patent medicine men did their miracle cures, he would make a fortune. Phinneas should know. He was a patent medicine man himself.

Lieta's warm fingers slid from Fargo's neck to his shoulders. Her body was strong and supple, honed by an active life spent mostly outdoors, and she forcefully steered him over to the bed. Her breath was hot on his cheek, her dark eyes glittering pools of smoldering passion. "I might not have much time," she whispered, which was fine by Fargo.

Kissing her, he pressed Lieta onto her back and slid his left leg up over hers. Her dress hiked well above her knees, revealing sleek, muscular legs most dance-hall girls would give their eyeteeth for. Placing his left hand on her knee, he caressed the inside of her smooth thigh.

Lieta whispered a few words in Pima, then gripped him by the hair and inhaled his tongue.

Fargo glided his hand higher. The heat she gave off surpassed any fire—nowhere more so than that radiating from her core. He brushed a finger across her wet mound, and her hips thrust toward him, her legs parting wide. Her lips traced fiery nibbles on his neck, his chin, his cheeks. Suddenly inserting his finger clear to the knuckle, he swirled it around and around. Another exclamation in Piman burst from her engorged lips as she dug her nails into his back deep enough to send spear points of pain knifing through him.

For some reason it reminded Fargo of an incident that took place several months ago when he overheard a bigoted blowhard in a saloon claim white women were better lovers than Indian women because they were more adept at pleasing men. But women were women. Some poured their hearts and bodies into making love, while others were as lively as lumps of clay. The color of their skin had absolutely nothing to do with it; it was the woman: her personality, her outlook, her passion for life that counted most.

Lieta was no lump. Her lips, her hands, were constantly in motion, arousing, inciting. Unbidden, she slid her dress up above her hips and wrapped her sturdy legs around his waist. When he inserted a second finger she started to cry out but bit her lower lip and groaned instead.

Pulling her dress higher, Fargo placed his mouth on her right nipple. A few flicks of his tongue and her hips began churning like a windmill in a thunderstorm.

Fargo knelt between her legs. Undoing his belt buckle, he set his gun belt within easy reach, then undid his pants. The moment his member slid free,

Lieta gripped him with both hands and made another comment in her language. She lowered his pole to her womanhood, rubbing the tip up and down, penetrating a fraction deeper with each stroke.

Fargo had to grit his teeth to keep from exploding before he wanted. Lieta had a way of stimulating him with her inner walls that caused his throat to constrict and his vision to blur. Soon he was buried to the hilt. They both lay still, immersed in bliss.

It was Lieta who began to grind herself against him with ever-increasing vigor, Lieta who mashed his chest against hers and writhed like she was trying to rub him raw, Lieta who slid her legs up over his shoulders.

Sliding his hands under her bottom, Fargo lifted her partway off the bed. His tongue found her other breast.

Lieta exhaled loudly and scraped her nails down across his arms. "Were you a Pima I would make you mine. We would have many children and grow old together, and you would have no regrets."

"But I'm not," Fargo reminded her. Yet another aspect of women everywhere: The belief that shedding their clothes for a man was the same as putting their brand on him. It never failed.

A tinge of sadness crept into her eyes but was dispelled the next instant when Lieta opened her mouth in a soundless cry and whipped upward so wildly the entire bed bounced and shook. She gushed in a torrent.

Fargo clung to her hips, his boots braced against the bed, stemming his own release for as long as he could. Until the moment came when there was no holding back and he battered her nether mount with an urgency she more than matched.

So powerful was his release, Fargo nearly cried out. The bed was thumping the floor with the impact of a blacksmith's hammer but he didn't care who heard them. He came and came, and afterward was cast adrift on a sea of tranquillity, floating in his own inner world where there were no vicious killers like Pike Thornton, no Black Sheaths with razor-sharp machetes, and no beasts in human flesh who schemed to turn the land red with spilled blood.

But the feeling wouldn't last. It never did.

The real world saw to that.

14

The plan was to slip quietly away, get the women, children, and civilians safely to Mesilla, and return to the fort by dawn with the Black Sheaths none the wiser. Since Colonel Fraco was northwest of the post, Fargo suggested to Lieutenant Jurgenson that everyone gather on the east side of the long barracks. Troopers brought horses from the stable, taking them out the back and working around in the shadows.

Lieta did not say anything but Fargo could tell she was upset at having to leave. She and Culazol were on the same horse, her brother leaning sleepily against her back. The boy smiled when Fargo drew rein and said something in their tongue.

"He says it is good to see you again," Lieta translated, "and to thank you for all you have done for us."

Fargo was surprised the boy remembered him. "Tell him I'm glad he's feeling better." He gave her hand a squeeze. "And let him know that as soon as I'm done here, I'll take you to your village."

Lieta would not meet his gaze. "Try not to get yourself killed. Those of us who are fond of you would not like it."

"Neither would I," Fargo said with a grin, but it failed to lighten her mood. Clucking to the stallion, he rode to the head of the line.

Lieutenant Jurgenson was overseeing the operation personally. Behind him, interestingly enough, was Juanita. She gave Fargo a peculiar sort of look and commented, "Here you are. I wondered where you had gone off to."

"I was with friends."

"*Sí*. I heard you. The lieutenant had just shown me to my room, and we thought the walls were tumbling down." Juanita's lips pinched together. "Tell me, *señor*. Is there a woman you have *not* bedded?"

"One or two," Fargo replied holding his own, and was treated to a disdainful toss of her head. Sighing, he moved up next to the young officer, who had overheard and was grinning in undisguised delight, now that his own prospects had improved.

"Sergeant McDermott had told me about you, scout. But I always chalked it up as another of his tall tales. I can see now I was wrong."

"Where is he, by the way?" Fargo changed the subject.

"He and four troopers are staying behind. They'll walk around a bit, turn out a few lamps, give the impression things are normal." Jurgenson touched a finger to his temple. "I do manage to come up with some ideas of my own, you know."

"A man should always use his head now and then for something other than a hat rack," Fargo retorted. "I'll take point. If you hear any shots, get everyone under cover." He jabbed his heels and trotted fifty yards, then slowed to a walk. He wasn't anticipating trouble. They hadn't made much noise. And Fraco was far enough away that in the dark it was unlikely the Black Sheaths had noticed anything out of the ordinary.

But when Fargo rounded the very first bend, up ahead, on a knoll by the side of the road stood a man holding the reins to a horse. The starlight did not reveal much other than that he wore a sombrero and he was gazing toward Jurgenson and the others. A second later he glanced at Fargo, swung astride his mount, and wheeled westward.

Fargo gave chase. It had to be a Black Sheath, and if the man made it back to Colonel Fraco and reported that all the women and children were being taken to Mesilla, the colonel would know something was amiss and alert Machetazo.

The Ovaro gained rapidly once they were over the knoll and on flat ground. Fargo saw a rifle slung across the Black Sheath's back but couldn't tell if the Black Sheath had a revolver. The man glanced back, his features inscrutable under the wide brim of his hat, and lashed his reins.

Within seconds Fargo was close enough to drop the man with his Henry but the sound of the blast would carry a long way—the same with the Colt. Colonel Fraco would hear, and send Black Sheaths to investigate. Fargo must tend to him quietly.

This Black Sheath wasn't a skillful rider. He slowed for obstacles seasoned horsemen would easily avoid. Again and again he glanced back, and when Fargo had reduced the gap to less than a dozen feet, his right hand swooped to his hip. Metal glinted dully in the dark.

One second they were galloping hell-bent for leather, the next the Black Sheath hauled on his rein and swung his horse broadside, simultaneously raising a machete overhead. Fargo had barely a heartbeat in which to rein to the left and duck. The machete whistled over his head, and before the man could swing again, Fargo wheeled the Ovaro, slipped his boots free of his stirrups, and launched himself through the air.

The man tried to jerk aside but he was much too slow. Fargo's shoulder slammed into his chest and they both tumbled, the man cursing vehemently in Spanish. As they fell Fargo threw himself to the right so when they hit the ground and pushed to their feet he was at arm's length. The precaution saved him. The machete streaked at his neck but he skipped back and the end of the blade missed by a cat's whisker. He tried to grab for his toothpick but the Black Sheath came at him like a man possessed, slashing and hacking in a fierce bid to slay him.

Fargo dodged the first few blows. Then his left boot slipped on a loose rock and he landed on his back, as helpless as an upended turtle. If the Black Sheath had stabbed at his chest he'd have died then and there. But the man raised the machete to chop at his neck. Rolling to the right, he heard the blade bite into the earth. He heaved upright, drawing the toothpick as he straightened, all done so swiftly the Black Sheath had time only to cock his arm.

For a few moments they stared at each other, their bodies coiled. "There's no need for you to die," Fargo said. "Not if Machetazo forced you to become a Black Sheath." He had no desire to kill some simple farmer.

The man lowered his weapon a few inches. "You think I am a conscript, is that it, *gringo*? But I wear my machete with pride. I like to kill, especially *norteamericanos* like you!"

With that, the Black Sheath cleaved the air in a downward stroke that would have separated Fargo's shoulder from his body had it landed. But, shifting to one side, Fargo not only caused the Black Sheath to miss, he opened the man's neck with a lightning slash of the toothpick.

The Black Sheath didn't seem to realize he had been cut. Pivoting, he swung the machete again, swinging low at Fargo's waist. Fargo countered, deflecting it, but nearly lost his grip on his knife.

Again the Black Sheath went to strike, then abruptly froze as blood spurted from the corners of his mouth. Gurgling and gasping, he looked down at a rapidly spreading dark stain on his shirt. His machete fell. Clutching his throat, he staggered toward his mount, one arm outstretched to grasp the reins, but the horse caught the scent of fresh blood and shied.

Fargo did nothing. There was no need.

The man tried to speak but all that came out was more blood. His knees gave way and he fell onto his backside and sat gaping in stunned disbelief at the world he would soon depart. His left arm rose to the heavens in silent supplication. Then his chin drooped to his chest, his whole body trembled, and he stopped breathing.

Waiting a few moments, Fargo walked over and nudged him with the toothpick. The Black Sheath plopped onto his side, his arms as limp as wet rags. Fargo took the rifle and a bandoleer and shoved them into his rolled-up blanket on the Ovaro. Then, stepping slowly and talking softly, he caught hold of the other animal's reins without any difficulty. But when he attempted to sling the dead man over the saddle, the horse nickered and pranced and wouldn't calm down no matter what Fargo did. Finally he hid the body in a patch of brush.

Lieutenant Jurgenson's detail was a mile north of the fort when Fargo overtook them. He handed over the Black Sheath's horse to a private. Jurgenson listened to his account, then commented, "Too bad you didn't kill all of them. There would be ten less to attack the fort."

Fargo gave that some thought. The missing Black Sheath would make Colonel Fraco suspicious. And Fraco, in turn, would relay his concern to the Beast. Since the element of surprise was no longer a sure thing, it made sense to cut the odds before Machetazo arrived.

The detail was halfway to Mesilla when Fargo reined around and rode back from point. "The women and children should be safe from here on," he informed Jurgenson. "I'm going to take you up on your idea and head for the post."

"What idea?" the lieutenant asked, then exclaimed, "Oh! But I should go with you. You can't do it alone."

That was the last thing Fargo wanted. "The colonel left you in charge, remember? You can't go running off on your men." He nodded at Juanita as he went by, but she still hadn't forgiven him, and turned away. A few seconds later Lieta saw him coming and went to say something but he went by so fast she didn't have the chance. He would apologize later. Right now he was pressed for time.

Three miles and a lot of hard riding brought Fargo to Fort Fillmore. It was as quiet as a tomb. The mess hall and barracks were dark; the compound deserted, as they usually were at that late an hour. Fargo reined up in front of the stable without being challenged and was debating where to look for the sergeant major when his name was whispered from over by the armory.

"Psssst. Boyo! This way!"

McDermott was crouched beside the building in a patch of inky shadow, two troopers at his side. "What are you doing back so soon, laddie? Is everything all right?"

Fargo related his run-in with the Black Sheath and what he had in mind.

"Go off by your lonesome against nine of the devil's own?" McDermott made a *tsk-tsk* sound. "That won't hardly do. I'm thinking you need one of the Emerald Isle's own to help pull it off."

"I was hoping you'd say that." Fargo clapped his friend's shoulder. "Can you be ready in five minutes?"

"Half that, if you promise the drinks are on you the next time we visit a saloon." McDermott turned to one of the privates. "Ross, I want you to tell Banner and Parker I'm going for a stroll with this buckskin lothario. The four of you are to lie low until the lieutenant returns."

"We wouldn't mind going with you, Sergeant," Ross said. "All we ever do is drill, drill, drill. I'd love to see some action for once."

"What a sweet sentiment," McDermott said in false praise, then growled, "but when I want the opinion of raw recruits, I'll post a notice on the bulletin board for everyone to read." He cuffed Ross across the back of the head. "Off with you before I forget myself and take you over my knee." The private dutifully obeyed, and McDermott grinned at Fargo. "I tell you, these lads worship the ground I walk on."

Aware they had only several hours until dawn broke, Fargo led the pugnacious Irishman on foot into the brush to the north. He remembered to remove his spurs first and left them in his saddlebags.

McDermott was a veteran of several campaigns against hostile Indians, and he could move almost as silently as an Apache when he had to.

A hushed expectancy seemed to grip the wilderness. Even the coyotes were silent. Fargo circled to come up on the gully from the rear, and they were still a good two hundred yards from where it should be when the stomp of a hoof let him know the Black Sheaths were a lot closer than he thought. He immediately hunkered.

In the dusky gloom it was hard to distinguish details. But after straining his eyes Fargo made out the silhouettes of picketed horses. He also saw sleeping forms spread out near them. Colonel Fraco had pulled back from the gully with the advent of night and bedded down where there was some grass for his animals.

McDermott crab-stepped closer and whispered, "Are those the very same nasties we're to dispose of?"

"The very same. Cover me." Fargo stalked forward, every nerve taut. Fraco didn't strike him as the careless type, so there had to be a sentry. But the man could be anywhere. Unless the Black Sheath coughed or moved or did something else to give away his location, spotting him would take some doing.

It helped that several of the sleepers were snoring

loud enough to drown out whatever slight noise Fargo made as he threaded through the vegetation. He counted seven, scattered at random. Which meant two were unaccounted for.

About to skirt a large tumbleweed, Fargo turned to stone on hearing a scrape from the other side. It was followed by a low grunt, and suddenly a Black Sheath stood up not six feet from him. It was the sentry. But one Black Sheath was still missing. There had been ten in that gully.

The Black Sheath yawned, cradled a rifle in the crook of his left elbow, and slowly strolled to the left.

Fargo set down the Henry and drew his Arkansas toothpick. Stealth was called for. He took a step but stopped cold as another Black Sheath emerged from the shadows.

"Were I any more bored, Alfonso, I would shoot myself for excitement."

The first sentry laughed. "You will get all the excitement you can handle when the general arrives tomorrow afternoon. The *gringo* soldiers are not cowards. They will put up a fight."

"I hope so," the other sentry said. "And I also hope I get my hands on a woman or two. It has been so long I have forgotten how."

Fargo dared not move or they might spot him. He waited for them to separate but they were in no hurry.

"A man never forgets a thing like that," Alfonso replied. "It is as much a part of him as breathing."

"But a man can hold his breath only so long," the second man argued, and frowned. "I envy Miguel. He gets to watch the road every night while we sit around doing nothing."

"You could have raised your hand when the colonel asked for a volunteer."

"Old habits are hard to break, *amigo*. He who volunteers least often lives the longest." The other sentry rested the barrel of his rifle on his shoulder. "We better break this up. You know how mad the colonel gets when he catches us talking."

The second man walked off but Alfonso dallied, his face upturned to the stars.

Uncoiling, Fargo pounced. He clamped his left forearm around the Black Sheath's throat, choking off any outcry, and plunged the toothpick into yielding flesh just above the left kidney. Once, twice, three times he stabbed, and as the blade pierced to the hilt on the third thrust, Alfonso dropped like a puppet with its strings cut. Fargo almost didn't catch him in time.

The other sentry was over by the horses. He hadn't heard anything and was patting one of the animals.

Easing the dead man down, Fargo turned to pick up the Henry.

"Look out, boyo!" Sergeant McDermott shouted, and two rifles boomed. One belonged to a Black Sheath who had sat up without Fargo's noticing, the other was the Irishman's .56-50 Spencer.

Shouts of confusion and the crack of more rifles blistered Fargo's ears as he dived. He came up with the Henry wedged to his shoulder and fired at a Black Sheath who loomed out of nowhere. Somewhere a pistol was added to the din. Slugs clipped the brush on either side and something brushed the crown of Fargo's hat. Hurling himself to the left, he banged off three shots from the hip. A Black Sheath cried out. Another cursed.

Then, incredibly, above the bedlam rose Sergeant McDermott's baritone voice in lusty song. He was singing as he fired—"Camptown Races," of all things— and punctuating each verse with a wild whoop.

Black Sheaths were trying to climb onto horses. Fargo squeezed off two swift shots and had the satisfaction of seeing two figures fall. From behind a cactus to the south a rifle spat flame and he answered in kind.

In the blink of an eye all was quiet except for the groaning of a wounded Black Sheath. Fargo was sure several were still alive and he wisely didn't move or make a sound.

McDermott, though, shed all caution and came barreling through the brush like a riled bear. His face creased in a broad grin, he declared, "We gave 'em hell, didn't we, boyo?"

Crouching lower, Fargo whispered, "Has anyone ever told you that you're an idiot?"

"Many a time. But it's a glorious idiocy. I can't help myself. All the Irish in my blood, you know." McDermott blasted off a shot and whooped for joy. "Give me battle or give me a discharge! Here I am, you renegades! Mrs. McDermott's pride and joy will pluck all your tail feathers!"

The Black Sheath behind the cactus fired again. This time Fargo saw him clearly and responded before the man could duck back. There was a shriek and a thud.

"That's showing these vermin!" McDermott roared.

"Keep them busy while I circle around," Fargo whispered, and darted off before his friend bellowed again. To some, the Irishman's quirk might seem the stuff of madness. But there was a method to it. Many Indians whooped and shouted to disconcert their enemies. A Sioux war cry was the most feared sound on the Plains. Comanche war whoops struck fear into the hearts of settlers all across Texas. All McDermott was doing was using the tactics of those he'd fought against his own enemies.

The wind had picked up, and from the northwest it brought the crunch of a twig. Fargo thought he saw someone, but the figure disappeared the instant he laid eyes on it. The wounded Black Sheath near the horses began groaning again, and for a while Fargo couldn't hear anything else. Then the man stopped. Faint rustling to the northeast gave him sudden cause for concern.

A Black Sheath was circling toward McDermott.

Fargo hoped his friend had heard the twig and the

other sounds but the Irishman was gazing to the west, not the northeast. Fargo had to warn him, but he had to do it without yelling or he would draw fire himself. Groping the ground, he found a rock about the size of a hen's egg.

Fifteen yards past the sergeant major, a shadow reared.

Quickly, Fargo threw the rock as near to the Black Sheath as he could. It crashed into the brush beside him and he recoiled. McDermott spun toward the noise just as the Black Sheath fired and apparently missed, because the brawny sergeant returned fire, hollering, "Sneak up on me, will you, you damned assassin!"

The figure dropped from sight but Fargo had a gut feeling the man wasn't dead. About to reverse direction, he saw bushes move a few yards west of where the Black Sheath had been. He crept west himself, paralleling his quarry, hoping in vain for a shot although twice he saw brush move against the wind.

The horse string came between them, and Fargo moved faster. Almost too fast. A revolver cracked down low to the ground, the slug passing within an inch of his face. A wounded Black Sheath was on his belly between two of the mounts, steadying a six-shooter with both hands.

Barely five feet separated them. Fargo had only to slant the Henry and squeeze the trigger. The impact flipped the man under the hooves of one of the horses, and the animal showed its displeasure by snorting and stomping. Bone crunched but the Black Sheath didn't cry out. He was already dead.

Other horses started whinnying and stamping. The racket prevented Fargo from hearing anything. Reaching the last animal, he glimpsed someone bolting to the northwest. McDermott's rifle spoke but the figure never broke stride. Fargo tried to fix a bead and couldn't. The man was weaving too wildly.

Fargo ran after him and had taken only four or five strides when another Black Sheath popped out of thin air not ten paces to his left. A rifle went off, clipping some of the whangs on his right sleeve. He fired twice, his first shot spinning the Black Sheath halfway around, the second ripping into the man's jawbone and tearing off part of his face.

The delay had given the figure to the northwest time to melt away. Fargo broke into a sprint. He suspected this was the last one. Alert for cactus he might blunder into, he went quite a distance. Thinking maybe the Black Sheath had gone to ground, he stopped and squatted.

Two minutes went by, then three. Fargo heard nothing, saw no one. He took a few steps to the northwest, a few to the northeast. In the belief the Black Sheath was long gone, he lowered the Henry and turned to go back.

"Twitch and I kill you!"

The harsh whisper was preceded by a gun barrel being jammed into the base of Fargo's spine. It was rare for him to be taken totally unaware, and Fargo mimicked a saguaro. A hand reached around in front of him and relieved him of the Henry.

"Call to your loud-mouthed friend over there. And no tricks, American. I speak excellent English."

Fargo shifted toward where he had last seen McDermott and bought himself a few second by whispering, "What do you want me to say?"

"I don't care so long as you get him over here." The Black Sheath jabbed the muzzle harder to accent his demand.

"Lieutenant Jurgenson!" Fargo shouted. "I need you a moment!" He hoped the Irishman would catch on that something was wrong and come to his aid.

"He is an officer?" the Black Sheath whispered. "Good. He will have valuable information General Machetazo can use."

Sergeant McDermott gave vent to robust laughter. "Was that an insult, boyo? Or your feeble attempt at a joke? Comparing me to that know-it-all tyke is like comparing a ripe apple to a green one."

"I warned you!" the Black Sheath hissed.

Fargo whirled just as the rifle discharged. How it missed him he would never know, but it did, and he found himself grappling with a husky Black Sheath who tried to bash his head in with the stock. They fought for possession, twisting and pulling and spinning around, neither gaining the upper hand until Fargo suddenly hooked his right foot behind the Black Sheath's ankle and pushed. They both went down. Fargo was on top and drove his knee into the man's gut.

The Black Sheath's grip slackened and Fargo tore the rifle free. He tried to knock the Black Sheath out, but the man jerked to one side and the next moment Fargo was pitched into the dirt, the rifle underneath him.

The man was fast. Springing onto Fargo's back, he clamped one hand on the barrel and the other on the stock and put all his strength into choking Fargo to death. The rifle barrel dug in to Fargo's neck, cutting off his breath and threatening to crush his throat. Fargo pushed against it but the Black Sheath had too much leverage.

Dimly, Fargo heard the Irishman calling his name but he couldn't respond. His chest began to ache but the pain was trifling next to his throat. For a second the world dimmed. Refusing to give up, Fargo heaved himself to the right. The Black Sheath's knees slipped and the pressure lessened. Not a lot—not enough for Fargo to pitch the Black Sheath off. But he could and did get his elbows under him and catapulted upward.

The Black Sheath tumbled, and Fargo was on him before the man could stand. He landed a left cross to the chin, a right to the cheek. The man lost the rifle but came up swinging. Fargo met him with an upper-cut. Crashing down, the Black Sheath weakly attempted to rise but a second uppercut stretched him out flat on his back, unconscious.

Boots drummed, and an open hand clapped Fargo on the shoulder. "Well done, boyo! There's nothing like a good donnybrook to clear the head and get the blood flowing."

The Irishman would never know how close he came to being slugged.

15

Lieutenant Jurgenson had the look of someone who had a chicken bone caught in his throat. "You did what?"

"We brought the bodies with us," Skye Fargo repeated. It was a little past five in the morning and the detail had just returned from Mesilla. Fargo and Sergeant McDermott were in the mess hall when the officer hustled in, Fargo working on his fourth cup of coffee since the "donnybrook."

"Why in hell did you do a thing like that?" Jurgenson demanded. "We don't have enough men to spare for a burial detail."

"I didn't bring them back to bury them," Fargo said. "I brought them to help us against Machetazo."

The young officer looked him up and down. "Did you receive a head wound I don't know about? What good will dead men do us? They can't shoot. They can't fight. You should have left them out there for the buzzards."

"That's exactly what I told him, sir," Sergeant McDermott mentioned. "But you should hear him out. He's damned tricky, our lothario. And when you're up against a wily blackguard like the Beast, you fight fire with fire."

"I swear, Sergeant. If you ever talk like the rest of us, the shock will kill me." Jurgenson took a seat across from them. "I'm listening, scout. And I hope this is good."

Fargo's initial plan had called for digging trenches at the northwest and southwest corners of the square where there were no buildings and the post was most vulnerable. Several troopers would man each, covered by others on the roofs and in windows, and fall back if the Black Sheaths threatened to break through. His new idea called for placing the dead Black Sheaths in the trenches, but when he was done presenting it, the lieutenant shook his head.

"The Beast is a lot of things but stupid isn't one of them. He'll see right through our ruse and break through sooner."

Sergeant McDermott came to Fargo's defense. "Think of it, sir. All the ammo they'll be wasting. And until they realize they've been hoodwinked, it'll be that much easier for our boys to pick them off."

Jurgenson wavered. "I hadn't thought of that." He dug out his pocket watch. "It's the time factor that bothers me. We have only seven or eight hours, maybe a bit more, and I can't see squandering any of it."

"We'll have plenty of time if we get to work right away," Fargo confidently predicted. He rose to get things rolling but the officer had another question.

"Where's this prisoner you mentioned?"

"Under lock and key in the guardhouse," Sergeant McDermott reported. "He won't tell us who he is or how long he's been with Machetazo or what part of Mexico he's from. Nothing." McDermott paused. "Mr. Fargo thinks he's none other than Colonel Fraco, the Beast's second in command."

"On what is this assumption based?"

"A hunch," Fargo admitted.

"Ah. Be that as it may, whether this man is or isn't Fraco has no practical bearing on our predicament. Machetazo isn't about to call off the attack because we have one of his men in custody. Quite the contrary. It might make Machetazo that much more determined to wipe us out." Lieutenant Jurgenson stood. "Fifteen against an army. Now I know how Travis and Bowie felt."

"Don't forget the trooper we sent to fetch Colonel Blanchard," McDermott remarked. "There's always a chance the colonel will make it back."

"You're deluding yourself, Sergeant. Our personal Alamo will be long over before help arrives."

Fargo agreed but refrained from saying so. It was up to them and them alone, and no amount of wishful thinking would change that. "Let's get to it."

Five troopers were assigned to dig each of the trenches, and while they toiled under the rising sun, Lieutenant Jurgenson and two others transferred crates and weapons from the armory to the stable, concealing everything under a mountain of straw. It was another of Fargo's brainstorms, in case Machetazo overwhelmed them.

Sergeant McDermott and the last of the troopers had the unenviable chore of stripping the dead Black Sheaths and dressing them in Army uniforms.

That left Fargo. He took a brass spyglass and rode to the highest point of land to the west. All their preparations would be in vain if they let the Beast take them by surprise, and his job was to see that that didn't happen.

Dismounting, Fargo sat on a boulder and swept the horizon from north to south and back again. Nothing moved in all that vast expanse. As he studied the lay of the land it occurred to him that the People's Army would arrive during the hottest part of the day. They wouldn't cross the plain to the southwest and be baked alive, nor would they try to negotiate the maze of ravines and gullies due west. They would choose the easiest route, through the hills to the northwest, which had the added benefit of screening them from the fort.

Knowing that, Fargo had a golden opportunity. He was still convinced that without Machetazo to lead them, the Black Sheaths would fall apart. The Beast was the glue that held them together. So if he stopped

Machetazo from reaching Fort Fillmore, the attack might never take place.

Turning the telescope on the hills, Fargo noticed that if the Black Sheaths took the route he suspected, they would pass within range of his Henry. It was a long, challenging shot, but he had made similar shots before.

Yanking the Henry out, Fargo propped it against the boulder and sat back down. The hard thing now was to stay awake. Almost two days without sleep was taking its toll. The hotter it became, the more sluggish he felt. Several times he rose and moved about to ward off fatigue.

Noon approached. Fargo opened the canteen he had brought, removed his hat, and filled it halfway. The water wasn't for him, it was for the Ovaro. Only after the stallion was done did he drink his own fill.

One o'clock came and went; two o'clock, then three. Fargo was beginning to hope Machetazo had been delayed when a column of dust marred the bright blue sky. He fixed his spyglass on it but another five minutes passed before a bedraggled column of Black Sheaths came into focus. They had been on the march all day and it showed. Men and animals were caked so thick with dust they gave the illusion of being statues. Those on horseback were slumped in their saddles, while those on foot trudged glumly along.

At the forefront rode General Vicente Machetazo. Head high, shoulders squared, he alone of all his army seemed impervious to the heat and the toil. Half a mile out he raised his right hand, bringing the column to a halt. Fargo wondered why, and didn't have to wait long to find out. Machetazo twisted, opened a saddlebag, and took out a spyglass of his own.

"Damn!" Fargo said out loud, and ducked behind the boulder. There was nothing he could do about the Ovaro. But it was far enough back from the crest, Machetazo might not spot it.

The Beast surveyed the terrain ahead, showing particular interest in the hills the column was winding through. His spyglass swiveled to the south, across the rise Fargo was on, and Fargo tensed. If Machetazo saw the stallion it would be obvious. But there was no reaction whatsoever.

The Beast moved the spyglass in a one hundred and eighty degree circuit, then lowered it. He pumped his other arm and the column lurched into motion again; an exhausted snake carried forward by the vitality of its head.

Fargo didn't lower his own spyglass until Machetazo was almost within range. The Henry to his shoulder, he placed his left elbow on the boulder for extra support and waited for Machetazo's torso to fill his sights.

Killing from ambush did not sit well with him. But if ever there was a man who deserved it, the sadistic fiend on the tired chestnut was the one. Ambushing him would save untold lives, avert untold suffering. As much as Fargo preferred to confront Machetazo man to man, there were innocent lives at stake.

The Beast was a few yards in front of the others, sitting tall, a perfect target. He had put his spyglass back in a saddlebag and was gazing toward Fort Fillmore.

Fargo elevated the barrel to compensate for the extreme range. There was no breeze to speak of so windage wasn't a problem. Scarcely breathing, he lightly touched his finger to the trigger. He would try to put at least three slugs into the chest, then light a shuck for the post.

The first inkling that something had gone wrong was a shout from a mounted Black Sheath. It was taken up by others. The entire column came to a halt and every head swiveled toward the rise.

Inwardly cursing, Fargo dashed to the Ovaro. He knew what had gone wrong and he was mad at himself.

Unique among rifles, the Henry sported a shiny brass receiver. Sunlight had a tendency to reflect off it as if off a mirror, and the flashes could be seen from far off. That was exactly what had taken place when Fargo elevated the barrel, but it wouldn't have if he had remembered to remove his bandanna and wrap it around the receiver earlier.

Eight Black Sheaths were racing toward the rise. But not Machetazo. He was back with the rest, his spyglass once again pressed to his right eye.

Fargo frowned, slapped his legs against the Ovaro, and went down the other side at a gallop. He had a long way to go but he had complete confidence in the pinto. Few horses were its equal.

The Black Sheaths reached the top of the rise and milled about a moment. Then one saw him and yelled, and on they came.

Fargo figured they would chase him almost to the fort but they gave up after only a few hundred yards and turned back. Under orders from Machetazo, he guessed. He didn't slow down, though. The troopers had to be warned.

Although the sun was well on its westward arc, there were four or five hours of daylight left. Fargo estimated it would take the Black Sheaths about an hour to get into position. Unless by some miracle Machetazo decided to hold off until morning, by nightfall it would be over. Tomorrow the buzzards would feast well.

A trooper on the roof of the sutler's spotted him and shouted down, and Lieutenant Jurgenson and Sergeant McDermott were both at the northwest trench when Fargo got there. It stretched from building to building, so there was no going around. Bending low over the saddle, he lashed his reins, and the stallion sailed up and over. For a few seconds they were airborne. Glancing down, Fargo saw four dead Black Sheaths dressed in spare cavalry uniforms, broomsticks and boards propped against their backs to keep them upright. He also saw a keg of black powder at the south end of the trench, with a trail of it leading to the front door of the sutler's.

Before the stallion came to stop, Fargo had swung off.

Jurgenson and McDermott rushed over, the young officer as anxious as a schoolboy on his first day of school. "Well, well? Out with it, scout."

"They're on their way or I wouldn't be here. Are our surprises set?"

Jurgenson nodded. "We've done everything you suggested. We even repositioned the cannons side-by-side over by the barracks."

Fargo looked. One cannon now pointed at the northwest trench, the other at the trench to the south-west. Two troopers manned them.

Sergeant McDermott grinned and rubbed his calloused hands together. "This will be a day my grandchildren will never stop hearing about!"

"Are you getting ahead of yourself?" Lieutenant Jurgenson said. "First get married and have some children, then start talking about grandchildren."

"Mere trifles, sir," the Irishman declared. "There isn't a wee lass anywhere who wouldn't give her wisdom teeth to snare the likes of Alphonsus Naal McDermott."

"Alphonsus?" Fargo said.

"To my shame and sorrow, boyo, yes. My father wanted to name me James. But my mother, who like all women has her daft spells, decided I should be named after an obscure great-uncle on her mother's side of the family." McDermott sighed. "I should be counting my blessings, though. She named my younger brother Bairrfhoinn."

Jurgenson's features were pinched as if he had been stung by a scorpion. "Enough about your silly names, for God's sake! I want to hear about the Beast and how long we have."

Fargo told them. The lieutenant rushed off to spread the word while he headed for the stable with the stallion. McDermott went with him.

"I have a favor to be asking of you, lothario."

"Name it."

The Irishman fished in a pocket and held out a sealed envelope. "If anything untoward happens to me, mail this to my parents. I've been a bit remiss in keeping in touch, and I want to go to my Maker with as few blights on my record as I can."

It was uncharacteristic of McDermott to be so melancholy. Fargo slid the letter into a saddlebag, saying, "I'll get it to them. But if you die on me, I'll send one of my own telling them how fond you are of Irish whiskey, poker, and fallen doves. Not in that order, either."

"You wouldn't!" McDermott exclaimed. "What a dastardly threat! And me, one of your boon partners. Why, who was it saved your scrawny hide that time a drunk tried to pigstick you in the back? And who was it lied to that filly in Denver and told her you'd lit out for San Francisco so she'd stop hounding you to tie the knot?" McDermott sniffed loudly. "You're an ingrate, boyo, and just to spite you, I won't let the Beast and his bullies plant me."

A yell from a trooper on the roof of the officers' quarters put an end to their banter. "There they are! They're spreading out in a skirmish line!"

Fargo hustled the stallion into a stall, shucked the Henry, and jogged to the northwest trench. Seven troopers were already there, watching as the mounted contingent of the People's Army formed into a long row from north to south. The infantry split in half, one column filing north around the fort, the other quick-marching to the south.

"They're surrounding us," a trooper said anxiously.

Lieutenant Jurgenson had risen to the occasion and stood with his chin high, a model of military authority. "What else did you expect, Private? But they'll try to break through here first." He glanced at the trench. "Let's hope our little ruse works."

The Beast and a pair of mounted Black Sheaths were conferring. One tied a strip of white cloth to the barrel of his rifle and spurred his horse toward them.

"No firing!" Lieutenant Jurgenson bawled. "He's our enemy but he's under a flag of truce."

Fargo stepped closer and said softly so only the young officer heard, "We don't want him to see our defenses, do we?"

Jurgenson started. "No, we don't. It wouldn't be prudent. I'll go out to meet him. Sergeant McDermott, should they not honor their own flag, you will assume command and resist to the last man."

"Permission to go with you, sir," the Irishman requested. "Those vipers aren't to be trusted, and that's no blarney."

"Permission denied." Jurgenson jumped the trench, adjusted his hat, and headed out to meet the emissary.

McDermott looked at Fargo but Fargo was already in motion. Springing across the trench, he caught up to Jurgenson and commented, "I hope you don't mind company."

"Not at all. To be honest, scout, I'm glad you're with us. You have more experience at this sort of thing than all the rest of us combined."

"It's Fargo."

"What?"

"My name's not 'scout.' My friends get to use my real one." Fargo said it because he was tired of the young officer's pompous attitude, as much as anything else, but damned if Jurgenson didn't blush.

"Why, thank you. I'm flattered. McDermott swears

by your integrity. He says you're the only man in the world he'd let marry his sister. If he had one, that is."

The Black Sheath had slowed from a canter to a walk and was waving the white cloth so no one would mistake his intentions. He was about the same age as Jurgenson, and just as pompous. "I am Lieutenant Lorenzo Guadalupe Alfredo of the People's Army for the Liberation of Mexico. General Vicente Machetazo has sent me to express his wishes."

"We're listening," Jurgenson said.

In a tone that made it sound like a pronouncement from the Almighty, Lieutenant Alfredo declared, "The general wishes to avoid bloodshed. He offers you and your command the chance to lay down your arms and surrender. In return, you have his solemn word no harm will befall you."

Lieutenant Jurgenson kept his composure. "Is that all?"

"The general also guarantees the lives of all non-combatants. Women and children will be treated with due courtesy." Alfredo paused. "In exchange for his generosity, he asks something in return."

"What would that be?"

"The general wants the *gringo* with you turned over to him to do with as he pleases. A small concession, he feels, for being so generous."

Fargo answered before Jurgenson could. "Go back and tell the Beast he can sit on his machete for all we care."

Lieutenant Alfredo bristled. "Who is in charge here, *gringo*? You or this officer?" He leaned forward. "The general was most surprised to see you. He thinks maybe the men he left to guard you are no longer alive."

"They're not," Fargo said. It wasn't true, of course, but now the farmers who had gone back to their homes would be presumed dead, and Machetazo wouldn't have them hunted down. "The same with Captain Ruiz and those your general left at the spring." He had saved the best for last. "And Colonel Fraco and his men."

The Black Sheath refused to believe it. "You killed them *all*? That is not possible."

"Tell it to their corpses." Fargo nodded toward where the Beast awaited the outcome of their talk. "And tell your general we're not buying his lies. His promises aren't worth a hill of beans."

"You dig your own grave, *bastardo*."

"Then I might as well dig it deeper." Fargo took a step, anger bubbling in him like lava in a volcano. "Let your glorious leader know that I warned the soldiers he was coming. We emptied the armory and hid all the guns and ammunition where he'll never find them. So even if he wins, it will all be for nothing."

The Black Sheath sat very still for all of ten seconds. "*Sí*. I will tell him. But I would not want to be in your boots for all the gold in Mexico when he gets his hands on you." Reining around, he trotted off.

Jurgenson let out a low whistle. "What were you thinking? Machetazo will be mad enough to skin you alive."

"The madder he is, the more reckless he'll be."

When they reached the trench, Sergeant McDermott had news to convey. "Their infantry has linked up to the east. We're hemmed in, but they're just standing there like so many dim-witted dominoes."

"The Beast won't commit his foot soldiers until he's softened us up with his cavalry," Lieutenant Jurgenson stated, echoing thought in Fargo's own mind. "Unwittingly, he's doing us a favor. We don't have enough men to fight on four fronts at once." He began barking orders: "Everyone to their posts! Don't fire until I say to! Remember your training and we'll make it through this alive."

"Anywhere special you want me?" Fargo asked.

216

"Technically, you're a civilian. I have no right to make you take part. You can climb on your horse and ride out if you want." When Fargo stayed where he was, Jurgenson smiled. "I didn't think so. Lend your support wherever you think we need it most at any given moment." He snapped a salute in respect, then hurried toward the sutler's.

"As shavetails go he has his moments," Sergeant McDermott remarked, and clasped Fargo's hand in his. "Give 'em hell, boyo. And know that whatever happens, Mrs. McDermott's wayfaring son is proud to have known your whiskey-guzzling self."

Fargo was left alone by the trench. He heard Machetazo bark orders, too, and the Black Sheath cavalry divided into two groups. It wouldn't be long now—time to do something else he had thought up, and maybe throw a scare into the enemy in the bargain.

Hastening to the stable, Fargo entered the tack room. On the ground lay one of Colonel Fraco's men. Beside him were a machete and a pitchfork. Leaning the Henry against the wall, Fargo set to work. It was grisly business, but the man was already dead and might as well be put to good use—or part of him, anyway.

The head was heavier than Fargo expected. He had to wriggle it back and forth to impale it on the blunt end of the pitchfork's handle. Placing the sombrero on top, he held the gory trophy aloft and strode into the sunlight. He hadn't told Jurgenson why he wanted one of the bodies left untouched, and now the young officer started toward him but stopped after only a few steps, overcome by horror.

Fargo was afraid the head would fall off when he leaped the trench but it didn't. A dozen yards out he halted, knelt, and imbedded the tines in the earth. The Black Sheaths were staring and muttering among themselves, trying to make sense of what it was. The truth hadn't dawned yet.

Machetazo resorted to his spyglass. Fargo stood there, and when he was sure the Beast had seen the head, he pointed at it, then at Machetazo, and sliced a finger across the bottom of his throat. His meaning could not be more clear.

Rage twisting his face, General Machetazo slowly lowered the telescope. Thrusting it under his belt, he bent and pulled a rifle from his saddle scabbard.

Fargo wondered what the butcher was up to. He was well beyond effective range of most rifles. Then Machetazo held it across the pommel and fed a cartridge into the chamber by levering the trigger guard. Only two rifles were loaded like that; the Sharps and the Spencer; this was a Sharps. Fargo had owned one for years and could easily tell them apart.

There was a crucial difference between the two models. Spencers were fine guns but savvy frontiersmen knew they lacked the power to consistently down big game like buffalo and elk or to shoot long distances. The large-caliber Sharps, on the other hand, was powerful enough to fell a bull buffalo with a single shot—or, in the hands of a marksman, to drop a man at more than five hundred yards.

Fargo was only three hundred yards from Machetazo. But instead of turning and running when the Beast took deliberate aim, he folded his arms across his chest.

"What in blazes are you doing, boyo?" Sergeant McDermott hollered. "Get out of there!"

Fargo did no such thing. He knew the Beast too well; knew Machetazo would never shoot him outright. In Machetazo's own words, "It would be too quick, too merciful." And there wasn't a merciful bone in Machetazo's body. Fargo had humiliated him—had escaped from Sergeant Gonzales, had slain Captain Ruiz and the others—and for that Machetazo would want him to suffer as few ever had.

The Sharps boomed.

For a sickening instant Fargo thought maybe he was wrong, maybe Machetazo's fury would get the better of his sadism. Then there was the *thwack* of a heavy slug striking flesh and bone, and the head on the pitch-fork handle went flying.

The Beast lowered the Sharps and grinned. He also did something else: He roared a command for the Black Sheaths to attack.

16

Skye Fargo turned and bolted toward the trench. He cleared it in a long hurdle and darting to the corner of the sutler's, drew his Colt. The first wave of Black Sheaths were charging at a gallop. He wouldn't be able to make it to the stable for his Henry, so the revolver had to do.

General Machetazo had drilled the Black Sheaths well. They held a tight formation, virtually shoulder to shoulder. They also were holding their fire until they were closer. Half made for the northwest trench, the rest were making for the trench to the southwest. Behind the first wave came another, just as disciplined.

Fargo heard Lieutenant Jurgenson remind the troopers that no one was to shoot until he gave the word. It was a smart thing to do. Except for Sergeant McDermott, they were raw recruits, as green as the summer grass in their home states back East. Their nerves were frayed to the breaking point, and in this high-strung state they might waste their initial volley by firing too soon.

The Beast had elected not to lead the charge. He was watching through his spyglass, the two lieutenants at his side.

Scores of hoofbeats rumbled like thunder, growing louder by the moment. The horses the Black Sheaths were riding had been taken from dead *Federales* and were trained for war. The sounds and sights of battle wouldn't send them into a panic and scatter them to the four winds.

Some of the Black Sheaths took aim at the decoy troopers in the trenches, and Fargo smiled grimly. Let them waste all the lead they wanted to on their dead companions.

Again Lieutenant Jurgenson's voice rang out. Rifles crackled all along the west side of the post. But the inexperience of the recruits showed in the pitifully few Black Sheaths they hit. Only one pitched from his saddle. The rest came on, in a sombrero-crowned tidal wave.

Fargo glanced down at the keg of black powder at the bottom of the trench, then at the doorway to the sutler's where McDermott was on his knee, matches in hand. Timing was everything—the slightest misjudgment and they would pay with their lives—but he trusted the big Irishman to get it right.

The Black Sheaths abruptly opened fire. Slug after slug thudded into the uniformed corpses, which refused to topple because of the boards propped against their backs. If the leading Black Sheaths caught on that something was amiss, it was too late to stem the charge. A few more were hit as the troopers steadied their nerves and their aim.

Fargo banged off two swift shots himself and a rider tumbled. Just as the Black Sheaths reached the trench, he hunkered lower so they would be less likely to notice him. His plan called for letting the first wave make it through. The kegs in the trenches were for the second wave.

Guns boomed fast and furious. Across the parade ground, the troopers at the cannons had lit matches and were crouched behind the big guns, awaiting the order to spring their surprise.

The Black Sheaths to the southwest were the first ones across a trench and into the square. They concentrated their fire on the officers' quarters, shooting out pane after pane. Not three seconds later the Black Sheaths to the northwest vaulted the other trench and the firing rose in an ear-blistering crescendo.

The second wave was fifty yards out and closing rapidly. If they made it through, the outcome was foreordained. Fargo marked the distance, and at twenty yards he glanced over his shoulder at Sergeant McDermott and nodded.

Instantly the Irishman applied a match to the trail of black powder that served as a fuse. In front of the sutler's, Lieutenant Jurgenson did the same to the powder leading into the southwest trench.

Wheeling, Fargo ran. Flame and smoke went flashing by, the powder hissing like a sidewinder. Bullets pockmarked the walls as Black Sheaths tried to bring him down. Another few strides, and he flung himself to the ground and covered his head, hoping to heaven he was far enough away.

The force of the explosion shook the very ground. Part of the building dissolved into bits and pieces which were swallowed up by a huge churning cloud of dust. Roiling outward and upward, it spread like fog. The screams of Black Sheaths and the whinnies of their mounts were smothered midcry.

Fargo could hardly see, hardly breathe. Debris began raining down—shards and fragments mostly, but larger pieces, too. A severed arm thunked him on the back, and the head and neck of a horse missed him by inches, splattering blood and gore all over his buckskins. Holding his breath, he rose onto his hands and knees and scrambled along the base of the building toward McDermott.

Rifles blasted continuously. Men were shouting and cursing in English and Spanish. Horses nickered and squealed.

Fargo burst out of the dust cloud only a few feet from the Irishman, who was working his carbine with

222

furious efficiency. Rising partway, he snapped a shot at one of the Black Sheaths in the square. There had to be ten or more. Sustained fire from the buildings had driven them to the center, and they were so preoccupied with picking off troopers in the windows and on the roofs, they hadn't noticed the pair crouched by the cannons.

Then, slicing through the riot of noise and confusion pealed the ringing command of Lieutenant Jurgenson. "Now, cannon crew! Do it now!"

Fargo and McDermott spun toward the doorway. Racing inside, they flattened onto the floor. The other troopers in the buildings were doing the same.

"Any moment, boyo!" McDermott exclaimed.

Fargo imagined what it must be like for the Black Sheaths: One second they were embroiled in a raging battle, the next, their enemies all vanished. They must be wondering why. Some might suspect that the kegs in the trenches were only part of the trap, but they could not begin to guess what was in store. They were doomed, every last one.

It had been Fargo's idea to load the cannons with grapeshot instead of cannon balls. It had been his idea to reposition them so they covered the parade ground. And it had been his idea to let the first wave of Black Sheaths through so they could be mowed down like ripe grain under a scythe.

Another heartbeat, and the cannons went off.

The wall above Fargo was struck by multiple heavy blows, as if by powerful fists. On the heels of the explosions came hideous screams and horrendous whinnies—cries that could send shivers down the spine. Fargo rose and peered out.

Seldom had he beheld anything so ghastly.

Grapeshot, at close range, was devastating. Similar to buckshot from a shotgun, only many times worse, it tore through flesh and bones as if they did not exist. The Black Sheaths and their horses had been ripped to ribbons. Not one man; not one animal was left untouched. All were on the ground, thrashing and convulsing and oozing bright scarlet from more wounds than anyone could ever count.

"Saints preserve us!" McDermott breathed. "They've been turned into sieves!"

Fargo warily emerged. A Black Sheath saw him but was in no shape to do anything. The left side of the man's body resembled paper cut into thin strips. His mouth moved but all that came out were tiny whimpers.

Jurgeson appeared, surveyed their handiwork with mixed awe and disbelief, and declared, "We did it! We really and truly did it!"

Fargo felt no elation at their victory. It was only half the battle. Machetazo still had more than thirty infantry at his disposal—more than enough, since the troopers were bound to have sustained casualties.

The lieutenant was thinking the same thing. "Sergeant McDermott! Round up all our men and have them fall in. The wounded go straight to the infirmary."

"And the dead, sir?"

"Can lie where they fell. We must prepare for the next attack."

As the Irishman jogged off, Fargo moved in among the Black Sheaths. A horse with its belly opened wide and its intestines coiled in a twisted pile was trying to get back up. The agony it was enduring had to be excruciating. Fargo ended its misery, then started replacing spent cartridges.

A few yards away lay a Black Sheath whose chest looked as if he had been stabbed a dozen times with a Bowie knife. Blood caked his chin and more pumped from his mouth with every breath. He shifted pain-racked eyes and gasped, "Kill me, *señor*. I beg you. Before I shame myself and scream."

Fargo raised the Colt.

"Hold on there!" Lieutenant Jurgenson huffed over. "What in God's name do you think you're doing? The United States Army doesn't condone the shooting of helpless prisoners of war."

"I'm a civilian, remember?" Fargo said, and put a slug between the Black Sheath's eyes. The man deflated like a punctured waterskin, a slow smile spreading across his grimy face.

"But—but—but—" Jurgenson stammered. He stared at a Black Sheath who had no arms and only one leg, who was flopping around like a trout out of water and blubbering hysterically. The man couldn't possibly survive. Jaw clenched, Jurgenson sighted down his carbine and blew the man's brains out.

"You're learning," Fargo said.

Jurgenson surveyed the slaughter they had caused. "I always thought war would be so glorious, so exhilarating. "But it's—" He seemed to search for the right word. "It's so ugly."

"Ever seen a trapper mauled by a grizzly? Or a mule-skinner tortured by Apaches?" Fargo gestured. "This is no worse—and it was done to save lives. That makes a world of difference."

"I know." Jurgenson took a deep breath and stood a bit straighter. "It's just that this is my first time."

"Be sure and have someone keep an eye on the Black Sheath infantry," Fargo advised, and ran to the stable to fetch his Henry. He did his best to avoid body parts and puddles of blood. As he came back out, he heard voices and spied Black Sheaths circling from the north side of the post to the west side, well beyond rifle range. The Beast hadn't wasted any time. Soon the fort would be surrounded once more.

Four troopers were standing at attention near the officers' quarters and Lieutenant Jurgenson was trying to pace a rut into the ground. Others were being helped toward the infirmary.

"We lost four and have two badly wounded," the

young officer stated. Taking his hat off, he swatted it against his leg. "All good men. What I wouldn't give for Colonel Blanchard to return along about now. But I know that's wishful thinking." He looked at Fargo. "Any more brainstorms, Trailsman? Thanks to you we've held our own so far. But the Black Sheaths won't be as gullible next time."

No, they wouldn't, Fargo mused. "It depends on what Machetazo decides to do. If he sends them against us before sunset, our best bet is to set fire to the stable and try to break through their lines to Mesilla."

"And if the bastard decides to wait until tomorrow?"

"Then maybe we can end this without much more bloodshed." But Fargo did not say how. It would remain his secret, and his alone, until later.

Jurgenson pointed at a private. "Baxter! Go up on the sutler's roof and observe the enemy without being seen. If it looks as if they're preparing to attack, let me know."

"Yes, sir." Baxter saluted and did an about-face.

Fargo scanned the post perimeter. "We need barricades where the trenches used to be. And at the southeast corner, too. The gap there isn't as wide but it's enough for foot soldiers."

"Consider it done." Lieutenant Jurgenson hustled the rest of the troopers off on the double.

Not a minute later Sergeant McDermott came from the infirmary, sorrowfully shaking his head. "It's a sad day, boyo, when those you've nurtured like wee chicks die in your very arms." His sleeves were speckled with blood. "The other wounded man won't last much longer, I'm afraid, without a sawbones." He glowered like a wild boar eager to rend and gore. "Damn the Beast and all his vile kind! Would that I could fight him one-on-one! I'd throttle him with my bare hands."

Fargo verified no one was within earshot. "We think alike, Irish. If I need someone later to back my play, are you in?"

"Boyo, I was born ready to romp and stomp. It's been the bane of my existence. Why, as a lad, I was forever getting my backside tanned for proving to the other whelps that I was tougher than any and all." McDermott leaned forward. "Why? What do you have in mind, exactly?"

A shout from the roof nipped Fargo's explanation in the bud.

"Sarge! A Black Sheath is approaching under a white flag! I think it's the same coon as before."

"And the lieutenant is nowhere to be found," Mc-Dermott said, looking all around.

Fargo had seen Jurgenson and the troopers enter the barracks. He reckoned they were after furniture to use on the barricades. Since he would rather talk to the Black Sheath without the lieutenant along, he nudged the Irishman and hurried to the gaping hole that had once been the northwest trench. Dead horses—and parts of horses, as well as dead men— and parts of men were knee-deep in spots.

Once again Lieutenant Alfredo had been chosen as Machetazo's emissary. Resentment radiating from every pore, he began by demanding, "Where is the *gringo* officer who spoke with me before? I would rather negotiate with him."

"Negotiate?" Fargo repeated. "We thought you wanted to surrender."

Alfredo was as humorless as he was hateful. "As you *norteamericanos* like to say, it will be a cold day in the *infierno* before that will happen. We still greatly outnumber you. Our illustrious general has only to say the word and we will crush you like bugs."

"You're welcome to try," Fargo said, and made as if to go back.

"Wait!" Alfredo said much too stridently. "Hear me out. The general is offering you one last chance to come to your senses."

Sergeant McDermott mentioned where Machetazo could stick his offer, which the Black Sheath chose to disregard.

"All General Machetazo wants are the weapons and ammunition from the armory. Tell us where they are and we will take them and go. No one else on either side need die." What do you say, *gringos*? Are a few guns and bullets worth your lives?"

"What about his demand that I be turned over to him?" Fargo asked.

Lieutenant Alfredo dismissed it with a flip of his hand. "The Great One is willing to forgo the pleasure it would give him to settle with you if you hand over the items he wants."

"The Great One can kiss my Irish ass," McDermott retorted. "The only way he'll get his hands on them is over our dead bodies."

Fargo was studying the Black Sheaths to the west and those he could see to the north. Few had guns. Most wore sandals instead of boots and had the rugged look of men accustomed to bending their backs to a plow. He had learned all he needed to. His new idea just might work.

"Insults will get you nowhere," Alfredo was saying. "You are being childish. Go back and talk it over among yourselves. See what the others think. Take a vote if you have to."

"A vote? You're talking about the U.S. Army, not a Sunday social." Sergeant McDermott held up a ham of a fist. "The only voting that will be done is by my knuckles."

"So I am to inform the general there is no deal?"

Raising his voice so the nearest Black Sheaths would hear him, Fargo responded. "Tell your general

I challenge him. I will meet him out here in the open whenever he wants. *Mano a mano*."

Alfredo glanced toward his lord and master. "What are you up to, *gringo*? No one said anything about challenges."

"Just the two of us!" Fargo shouted. "If I win, the Black Sheaths disband and those who want can go back to their homes. If he wins, the soldiers will leave Fort Fillmore."

Sergeant McDermott almost spoiled everything. "What are you on about, boyo? You don't have the authority to make a promise like that."

Whatever else Lieutenant Alfredo might be, he was no fool. He saw other Black Sheaths were listening, and he raised his reins to go. "Clever, *gringo*. Very clever. But it will not work. They are too afraid of the general and his demons."

Fargo was suddenly reminded of a wild card in the deck—or, specifically, three wild cards. There had been no sign of Antonio, Manuelito, and Amarillo. Yet Machetazo wouldn't let them stray too far off. Fishing for information, he commented, "The demons are nothing to worry about. I doubt they're even here."

Alfredo swallowed the bait. "They are always around. But like the wind they are invisible." He paused. "General Machetazo uses their talents wisely. They are hunters, not *soldados*, and are on the scent of prey even as we speak."

Fargo hoped it wasn't the Southerners he left at the spring. It might have been a mistake on his part to reveal he had disposed of Ruiz's bunch. "Tell your general he has until sundown to accept my challenge."

"I already know what he will say. He will refuse to soil his hands on so lowly a nuisance. He has more important things to do, such as plotting the downfall of your companions. Tell them to enjoy this night. Tomorrow is their last day of life."

Unwittingly, the Black Sheath had revealed important information. Fargo turned to go and was puzzled by a comment Alfredo threw after him.

"Besides, *gringo*. There is no need for the Great One to accept a challenge from someone who is already dead. Your death will do more to assure our victory than that of any other." Alfredo reined his mount westward.

"What do you suppose he was blathering about?" Sergeant McDermott wondered.

Fargo shrugged. It made no difference. By morning it would all be over, one way or the other. They hiked back to the fort.

Lieutenant Jurgenson alternated between irritation and relief when he heard their account. "You went out there without me? I'll remind you I'm still in charge. And while I expect such behavior from you, scout, the sergeant should know better."

Fargo wryly grinned. They were back to "scout" again.

"I don't find this at all amusing," Jurgenson misconstrued. "While I consider your advice invaluable, I will not have my authority usurped. If Machetazo tenders a white flag again, I insist on being notified immediately."

"Will do, sir," McDermott said apologetically.

"With that out of the way," Jurgenson went on, "and now that we know we have until morning, find a trooper who can make a decent cup of coffee and have him whip up a meal. It doesn't need to be fancy so long as it's filling."

"Yes, sir." The Irishman pivoted but his superior wasn't finished.

"Once it's ready the men will eat in shifts, half at a time—just in case the information you were given is false. It'll be dark soon and I wouldn't put it past the Black Sheaths to attack."

There was always that possibility but Fargo doubted

the Beast would risk it. Machetazo had lost too many men as it was.

The officer turned to him. "Have you come up with any more devious tactics for us to use?"

"I'm working on it," Fargo replied. Jurgenson would try to stop him if he told the truth and there was too much at stake.

"For what it's worth, I have every confidence in you."

For the next half hour Fargo lent a hand building barricades. Chairs, tables, a desk—anything and everything that wasn't nailed down was heaped high. The troopers were bone-weary but labored without complaint.

Sundown neared. The Black Sheaths kindled cooking fires and huddled around them in small groups. Machetazo and the two lieutenants had a fire of their own apart from the rest. Their pack animals and the few mounts they had left were tethered close by, and sentries were posted.

Fargo was famished. When a trooper informed him he could go eat if he wanted, he made a beeline for the mess hall. Since it was on the east side of the square it hadn't sustained damage. All the lamps were lit and silverware had been laid out. The troopers joked and laughed but it was halfhearted.

The man chosen to prepare the meal had done an admirable job on such short notice. Slabs of beef recently acquired from a rancher and corned to preserve it were cut, roasted, and set out. The potatoes were underdone but adequate. Saratoga chips shipped in from New York and dodgers made by the cook before the command moved out completed the selection.

Fargo helped himself to some of each and took his sweet time eating. After the events of the day he owed it to himself. Half a pot of hot black coffee washed it down, and, sitting back, he patted his stomach. He was fit to burst and felt sluggish.

Sergeant McDermott joined him just as Fargo pushed his chair back. "You're not leaving, are you, boyo? I wanted to find out what you have in mind for tonight." His tray was piled with a mountain of food—particularly dodgers, which were tasty loaves of corn bread.

"It's risky," Fargo admitted.

"What isn't in this world? Hell, getting out of bed is a throw of the dice." The Irishman crammed half a dodger into his mouth and chomped like a ravenous wolf. "And it's not as if I've ever shied from danger. Were I the timid type, I'd take up tailoring like my mouse of a brother."

"To each their own."

"That's what my mother always said. But I thought it a shame to waste so much good Irish blood in a profession fit more for grannies. I mentioned that to my brother once and he showed he had true McDermott spirit after all. He up and punched me." McDermott rubbed his chin. "Not a bad blow, either, for so puny a lad."

Lieutenant Jurgenson entered. He had changed uniforms and brushed off his hat and boots. "Gentlemen! I trust you won't mind my company?"

"Not at all, sir," Sergeant McDermott said.

Fargo was inclined to leave but he stuck around long enough to savor another cup of coffee, then excused himself and walked to the stable. He hadn't fed or watered the Ovaro all day, a lapse he had to correct. After leading the stallion to the water trough, he fed it enough hay to last the night. He had to use his hands since there wasn't another pitchfork. When he was done he had bits of hay clinging to his buckskins, and as he was brushing them off, the Ovaro raised its head and nickered.

Fargo looked up. The stable was quiet and still. Some of the other horses were dozing. The pinto, though, was staring at a knee-high pile of straw a few

232

stalls down. He figured a rat or mouse must be scurrying about. Then he spotted a patch of black amid the yellow and, placing his hand on the Colt, he crept forward. Mice he didn't mind, but rats were another story. He was only a few feet away when the black patch moved—it was hair but it didn't belong to any rodent. It was atop a man's head.

One of the demons had been hiding in the pile, waiting for just that moment to spring.

Simultaneously another came rushing from an empty stall and the third dropped from the loft, cutting off any possible escape.

Fargo was in for the fight of his life.

17

Antonio was the one hiding in the hay, but as quickly as he struck, Skye Fargo was a shade quicker. Side-stepping, Fargo whipped out his Colt and slammed the barrel across the 'breed's temple. Antonio pitched to his hands and knees, dazed. Before Fargo could finish him off, Manuelito and Amarillo converged, Manuelito swinging a machete. It would have cleaved Fargo like a melon had he not leaped aside. In doing so he put himself within easy reach of Amarillo, whose own machete smashed against the Colt and sent it skittering across the aisle.

Fargo retreated a few steps. His back was to a corner and he could go no farther. The brothers had him trapped.

For a few moments no one moved.

It was then that the comments Alfredo had made to Fargo earlier took on a whole new meaning. Alfredo had come right out and stated the demons were on the scent of prey, as he had put it. Little had Fargo suspected it was *his* scent. And then there had been that last puzzling comment. "There is no need for the Great One to accept a challenge from someone who is already dead." Now it all made sense.

Fargo wasn't surprised the demons had slipped onto the post unseen. As clever as they were deadly, they had chosen the stable to jump him because they knew he would eventually show up to tend his horse. Now here he was, his back literally to a wall, the Colt out of reach, his Henry over against the Ovaro's stall, and unarmed except for the toothpick, which he didn't dare try to grab or he would lose his head.

Manuelito and Amarillo might as well have been tree stumps. They were waiting for Antonio to recover, which he did with dismaying swiftness. Pressing his left hand to a welt on his temple, the most talkative of the brothers hissed, "For this your death be slow, white-eye. Be painful. We take you in hills. Cut you till dawn come."

"It won't be easy," Fargo vowed, glancing at the open doors. The parade ground was deserted. Almost all the troopers were in the mess hall.

Antonio edged closer, his machete arm poised. "We see how easy, eh?" And at a word from him, all three attacked.

By rights Fargo should have died. He was empty-handed against a trio of the worst killers on the frontier. But they blundered. In the confined space they couldn't all close in at once. In their bloodthirsty eagerness they jostled one another. It threw Antonio off stride and his swing missed by a whisker.

Grabbing Amarillo's wrist as his machete descended, Fargo rotated on the heels of his boots, swiveling Amarillo between him and Manuelito. Almost too late Manuelito checked his swing and his machete glanced off Amarillo's shoulder, cutting deep enough to draw blood.

Exerting every ounce of strength in his sinews, Fargo shoved Amarillo against the other two, spun, and dived for his Colt. His fingers were inches from it when a thrown machete thudded into the dirt, nearly shearing off his fingertips and preventing him from grabbing it. He sensed one of the brothers was almost on top of him and rolled onto his side just as Manuelito launched himself into the air.

Snapping up his left leg, Fargo caught the half-breed

full in the face. Manuelito tumbled against a stall. His head bore the brunt of the impact. He fell flat on his stomach and was momentarily still.

Antonio and Amarillo didn't give their fallen brother a second glance. Machetes upraised, they lunged.

Fargo scrambled backward and felt his right hand brush some straw. Clutching it, he flung it at Amarillo's face and the 'breed instinctively jerked back.

That left Antonio. Snarling like a wild beast, he streaked his machete in a glittering arc. Fargo saved his legs from being chopped off at the knees by tucking them to his chest. Antonio overextended himself, and before he could straighten, Fargo slammed both boots into the renegade's sternum.

Levering himself erect, Fargo started to glance over his shoulder to see how close he was to the Henry. Amarillo seized the moment and came at him in a coldly methodical bid to inflict a crippling wound. Fargo dodged a thrust aimed at his chest, another speared at his groin. He narrowly avoided having his head opened up. The next swing was at his shoulder.

Suddenly reversing direction, Fargo gripped the 'breed's wrist, wrenched it with all his might, and drove his knee into Amarillo's elbow. A loud *crack* resulted. Amarillo threw back his head but didn't cry out, his machete slipping from fingers gone numb.

Fargo caught it by the handle, shifted, and slashed the razor edge across the demon's exposed throat. It bit clean to the spine. A crimson geyser spurted as Amarillo's head flopped back, dangling like a loose rein. The headless body actually took a faltering step, then collapsed in its tracks.

Antonio was in shock—but only for a few seconds. With a rumbling deep in his chest, he attacked with a fury born of a red-hot lust for revenge. His right arm flashed right, flashed left, and it was all Fargo could do to stay one step beyond his reach. Skipping backward, he felt his right foot snag on something. He clutched at a stall but gravity had taken over and he wound up flat on his back.

Antonio reared over him.

The object Fargo had tripped over was the Henry— it was right next to him. Dropping the machete, he snatched up the rifle in time to block a blow that would have split his chest from chin to navel.

A round was already in the Henry's chamber. Thumbing back the hammer, he fired as Antonio slashed at his face; fired as Antonio staggered back; and fired as Antonio howled in baffled rage and toppled.

Out of nowhere flew Manuelito, his machete on a downward arc intended to shear into the junction of Fargo's neck and shoulder. Fargo had no chance to react, no hope of warding it off.

From the front of the stable four shots rang out. Each one jolted Manuelito back a step. The feral gleam in his dark eyes died, his arms sagged, and he keeled over without uttering a peep.

Slowly pushing to his feet, Fargo leaned against a rail. "I should have known it would be you."

"I heard a war cry and it sort of piqued my curiosity." Sergeant McDermott scrutinized the bodies with interest. "Are these the devil's demons you were telling me about? They don't look so all-fired fearsome now. It goes to show you my grandpa was right. He was forever fond of saying that in death all men are equal."

No one knew that better than Fargo, who had seen more than his share. Stepping over a machete, he walked to where his Colt lay.

A loud commotion presaged the arrival of Lieutenant Jurgenson and three troopers. Several horses were stomping and kicking their stalls, and at Fargo's urging, Jurgenson ordered his men to drag the bodies out and cover the pools of blood with dirt and straw to mask the scent.

"Then I want sentries posted on roofs on all four sides of the square," the officer instructed McDermott. "I realize that stretches us thin but we can't have our enemies sneaking in and out at will."

When they were alone again, Fargo turned to the Irishman. "I need some shut-eye. Will you see to it someone wakes me at midnight?" He had gone so long without rest, he couldn't guarantee he wouldn't oversleep.

"I'll rouse you myself just as I used to rouse my sweet, doting mother, with a stirring song about the blessed Emerald Isle."

"A holler will do," Fargo said. He climbed the ladder to the loft and pulled it up after him so no one could take him by surprise. Tunneling into the hay, he curled up with his rifle and was asleep the instant he closed his eyes. It seemed like only minutes later that a thump and a hail dragged him reluctantly from his rest.

"Are you still up there, boyo? I hope you didn't traipse off on me, because I have my heart set on doing unto some riffraff as they've been trying so industriously to do unto us."

Sliding out from under the hay, Fargo blinked in the lantern light and crawled to the edge. "It's not the same riffraff."

The Irishman's eyebrows pinched together. "How can that be? Are you so befuddled by sleep you're not thinking straight?"

"Most of the Black Sheaths who are left were forced to join Machetazo's army," Fargo explained. "Farmers and the like. They would just as soon throw down their machetes and go home."

"Are you telling me that when Machetazo gives the order tomorrow, they won't attack us?"

"He's not going to give the order." Gripping the top of the ladder, Fargo climbed down and began brushing off hay.

"I think I see where this is leading," McDermott remarked, "and if you're about to do what I think you're about to do, you could get us both riddled with lead."

"You don't have to come."

Stepping back, McDermott placed a hand to his chest. "That wounds me to the quick, lothario. How can you say that after all we've been through together? You can count on me, thick or thin, and you damn well know it."

Fargo clapped him on the arm. "As temperamental as you Irish are, it's a wonder any of you live to old age."

They moved along the aisle, McDermott gnawing on his lower lip like a beaver on wood. "I want to be clear on something, boyo. You're saying the worst of them were the ones we've wiped out?"

"Machetazo started his army with all the bandits and hard cases he could round up. But that wasn't enough so he took to having *peóns* join his cause whether they wanted to or not. Decent family men who did it out of fear their loved ones would be harmed if they refused." Emerging into the night, Fargo paused. "But Machetazo has never fully trusted them. To keep them in line, he picked the worst of his killers as officers and sergeants." He had Juanita to thank for that information.

"Why, that's blasphemy!" McDermott declared. "Besmirching sergeants is the same as besmirching the pope."

The comparison eluded Fargo. "Machetazo rewarded the *bandidos* in his army by giving them guns and horses, which were always hard to come by. Most of the farmers have only machetes."

The Irishman stared at the dead littering the square. "With his cavalry disposed of, why haven't the rest thrown down their weapons and left?"

"So long as Machetazo is alive they know their families will never be safe." Fargo headed for the sutler's. "We're going to remedy that." The building was black as pitch inside, and he had to grope his way down a hall and into a room with a window facing west. The glass was dotted with holes but intact. Unfastening the latch, he raised the window and slid a leg out.

"The lieutenant will throw a hissy fit when he hears what we've done," McDermott mentioned.

"It will be a short one when he learns the Beast is dead." Fargo eased his other leg over. "Hell, the Army might even pin a medal on you."

"Wouldn't that be grand? I had to pawn the last one they gave me for poker money." The Irishman unfurled and craned his neck toward the roof. "Before we go any further I'd best protect our backs." Putting a hand to his mouth, he whispered loudly, "Private Baxter! Can you hear me?"

After a few seconds an anxious answer was whispered, "Is that you, Sergeant Major?"

"No, it's a leprechaun." McDermott swore lustily. "Of course it's me, you dunderhead! Mr. Fargo and I are about to go for a wee stroll. You're not to call out or tell anyone. Is that understood?"

"Including Lieutenant Jurgenson?"

"*Especially* him! We don't want to be giving an officer indigestion, now, do we? Be on the lookout for us when we return so you don't shoot us by mistake. I know how itchy a trigger finger can get."

"Don't you worry, Sarge. I could never forgive myself if I killed you. I happen to think you're aces."

"Really? I don't suppose you have a pretty sister back home who is fond of men in uniform? One who can cook and sew and doesn't have a habit of sassing back every time she opens her mouth?"

Fargo poked McDermott in the ribs. There were times when the Irishman tended to get carried away with himself.

"We'll talk more later about your sisters," McDermott whispered up ro him. " Just remember. Not a word to the lieutenant or you'll be shoveling out the stable for a month of Sundays."

"You can count on me, Sergeant."

McDermott winked at Fargo. "You've got to love the puppies they send us these days. They're as eager to please as politicians stumping for votes."

Fargo took a few steps and sank to one knee. Six hundred yards from the fort glowed four campfires, staggered at regular intervals. The northernmost one, he knew, was where he would find Machetazo and the lieutenants. But they could wait. Bent at the waist, he stalked toward the second fire, the Irishman right behind him.

When they had only thirty yards to go, a shadow separated itself from the murk, moving slowly toward them. Thinking they had been seen, Fargo squatted behind some bushes and brought the Henry to his shoulder. But there was no outcry.

The sentry was staring down at the ground. Even in the dark it was plain he was as unhappy as a person could be, and paying no attention whatsoever to his surroundings. His only weapon was a machete.

Handing the Henry to McDermott, Fargo palmed the Arkansas toothpick. As the unsuspecting Black Sheath trudged by, Fargo leaped. Jabbing the tip of the toothpick into the man's neck deep enough to show what would happen if he didn't cooperate, Fargo clamped his other arm around the man's chest and whispered, "Not a sound, or you're dead."

Over at the fire other Black Sheaths were talking in hushed tones and sipping coffee. They looked about as happy as the sentry.

"Are you a conscript?" Fargo whispered.

"Sí, señor."

"Where are you from?"

"Outside a small village in Sonora. Please do not kill me, *señor*. I have a wife and nine children I dearly want to see again."

"It might be sooner than they think." Fargo relaxed his grip but didn't lower the toothpick. "What's your name?"

"Carlos Ramirez, *señor*. I know who you are. The general has been bragging that by morning you will be dead."

"The general is in for a surprise." Fargo indicated those at the campfire. "Are they conscripts, too?"

"*Sí*. And like me, they would give anything to be with their families again. We do not want to fight. This is Machetazo's war, not ours." Carlos glared at the fire to the north. "But we are afraid of him, *señor*—him and his demons."

"The demons are no more."

Carlos snapped his head around, nearly impaling his neck on the toothpick. "You saw this with your own eyes?"

"I killed two of them myself." Fargo beckoned to the Irishman, then replaced his knife. "Go tell your *compañeros* what I've told you. Have them spread the word to those at the other fires. Any who are brave enough can join my friend and me at General Machetazo's fire in half an hour."

"And then what, *señor*?" Carlos asked in budding hope.

"The day of the Beast will end."

Joy blossomed on the farmer's haggard face. Clasping Fargo's hand, he pumped it and whispered, "If you do this thing for us, *señor*, we will forever be in your debt. You will be welcome at any supper table in northern Mexico." Barely able to contain himself, he bounded toward his friends.

"Taking a bit of a chance, aren't you, boyo?" McDermott asked. "If one of them takes it into his misguided head to warn the general, what then?"

"We get there first and make damn sure Machetazo doesn't slip away." Accepting the Henry, Fargo worked his way around so that they approached the Beast's campfire from the north. Vegetation was sparse but there was enough cover for them to slink to within twenty feet without being discovered.

Vicente Machetazo sat with his right arm propped on his knee, his chin on his fist, glowering into the fire. With his other hand he fingered the hilt of his machete as if he could not wait to use it. He was as tense as a cornered jaguar and kept glancing toward Fort Fillmore.

The two lieutenants could not hide their nervousness. Alfredo coughed lightly and said, "No one can get the better of your demons, Great One. They will return any moment. Wait and see."

"You heard those shots, that yell," Machetazo snapped. "Had they succeeded, they would have been here by now." Growling, he kicked at a rock. "Half my army is dead. All my officers but you two have been slain. Most of our guns, most of our horses, are gone. And now my demons are missing."

"Antonio and his brothers do not die easily, sir." Alfredo tried to cheer him up.

Machetazo wasn't listening. He kicked another rock, then declared, "It's all because of that *gringo*. The one they call Fargo. It was foolish of me not to slit his throat when I had the chance. But who knew?" He said it again, more to himself than to them: "Who knew?"

They fell silent and did not speak again until Lieutenant Alfredo glanced to the south and asked, "Why are those men coming this way? We did not give them permission to move about."

It was a few seconds before Machetazo lifted his head. When he did, he sprang to his feet. "How dare they disobey me! Have they lost their senses?"

Fifteen to twenty conscripts materialized out of the

darkness and stopped just within the circle of firelight. Wearing expressions of open defiance, they stared in icy silence at the would-be ruler of Mexico.

The two lieutenants stood. Alfredo asked harshly, "What is the meaning of this? Haven't you learned by now to do as you are told?"

None of the conscripts responded.

"Are you hard of hearing as well as brainless? You have invited the wrath of the Great One and will suffer the consequences."

Carlos Ramirez shouldered to the front and announced, "Your days of threatening us are over. From this moment on we are masters of our lives again."

Lieutenant Alfredo was going to reply but Machetazo shoved him aside. "You could not be more wrong, dirt farmer. Your paltry lives are mine to command. Or have you forgotten that all I need do is give the word and my demons will pay your families a visit?"

"Your demons are no more," another man said.

"Who told you that?"

Fargo leveled the Henry and strode from concealment. "I did." He expected one or both of the lieutenants to resist, and they didn't disappoint him. Alfredo swooped a hand to his revolver and Fargo sent a slug through his chest that spun him halfway around. The other one had a rifle but it wasn't cocked, and in the second it took him to cock it, Fargo shot him through the forehead. The blasts rolled off across the hills and echoed in the distance.

Machetazo seemed stunned by the suddenness of it all. He tore his gaze from Alfredo, started to draw his machete, and roared, "You!"

"I wouldn't," Fargo said.

The Beast drew up in midstride, his mouth twitching from the violence of his emotions. "I should have known you put these spineless jackals up to this. They do not have the backbone to do it on their own."

"They might surprise you with what they have the backbone to do before we're done," Fargo predicted.

Machetazo drew himself up to his full height and puffed out his chest. "What now, *gringo*? Will you turn me over to the Army to face a firing squad? Or will the civilian authorities put me on trial and make a spectacle of sentencing me to hang? Perhaps they will sell tickets as I hear they sometimes do."

"I have something else in mind." Fargo motioned at McDermott, who warily disarmed Machetazo and stepped back again.

The butcher was amused. "All of you can breathe easier now. The dreaded Beast has been deprived of his fangs."

Carlos and those with him came closer. "You will soon be deprived of something much more precious. And you will not find it so humorous."

"Spare me your threats, you miserable slug," Machetazo rejoined. "What do you know? You should be grateful to me for giving meaning to your pointless existence. Before you enlisted in my glorious cause your life was empty and shallow. I made you someone special. As a Black Sheath you are feared and respected from one end of Mexico to the other. As a dirt farmer you were nothing."

"That is where you are wrong," Carlos said. "As farmers we grow things to feed ourselves and others. We create new life so that many might live. But Black Sheaths only take lives to feed your ambition."

"Do my ears deceive me?" Machetazo laughed. "A miracle has occurred. Dirt farmers can now think on their own."

"We always could. You simply refused to admit it."

Sergeant McDermott tapped Fargo's arm and pointed. Off in the night figures moved. Lots of them. They came singly and in pairs and clusters—not just the Black Sheaths on the west side of the fort but those from the north, east, and south, as well. Many were running. They did not want to miss it. After the nightmare they had endured they needed to be there. It was important that they see the devil fall with their own eyes.

Machetazo became aware of them. His smug smile died. For the first time uncertainty crept over him. His arrogance had developed a crack that grew wider and wider as more and more of those he had trampled under his boot heels arrived. Their ranks swelled until they formed a solid ring with him at its center.

A hush fell.

Carlos raised his arms to get their attention, then nodded at Fargo. "Do you see this man? He is the one who has done this great thing for us. He has slain the demons and now gives us that which we desire most in this world. Remember him always."

Comprehension sank into Vicente Machetazo, and his scar drained of color. "I demand to be taken to the officer in charge at the fort so I can surrender myself to him."

Fargo turned. The Black Sheaths parted to let him and the Irishman through, many nodding or touching his arms in gratitude as he passed.

"Where are you going, *gringo*?" the Beast demanded. "You can't leave me like this! Do you hear me? I deserve better!"

The ring closed again.

Fargo did not look back. His ears sufficed. He heard the rustle of machetes being slid from their sheaths, heard a whimper drowned out by the swish of dozens of steel blades. Last came the best sounds of all: the unforgettable ripping and rending of human flesh being hacked to pieces, and a scream that went on and on and on.

Sergeant McDermott was unusually quiet until they reached the barricade, and then he had only one comment: "Remind me never to get you mad, boyo."

18

At first light Private Baxter reported that there was no sign of life anywhere near the fort. Lieutenant Jurgenson asked Fargo to ride out and investigate.

McDermott had been right about the fit Jurgenson would throw when he learned what they had done. But he was madder about them going off again without consulting him than he was about the outcome. "What's done is done," Jurgenson summed up his sentiments. "And while I don't agree with your methods, scout, I won't make an issue of it."

"Does that mean I'm off the hook, too, sir?" McDermott had asked.

"No. Twice you have disobeyed me. I won't condone insubordination, Sergeant Major. Consider yourself confined to the Territory for the next month."

"The *Territory*, sir?" the Irishman repeated. "But that means I can still go to Mesilla or Albuquerque and have me a lively time."

A grin had spread across Jurgenson's face, but he adopted a stern air and responded, "When I say the Territory, Sergeant, I damn well mean the Territory."

McDermott had watched the shavetail walk off and said to Fargo: "Don't ever tell him I said this, but that lad has the makings of a damn fine officer."

Now, with the Ovaro saddled, Fargo moved to a gap the troopers had made in the southwest barricade. Pulling on the Henry, he fed a cartridge into the chamber.

"Watch your back out there, boyo," the Irishman

advised. "There might be a few diehards left who want revenge for Machetazo."

Lieutenant Jurgenson agreed. "We'll keep you covered as best we can. If you run into trouble get back here on the double."

Fargo rode out.

The Black Sheaths, their supplies, and the few remaining horses were gone. In the ashes of every campfire were the charred tatters of machete sheaths. They were a symbol of the Beast and all he stood for, and the farmers wanted no part of them.

Near the embers of the northernmost fire was a sight Fargo would never forget. Bits of flesh and bone no bigger than his thumbnail were scattered like grass seed. Alfredo and the other lieutenant, though, hadn't been touched.

The news that the People's Army for the Liberation of Mexico was no more elicited whoops of joy from the troopers, but their celebration was short lived. Jurgenson set them to work burying the dead and cleaning up the blood and debris.

Fargo helped out. There was only one loose thread left to wrap up, and he was in no hurry. Susannah and the rest of the Southern sympathizers weren't going anywhere.

It took four days to restore Fort Fillmore to some semblance of normalcy—enough for Lieutenant Jurgenson to order the women and children be brought back. McDermott was assigned the detail, and Fargo tagged along. He wanted Lieta and Culazol to know that in a few days he would be ready to escort them home—only they weren't in Mesilla. They had left the morning after they'd arrived without saying a word to anyone.

Juanita wasn't her friendly self, either. She rode beside him on the way back and was polite enough, but Fargo sensed an aloofness that had not been there before. At the fort she sought out Lieutenant Jurgenson, and the radiant smile she bestowed on him showed where her sights were set.

The very next day Fargo rode out to bring the Southerners in. He wanted to go alone but Jurgenson insisted on sending Sergeant McDermott and two troopers.

They were a couple of miles from the spring when Fargo noticed the buzzards. Clucking to the pinto, he pushed on at a trot until they came to the dry wash. Entering it at the south end, they dismounted and advanced on foot.

The stench hit them long before they saw the decomposed corpses. Rotting bodies were everywhere, swarming with vultures. In addition to those of Ruiz and the Black Sheaths, Tarleton Wilkes and Tyrel and Elwin Owensby lay where Fargo had seen them last.

Four more bodies had been added. The men from the Conestogas had been staked out and brutalized. Susannah and the two women, though, were missing. So were the wagons—and the gold.

"Do you think Apaches got to those four?" Sergeant McDermott wondered.

Fargo shook his head. Apaches struck swiftly and retreated into their mountain haunts before anyone could catch them. They wouldn't take wagons. It would slow them down too much. He climbed out of the wash, saying, "Don't show yourselves until I've had a look around."

The buzzards resented his intrusion. They hissed and flapped their wings but when that failed to drive him off they lumbered into the sky and circled in a cloud of feathers and beaks.

Tracks confirmed Fargo's hunch about the culprits. He roved from the spring to where the wagons had been, then over toward the hills and back again. When he was done he had a fairly good notion of what had happened and who was to blame. He waved the others over, and while the troopers guarded their horses, he walked McDermott through the sequence of events.

"It wasn't long after Juanita and I left. Six riders came in from the east. Either they were trailing the wagons or they heard the shots I swapped with Ruiz and his men." Fargo showed the Irishman six sets of hoofprints. "They came in on the far side of the wagons, climbed down, and took the Southerners by surprise."

"And you're positive they weren't Mescaleros."

Fargo hunkered and tapped the imprint of a high-heeled boot. "There were three whites and three Mexicans—"

"Hold on, boyo. How can you tell that? One track looks pretty much the same to me."

"The shapes of the soles and the heels are different." Fargo traced a line of faint tracks. "They staked out the four men and one of the whites carved on them while the rest watched. At some point the man doing the carving ran over to the wagons." Fargo led McDermott toward where the wagons had been parked.

"He found out about the gold?"

"That would be my guess. The Southerners tried to buy their lives." Fargo touched a set of footprints that was more clearly defined than most. "See here? This is where the one who climbed in the wagon jumped back down. He went over to the Southerner he had been cutting on and slit the man's throat."

"So much for gratitude." Sergeant McDermott scratched his chin. "It beats me, boyo, how you read sign like you do. You're the best there is or I'm not Irish."

Fargo wasn't done. "After killing the four men, the outlaws forced the women onto the wagons and headed east."

"That much I can see for myself. Wagon tracks are

hard to miss." McDermott paused. "Wait a second. You said 'outlaws.' "

"Pike Thornton and his bunch."

McDermott arched an eyebrow. "Either you're a wizard with magical powers or you're guessing."

"I'm no wizard," Fargo said with a grin. "I tangled with Thornton the day Jurgenson and you bumped into me on the road, remember? And I have a score to settle with him." He hurried toward the Ovaro.

"Not so fast. Thornton's had a week start or better, hasn't he? You can't catch him now."

"You're forgetting the gold. Those wagons are so weighed down, Thornton can't travel more than ten miles a day. I'll have Thornton and his curly wolves in my gunsights before you know it."

"In *our* gunsights," Sergeant McDermott amended.

So off they trotted, paralleling the wagon ruts until they came to where Pike Thornton had made camp for the night. There they made another grisly discovery. Fargo saw hundreds of flies buzzing above a nearby draw and, venturing over, he had to cover his nose and mouth with his shirt to keep from gagging.

"Begorra! Is that a woman?"

"It was." Fargo backed away and took deep breaths of untainted air. "They had their way with her and left her for maggot bait."

McDermott smashed a burly fist against his other palm. "The sons of bitches! Do you think they'll do the same to the other lasses?"

"Only time will tell."

Sunset came and went but Fargo forged steadily east. A sliver of moon provided the light they needed, and by midnight, when they stopped, they were half-way to Mesilla. Five hours of rest was all Fargo allowed. Before sunrise they forked leather, and by eight that morning they reached the Albuquerque-Mesilla road, where they made a surprising discovery. The wagons hadn't turned north toward Albuquerque nor south toward Mesilla. They had crossed the road and continued east.

"What the hell?" McDermott exclaimed. "Are they addlepated? There's not another settlement for hundreds of miles."

Fargo had an idea what the outlaws were up to. Thornton's likeness was plastered on Wanted circulars from Texas to California, so he couldn't very well go barreling into a town and deposit that much gold in a bank. It would have excited too much attention. The smart thing for the outlaws to do was cache the gold and get rid of the wagons. He figured they would head for one of the fords across the Rio Grande, but they had stopped in a clearing not far from where he had encountered them initially. Mounds of ashes and metal parts were all that remained of the two Conestogas. They had been set alight and burned to the ground, contents and all.

Sergeant McDermott was stumped. "This is making less sense by the hour. What did they do? Switch the gold to their saddlebags?"

"They'd need enough pack animals for the entire Third Cavalry," Fargo replied, which wasn't much of an exaggeration. Dismounting, he prowled the clearing. Beside a thicket within sight of the river was a five-foot-square area where the earth had recently been disturbed. Leaves and grass had been scattered over the spot to hide the fact. Finding a suitable downed branch, he began digging.

McDermott and the troopers helped.

Fargo knew all too well that outlaws were lazy by nature. They rode the owl-hoot trail because it was easier than working for a living, and they never exerted themselves more than they had to. So it came as no surprise that he had to dig only two feet down before he struck something hard. Brushing off a little more dirt, he exposed part of a yellow metal bar.

Sergeant McDermott uncovered another. "Saints preserve us! They buried the gold rather than take it with them! I've heard it said Pike Thornton is a shrewd coyote but it seems to me he's six bullets shy of a full cylinder to just leave it here like this."

"He didn't know we were after him," Fargo mentioned. "And this is as safe a place as any until he can come back for it."

McDermott held one of the bars up and it gleamed like a miniature sun. "Begorra. It's enough to set a man to looking for that fabled pot at the end of the rainbow."

Fargo straightened. "From here on I go alone." He held up a hand when the Irishman went to protest. "I can make better time by myself. And you need to get to Mesilla and bring back a couple of wagons to transport the gold to the fort."

"I don't like your going off by your lonesome," McDermott said, "but you're right. We can't leave this gold here." He followed Fargo to the Ovaro. "Be careful, boyo. I don't have so many friends that I can afford to lose one."

From the clearing, Thornton's pack had headed north. Fargo did the same and soon found where they had turned to the northwest, toward far-distant Albuquerque, but not before they watered their horses at the Rio Grande. They also murdered the second woman and partially covered her with uprooted weeds. Blood under her broken fingernails showed she had fought fiercely for her life—in vain.

Now only Susannah Wilkes was left.

Toward the middle of the afternoon Fargo spied more buzzards circling an arroyo. One swooped low and was driven off by a weakly thrown rock. Drawing rein at the rim, he jumped down. At the bottom a naked figure with disheveled blond hair was slumped in the shadows. "Susannah?"

Wilkes's once lovely face tilted toward him. Her cheeks were pulped, her lips puffed up like sausages, and one eye was swollen shut. "Who?" she croaked.

"It's Fargo." He started down.

"Don't!" Susannah cried. Her chin drooped and she said softly, "You're too late, handsome. I'm done for. Go away and let me die in peace."

Fargo continued down anyway but she heard a stone rattle from under one of his boots, and her head snapped back up.

"No! I mean it!" Susannah pleaded. "I don't want you to see what they've done to me."

"I can take you to Mesilla," Fargo offered.

"Please do as I ask!" It was more a wail than a request. Susannah tried to slide into deeper shadow but slipped and sprawled on her side in the sunlight.

It took a lot to shock Fargo. He had seen horrible things in his travels. This ranked with the worst. A deed only the sickest of minds could contemplate and the wickedest of hearts could carry out. "Susannah?" When she failed to respond he hurried on down.

Gently placing a hand on her shoulder, Fargo leaned closer. Her eyes were glazing over. He felt for a pulse, rolled her onto her back, and folded her arms across what was left of her chest.

The arroyo was a ready-made grave. All Fargo had to do was kick enough dirt down to cover her and add a layer of rocks and small boulders to discourage predators. Then he stepped into the stirrups and resumed the hunt with newfound purpose.

Miles later the sky gave birth to yet more buzzards. This time the carrion-eaters were pecking and tearing at three bodies. A pair of *pistoleros* and a lanky gunman had died in a pitched gun battle and been left where they had fallen. Two surviving gunmen had then fled, pursued by the sole surviving Mexican. Drops of blood hinted he had been wounded. Deducing the cause of the gunfight wasn't difficult. Outlaws were not only lazy, they were greedy, or they wouldn't be outlaws to begin with.

Vegetation became sparse; the ground rocky. The ring of the stallion's hooves carried quite a distance but Fargo refused to slow down. There was no way in hell he was letting Pike Thornton get away.

The tracks became fewer and farther between. Several times Fargo had to stop and climb down to search for sign. Another hour and a half brought him to boulder-strewn hills, and he had just begun to wind through them when he came upon a dead horse. It hadn't been there long. The pool of blood rimming it wasn't completely dry.

Wheeling the Ovaro into cover, Fargo grabbed the Henry and took a closer look. The silver-inlaid saddle was Mexican. From it, bloody footprints pointed up a hill to the left. The man was bad hit. He had staggered as if he'd had too much tequila, and twice he sagged against boulders, leaving scarlet smears.

Toward the top lay a rifle. A few yards more, propped against a slab of rock, was the one Fargo thought it would be. His eyes were closed and his slow breathing had a raspy quality typical of punctured lungs. "Cipriano?"

The Mexican's eyes snapped open and he tried to draw a pearl-handled Remington from a silver-studded holster on his right hip but he lacked the strength.

Fargo relieved him of it and wedged the revolver under his belt. "They ambushed you, didn't they?"

Cipriano peered up quizzically. "I remember you. You are the one who outfoxed us by the river. What are you doing here?"

"I'm after Pike Thornton."

Lurid oaths gushed from Cipriano's mouth, along with drops of blood. "I hope you catch him! The pig! He knew I am too fast for him so he shot me and my horse from far off, then rode away laughing."

Fargo took a seat. "He wants all the gold for himself. Whoever is with him will be next."

"You know about the gold?" Cipriano licked his parched lips. "*Sí*. Dinsdale is stupid enough to trust Thornton. But he will learn."

"You shouldn't have done that to the women."

Indignation blazed from Cipriano's dark eyes. "You think that I, Cipriano, would do such a thing? It was Thornton, and he alone. I am a *pistolero, hombre*. I shoot men who try to shoot me. I do not hurt women or children."

"Or men of God."

Cipriano was astonished. "Is there anything you do *not* know?" He stared off across the barren wastes. "My greatest sin is that I didn't stop Thornton from dragging them off. I will hear their screams in hell."

"Can I get word to anyone for you?" Fargo asked.

His features softening, Cipriano smiled. "*Gracias*. That is decent of you. I have a sister in Nogales. Ramona Vega is her name. She knows what I am and how I have wasted my life, but she still cares." A violent spasm shook him, and when it was over he was on his back, staring at the sky, and he had only breath enough left to say, "Kill him, *hombre. Por favor*."

Fargo sat there a minute, then started down. He took a different route to reach the Ovaro quicker, and halfway to the bottom a peculiar buzzing brought him to a stop. The source was a crack in the ground, a crevice three feet wide and eight feet long. He dropped a rock into it and the buzzing grew, mimicking a swarm of locusts.

Pike Thornton and Dinsdale were now heading west toward the Albuquerque-Mesilla road, only at a much slower pace. With Cipriano no longer after them, they had no need to hurry.

Thornton didn't wait long to dispose of Dinsdale. Only a few miles on, Fargo crested a rise and saw the body of the young outlaw facedown in the dirt. He had two bullet holes between his shoulder blades.

The sun was blistering hot but Fargo no longer felt it. The wind on his face, the rolling gait of the Ovaro—he was oblivious to it all. He concentrated on the horizon and only the horizon. Toward sunset tendrils of smoke marked the end of his hunt, and he slowed to a walk. Twilight had fallen when he came within sight of the fire and drew rein. He had an easy shot but he left the Henry in the saddle scabbard and drew the Colt instead.

Pike Thornton was leaning back against his saddle and caressing a gold bar as if it were a lover. He kept chortling as if at a private joke. He also had a habit of talking to himself. "They're all mine! Every last one. I'm richer than old King Midas." He lifted the bar to his lips and kissed it—not once, but many times. "Only the best will do from here on out. A mansion in New Orleans, maybe. Servants to wait on me hand and foot. Tailored clothes and a fancy carriage. What more could a person ask for?"

"Life," Fargo said, and jammed the Colt against the back of the outlaw's head.

Thornton dropped the gold bar and recklessly stabbed for his hardware but thought better of the idea and froze. "Who are you?" he demanded. "What do you want?"

Reaching down, Fargo relieved the killer of his six-gun and moved around in front of him. "Cipriano sends his regards."

"You!" Thornton blurted. "What the hell do you have to do with that uppity Mex? He's long dead by now."

"Susannah Wilkes sends her regards, too."

"How can that be? She's dead as well. I should know. I—" Thornton clamped his mouth shut, realizing he had said too much. He waited for Fargo to say more, and when all Fargo did was stare, he shifted uncomfortably and spat: "Don't just stand there, damn you! I want to know what this is all about."

"We're taking a ride, you and me."

"Like hell. I don't have to go anywhere I don't want to. Unless you start explaining, I'm not budging."

Fargo shot him in the right leg.

Howling like a gut-shot mongrel, Pike Thornton clutched his shin and rolled back and forth. After a while his fury eclipsed his pain, and rising on an elbow, he snarled, "Mister, you just made the biggest mistake of your life."

"Get on your horse."

Thornton was incredulous. "How am I supposed to ride with a hole in my leg? Hell, I can't even saddle up."

"Ride bareback." Fargo aimed at the outlaw's other shin. "Or I can tie you on belly-down. Your choice."

His teeth clenched, Thornton pushed up onto his good leg and hobbled toward his mount. Gripping the saddle horn, he hesitated. "Let's talk about this. What do you want? The gold bar? It's yours."

"Climb on." Fargo waited until the outlaw obeyed, then scooped the bar off the ground.

"I knew that's all you wanted. So why not let me go? I'm not about to report you to the law. They'd throw me behind bars the moment I showed my face."

Saddle leather creaked under Fargo as he straddled the pinto. He crammed the gold bar into a saddlebag, then said, "Head back the way you came. I'll let you know when to stop."

For most of the ride Pike Thornton was quiet. But as they neared the hills where he had ambushed Cipriano, he fidgeted and declared, "If you'd just say what this is all about, maybe we can work out a deal. I have more gold where that bar came from. Enough to last you the rest of your life."

Fargo let him stew. In the dark they were almost on top of Cipriano's dead horse before they saw it.

He instructed Thornton to dismount, then slid down and gave him a rough push. "Head on up. I'll tell you how to go."

Thornton's wound slowed them. So did the press of boulders. But at length they neared the crevice, which in the cool of the night was quiet. A dozen feet below it Fargo commanded, "Stop and sit."

"And then what?"

"We wait." Sitting cross-legged on a boulder the shape of a washtub, Fargo didn't say another word until sunrise.

Pike Thornton cursed him. Pike Thornton railed to high heaven. And as dawn painted the eastern sky pink, Thornton began to plead to be let go.

The sun rose on a nervous ruin. Caked with sweat, constantly wringing his hands, the outlaw asked, "*Now* will you tell me what the hell is going on?"

"Soon," Fargo said. The temperature had to rise before the creatures in the crevice became active enough.

Exhaustion took its toll on Thornton. Unable to keep his eyes open, he dozed off. But he didn't get to sleep long.

The buzzing Fargo had heard the day before started up again about nine. Standing, he nudged the outlaw. "Wake up and take off your clothes."

Thornton sat up and blinked in confusion. "What did you just say? I don't think I heard you right."

"Take off your clothes."

"Like hell I will! I've put up with this long enough! If you're going to kill me, shoot me and get it over with."

With lightning swiftness Fargo smashed his Colt against the outlaw's temple. He stepped aside as Thornton pitched forward, then stooped and did what needed doing. Dragging Thornton to the edge, he picked up handfuls of rocks and tossed them into the crack one by one. The buzzing changed into an ominous rattling, proof the occupants were sufficiently stirred up.

Hunkering, Fargo slapped Thornton's cheek a few times. This time when Thornton's eyes opened, they were filled with fear. "Hear that?" Fargo said. "Some people think snakes den up only during the winter but that's not true." He slowly rose.

"Snakes?" the outlaw said, cocking his head.

"Rattlers." A push of Fargo's boot was all it took. Thornton tumbled into the crevice, and almost instantly the rattling rose to a feverish pitch. The screams came next. Shrieks of terror like those the women must have made when they begged for their lives.

Dirt cascaded down the sides and a hand appeared, desperately clawing toward the top. Blubbering incoherently, Pike Thornton clutched the rim. His body crawled with rattlesnakes. A small one had its fangs buried in his face. Three larger ones hung from his neck. And his chest and back were a writhing mass of reptiles. For a few moments Pike Thornton clung on. Then the venom took its toll. Losing his grip, he slid back down, disappearing into the shadows at the bottom. The rattling went on and on.

Skye Fargo holstered his Colt and bent his steps toward the Ovaro. It had been a long night and he could use some hot food and plenty of rest. Mesilla wasn't all that far away. He thought of Chico's cantina, and the two lovely women upstairs, and he smiled.

No other series has this much historical action!

THE TRAILSMAN

To order call: 1-800-788-6262

JASON MANNING

Mountain Honor   0-451-20480-8
When trouble arises between the U.S. Army and the
Cheyenne Nation, Gordon Hawkes agrees to play peace-
maker-until he realizes that his Indian friends are being
led to the slaughter...

Mountain Renegade   0-451-20583-9
As the aggression in hostile Cheyenne country escalates,
Gordon Hawkes must choose his side once and for all-and
fight for the one thing he has left...his family.

The Long Hunters   0-451-20723-8
1814: When Andrew Jackson and the U.S. army launch a
brutal campaign against the Creek Indians, Lt. Timothy
Barlow is forced to chose between his country and his
conscience.

To Order Call: 1-800-788-6262